WILD EVER AFTER

USA TODAY BESTSELLING AUTHOR

REBECCA JENSHAK

Copyright

Copyright © 2023 by Rebecca Jenshak

Rebecca Jenshak
www.rebeccajenshak.com
Cover Design by Lori Jackson Designs and Books and Moods
Cover Photo by Wander Aguiar
Editing by Edits in Blue and Fairest Reviews Editing Services
Proofreading by Sarah at All Encompassing Books
Formatting by Books and Moods

CHAPTER ONE

Jade

BIG DREAMS

"I thought you weren't wearing a veil for the reception?" Melody purses her shiny lips as she scrutinizes my look from head to toe.

"I changed my mind." I smooth a hand over the lace, admiring the soft, intricate material. "What do you think?"

My nerves ramp up as I wait for her answer. Melody is my boss and also sort of my hero. At thirty-five, she's one of the youngest editors in chief of *I Do* magazine. She's known for having her finger on the pulse of the wedding industry and generally being well liked and respected—a tough combination to pull off.

My little monthly column, Cocktail Hour with Jade, went from a few hundred views to a few million in the course of just nine months. Brides and couples planning or just dreaming of their future weddings have been following my wedding planning journey. I've covered everything from how to find the perfect wedding planner to current bouquet trends, to wedding cakes, and finally...dresses.

I Do is paying for my wedding, so I can't really blame them for wanting Melody to sign off on the purchases. And I agreed to it. Is it weird that my wedding involves a contract a mile long? Probably, but since I never planned to get married anyway, I'm okay with it. It's almost like my childhood not-so-dream wedding come to life. By the time I was ten, I'd seen my mom get divorced three times in those years and I realized that marriage wasn't some sacred union of two people. Half of the time, or more if you're my mom, it ends in tears and moving to yet another new home.

"I don't know." She tips her head side to side as she walks a circle around me. "Can I see something shorter?"

"Of course." The shop owner, Patrice, who has been hovering nearby, jumps into action.

While she and Melody look at veils of all lengths and layers, I step off the platform and grab my phone from my purse on a chair nearby.

My brows knit together at the sight of three missed calls from my fiancé. Sam isn't the kind of guy to randomly call during the day, let alone three times. Before I call him back, I snap a quick selfie for my best friends Scarlett and Piper. They helped me pick out the dress, but they'll be pumped to know Melody gave it her blessing. I can't believe I'm actually getting married in less than a week. I thought I'd be traveling to Mars before I walked down the aisle.

As I'm returning Sam's call, the bell on the front door jingles and my fiancé steps inside. His light brown hair is messy, and his Imagine Dragons T-shirt is wrinkled, but even so, Sam is still handsome. He's tall and wiry, with a vibe that's somewhere between rockstar and preppy. He grew up with money and visits to the country club for brunch. His scruffy appearance isn't fooling anyone. That kind of thing is always visible on a person. Or maybe just to me.

Sam scans the wedding dress boutique until he finds me. I raise a hand in a hesitant wave. The man hasn't been interested in a single wedding plan, but, of course, he would show up and see me in my dress. At least it isn't the one I'm wearing for the ceremony. That one is going to knock his socks off.

Instead of waving back, he heads toward me at a pace that means business.

"Hey," I cross the small sales floor to meet him, "what are you doing here? I wanted both my dresses to be a surprise. Do you like it?"

"I've been trying to call you all morning." His exasperated tone puts me on edge. He doesn't even offer so much as a glance down at the short, white dress with its cute tie straps at each shoulder and flouncy skirt.

"It's a Monday morning, Sam. I'm at work."

"Work?" One brow arches, and he mutters, "Our wedding is work."

"I didn't mean it like that, but—"

He cuts me off. "We need to talk."

"Okay. I should be done here soon. Do you want to grab lunch?" I mentally scroll through my calendar for the rest of the day. "It'll have to be quick. I have to finish edits on my article for Friday, and triple check a million other details. There's so much to do before Saturday. Oh, did you pick up your groomsmen gifts from the jewelry store?"

He lets me rattle on without interrupting, but as soon as I'm done, he shakes his head. "This isn't working for me."

"I thought you liked the cuff links." Liked might be too strong of an emotion for the passing nod he gave them. Though to be fair, our opinions were mostly disregarded in favor of what the magazine thought was sellable. Every single detail made an appearance in one of my articles. Weddings are a business, after all.

"Not that. This." He points between us. "I don't think I can go through with this."

I whip my head around to find Melody. She's still with Patrice, so I pull Sam into one of the little dressing rooms.

"What are you talking about? The wedding is in five days." My voice is a panicked whisper.

"It's too much," he says. "We've only been dating for…" He trails off, clearly clueless on the actual amount of time.

"Twelve months," I fill in for him. An entire year I've been with one guy. It's my longest relationship, by far. "What does that have to do with anything? You love me, I love you. What's the big deal?"

"You're talking about marriage, Jade. *Marriage.* I don't want to be one of those guys who gets divorced."

"O-kay. Me neither."

"I don't think you're taking this very seriously. You let the magazine set our wedding date for Christ's sake."

"Is everything okay in there?" Melody asks.

I suck in a breath and slap a hand over Sam's mouth. Too little, too late.

Melody's Louboutin shoes are visible under the black curtain. I spend a few seconds considering that maybe she didn't hear us arguing, but I know I'm not that lucky.

Crap, crap, crap.

"Yeah. I'll be right out." I try for calm and upbeat, but even I hear the slight edge of panic in my voice. I remove my hand from Sam's mouth and whisper, "Can we talk about this later? That is my *boss* out there."

"I don't think there's anything else to say, Jade. I'm heading out of town for a few days. It'll give you time to clear your stuff out of the apartment."

"Wait. You're breaking up with me?" I forget to keep my voice low and then take a deep breath and speak in a soft, but firm tone. "Don't do this. We'll figure out a way to make this work. I know it's been a lot lately, but it's almost over. After the honeymoon in St. Lucia, I'll take a few extra days off and we can relax, kick-back, and do whatever you want."

We have fun together—maybe not recently, but that's because wedding planning is my literal job right now. It's going to be back to normal soon.

"God. Why am I even surprised you're trying to bargain your way to having this wedding?" The disappointment in his eyes has my hackles rising. He agreed to this. Besides, it's too late to back out now.

"It's called compromise."

His voice booms now as he speaks, "Nothing about this is a compromise. The whole wedding is a sham. I never even proposed."

He's right. I proposed to him. We were already living together and talking about our future. Sure, I didn't imagine marriage in that future, but he did. Sam has been talking about marriage with two kids and a golden retriever since I met him. I assumed he hadn't asked me to marry him yet because he knew how hesitant I was after watching my mom do it unsuccessfully three times.

Then I saw an amazing opportunity at work. We got engaged, and I got a promotion. Maybe that doesn't sound like a fairy tale, but it's everything I wanted. Except the ring. I glance down at the beautiful round-cut diamond on my left ring finger. It's elegant and totally on trend this year, but I always pictured an oval or emerald cut. It's the first thing that Melody vetoed, but it's still the thing that hurts the most.

The wedding was supposed to be years off. I thought maybe then I'd be ready. A month ago, Melody set the date to cash in on all the interest my articles were getting. Maybe I should have fought harder to give us more time, but I have big dreams and I'm willing to sacrifice for them.

Something Sam doesn't understand. He isn't the most ambitious guy. He's perfectly content to let life pass him by. I always kind of liked that about him. Always in the moment, enjoying life. He's had everything he's ever wanted given to him. And I've had to claw every step of the way. It's a fundamental difference between us, but I've never resented him for it. Not until right this second, when he's trying to destroy months of me working my ass off for my dreams. My dream job and my dream wedding.

"You said the engagement was just for the magazine articles and we could continue our relationship on our terms. You said we would decide if and when we got married and the rest was just for show. It wasn't supposed to go this far." His voice keeps getting louder until I take a step back.

Sam hardly ever raises his voice, but he's reached a breaking point. I don't feel good about what this wedding has done to him, but he's freaking out with my boss right outside. Blood pounds in my ears and my breakfast threatens to make another appearance.

"Well?" He's staring at me, waiting for me to say something to defend myself, I guess.

Instead, I flee. I push out of the tiny dressing room. Melody and Patrice are watching wide-eyed, but neither says a word. Instead of trying to explain the completely unexplainable situation, I grab my purse from the chair and then I do the only thing I can think to do: I run.

CHAPTER TWO

Declan

DID MAVERICK JUST OUTSMART US?

I'm working in the driveway, painting the shutters I made yesterday, enjoying the quiet of the neighborhood and the feel of the sun on my back, when a red Volkswagen Beetle flies past me. I don't see a lot of the woman behind the wheel, just her red hair and something white flying out the driver's side window. She slams on the brakes in front of the house next door, making the tires squeal on the pavement.

I pause, with the brush still in my hand, when Jade gets out and does some sort of run-jog-limp up the driveway to my buddy Leo's house. He and his fiancée Scarlett left a while ago, so maybe Jade is just here to pick something up.

Except, she looks like she's about to walk down the aisle, not run an errand. She's a bridal vision from the veil flowing out behind her to the stark white dress that molds to her curves. She stops and reaches down to remove the shoe on her left foot. The right one is missing. Where it went…I can only guess.

I can hear her pounding on the front door. And the exasperated groan she lets out when no one answers.

Setting down my brush, I take two steps toward her. I don't know Jade that well. She is best friends with my buddy and teammate's fiancée, so we've spent some time together at parties and such.

Jade is the kind of woman who walks into a room and is immediately the center of attention. She's got that something that makes people want to know her. Guys, especially. She's totally hot and seems cool. She's not exactly my type, but I can't deny that I find her interesting. Actually, I wouldn't say she's not my type. I don't think I really have a type, but she's had a boyfriend, now fiancé, for as long as I've known her, so we've never really talked beyond casual conversation amongst a group of our friends. And she's out of my league. Like way out. I prefer anywhere but the center of attention.

She continues to pound on the front door as she takes out her cell phone, taps on it a couple of times and then holds it to one ear, all while muttering something unintelligible under her breath.

As I get closer, I'm better able to take in the vision that she is in white. The veil hangs over one shoulder and the wind keeps blowing it around her head. She doesn't have enough hands to fight with it, knock on the door, and hold up her phone. Even with exasperation written all over her face, she's still gorgeous.

I approach cautiously. "They aren't home."

At my words, she spins and lets both hands drop to her sides. "Declan."

I jut my chin toward the house. "They left about an hour ago."

She scans the neighborhood. The small cul-de-sac is filled with houses owned by Wildcat hockey players like me. Ash's house is across the street. He lives there with Tyler and Tyler's fiancée, Piper. Our

14

team captain, Jack, lives at the very end of the subdivision. A block over Johnny Maverick and his wife just bought a house. And last week, I closed on my place.

It's a blast living so close to my teammates. Practical, too, since we hang out so much. We're friends above everything else. Plus, the houses on this street are awesome. They're close together, but still have a decent-size yard, and we're not far from the arena.

"Did you need something?" I ask, since, after my name, she hasn't spoken another word.

"Yes. No." She shakes her head. The light red strands of her long hair catch the sunlight. "I don't know."

She gives me a sad smile and then starts for her car. Except, instead of getting in, she sits on the curb in front of it.

I stand frozen, trying to decide if I should engage or head back to my place, but when her shoulders start to shake and I realize she's crying, I move toward her before I even comprehend what I'm doing.

Taking a seat next to her, I let my long legs stretch out in front of me.

"I'm sorry." She sniffles and keeps her head down, so I can't see her face. "I'm okay. You can go. I just need a minute."

"I needed to take a break anyway."

She sniffles again and looks up. Jade has these big brown eyes that stand out against her fair complexion. Her eyes are one of her best features — though if I'm completely honest, she has a lot of best features — but right now with those wide, tear-filled eyes aimed at me, I feel way in over my head. She obviously needs comforting, but I don't know if I should ask what's wrong or just sit here. Let her cry in peace? Maybe offer her a beer? I decide doing nothing is the least risky course of action.

15

"How's the new house?" she asks after a few minutes of silence.

"It's good." I clear my throat and rub my palms together. I'm thrown by the change in topic, but happy for something to say. "I got the carpet removed and new flooring put in, new windows —" I stop. "Do you really want to hear about this right now?"

She inclines her head. "Yes, please. I need a distraction or I'm going to have a nervous breakdown."

"It can't be that bad. You're getting married this weekend."

She cuts me a glance that has me removing my foot from my mouth.

"Oh shit. I'm sorry." I should have let her cry in peace.

She swipes at the tears tracking down her cheeks and sits a little straighter. "It's fine. I'm going to figure this out. I'm sure he just needs a few hours to cool down. We've had so much going on these past couple of weeks, getting ready for the wedding. Or maybe it's cold feet. That happens, right?"

The hopeful look on her face keeps me from saying what I'm really thinking – you have to be some sort of soulless bastard to break up with a girl while she's wearing her wedding dress. "Yeah. I think it does."

Her phone vibrates in her hand, and she silences it.

"I take it that's not him?"

"It's my boss calling. She was there when Sam called things off and called our engagement a sham."

Damn. That sounds like more than cold feet. I don't know all the details about her relationship with Sam, but I know that Jade's been writing about their upcoming wedding for the magazine where she works. It's supposed to be a pretty big deal—a feature story in their print magazine showcasing their big, fancy wedding. Or that's what

I've heard from the tidbits Leo's shared.

She invited the entire team, even though only a few of us have spent any time with her. I guess having a bunch of pro hockey players on the invite list was an interesting angle to someone. I don't get it, but I agreed to go. She's always been friendly and nice, and Leo said it would mean a lot to her.

"He has to change his mind," she says, more to herself than me. "I can't be this close to having everything I want for it to blow up in my face."

In my experience, that's exactly when things tend to blow up, but pointing it out seems less than helpful. And I've already put my foot in my mouth enough for one day.

A truck slows and pulls into my driveway. The HVAC guy I called earlier waves through the open window. I return the gesture and then stand. "Do you want to come wait at my house? It's kind of a disaster from all the remodeling I'm doing, but it beats sitting on the curb."

"No. I should go." She rubs the lacy material of her veil between her finger and thumb and glances over at my place. "That's always been my favorite house on the block. I love the stonework and how the garage is separate from the house."

The corner of my mouth pulls into a smile. "Thanks."

The bones of the house are great, but the inside is stuck in the nineties. It's going to take all summer to get it into the twenty-first century, but since I recently signed a seven-year contract with the Wildcats, I finally felt ready to put down some roots.

I offer her my hand. After a beat, she slides her delicate fingers over my palm, and I help her up.

"Thank you."

"I didn't do anything." I'm still holding her hand, and it's damp.

Probably from her tears.

"You do that a lot," she says, taking her hand back and rounding the front of her Beetle.

"Do what?"

"Dismiss the nice things you do for people."

Her statement leaves me with nothing but questions. Like what nice things? And how did she notice? But she ducks into her vehicle before I can ask them.

A couple of days later, I meet up with the guys at the rink to do some skating. We're in the off-season, but after a blowout loss in the final round of the playoffs, we're all itching to get back to work. It's the second year in a row we've gotten so close that we could taste it.

I'm not getting any younger. At twenty-eight, I just inked what could very well be my last NHL contract. I spent so many years digging in, proving my worth as a player and a leader, that I never considered what comes next. But now, I'm beginning to wonder what I'll have waiting for me when it's all over.

A lot of guys start side hustles at this point in their career. They invest in real estate, sign lucrative endorsement deals, or make connections with all the right people. I've stayed out of the limelight. My reputation is mostly good and mostly centered around hockey. I don't date (not anything high profile enough to earn me a spot in the tabloids—not anymore, at least), I don't show up to high-visibility events, and I don't generally talk to the media, unless it's sound bites before or after a game.

I'm not good at all the extra stuff that comes with being a hockey player. There are so many interviews—before the game, after, pre-season, post. Not to mention the media outlets hungry for some juicy new headline. And don't even get me started on the events. Most of them are for a good cause, but the sheer number of invites to charity auctions and grand openings for bars and other local small businesses blows my mind.

My game has always spoken for itself. I'm lucky that way, I guess. But as I think about starting my eighth year in the league, those 'what's next' questions are starting to plague me. Maybe if I put myself out there more, I'd get more endorsement opportunities. The thought is tempting, but not enough to make me say yes to any of the invites sitting in my inbox.

"You guys want to grab a beer tonight?" Leo asks when we exit the ice.

"Definitely," Tyler says.

The six of us get together at least a few times a week: Leo, Ash, Jack, Tyler, Maverick, and me. A few other teammates come out occasionally, but these are the guys that I know have my back no matter what.

I drop onto the bench as I catch my breath and use the hem of my jersey to wipe the sweat from my brow. "I'm in."

"Hold up." Ash runs his fingers through his wet hair. He's been letting it grow the past two years and it's long enough that he pulls it up into a little man bun, which he does now, using a hot pink hair tie. Then he points to Leo and Tyler as he narrows his gaze. "The two of you are the last to suggest a guys' night these days."

"It's Jade's bachelorette party," Jack pipes in. "The girls are out of town tonight."

Jade's bachelorette party. I guess it was cold feet. I consider asking

Leo for details about what happened and how they worked it out. He'd know, but it feels weird to pry.

"Kota is pumped." Maverick takes a seat next to me and nods to Leo. "Thank Scarlett for me. It was nice of them to invite her."

"Yeah, man. Of course." Leo waves him off.

"Kota, we all like," Jack says. "It's you we want to trade."

Maverick chuckles. "I'm too tired to kick your ass right now."

"Sure, Rookie." Jack grins.

"We're not rookies anymore," Tyler says, with a hint of pride—well-deserved at that, he and Maverick both had great first seasons.

"You're rookies until training camp," Ash tells them. He's been in the league almost as long as me and Jack.

We hit the locker room to change and then head to our favorite bar down the street, Wild's. Jack grabs the first round and the rest of us get a table in the back.

"How's the house coming along?" Leo asks me.

"Good. Floors and windows are done. HVAC is getting replaced today and next week I'm tackling the guest bathroom."

"Getting rid of that ugly-ass hunter green tile?" Ash asks.

All the guys came over the night I got the keys. We christened the place with beer and pizza.

"What about the gold-plated hardware?" Jack asks, as he sets our drinks down on the table.

"It's all going," I say. "I'm taking it down to the studs."

"Impressive," Maverick says. "I hired a guy to do all the renovations on mine."

"I've got the summer." I shrug one shoulder. I've enjoyed working on the house so far.

"I plan on spending my summer in bed with my gorgeous wife."

He takes a long pull from his beer and then picks up his phone. He turns the screen toward us. "What's the plan for phone sex? Are they calling us for that before or after they go out?"

Leo and Tyler give him a long look.

"You two didn't plan ahead for this?" Mav asks.

"No," Leo says.

"Chumps," he says. "Always lock in phone sex."

He stands. "I gotta take a piss."

We chuckle as he heads off to the bathroom. Tyler rests his elbows on the table and leans forward. "I'd never say this to his face, but did Maverick just outsmart us?"

"Can you fools really not go one night without your women?" Jack raises a brow as he takes a swig of beer.

"Of course, we *can*," Leo says.

"But why would we want to?" Tyler adds.

Watching my buddies fall hard has been a trip. I'm happy for them. And lately, it's been on my mind. Another side effect of seeing the end of my career in the distance, I guess. Who is going to be there when it's all over?

While the guys continue to give each other shit, I slide from my seat and head to the dart board. I grab the darts and set the game, but before I throw, my phone buzzes in my pocket.

Maverick comes back out from the bathroom. "Can I get in on this?"

"Definitely. You throw first," I say as I unlock the screen and read the text from Crissy, *Hey, busy tonight? xo*

I start to respond but then delete it and shove my phone back in my pocket.

"Everything okay?" Mav asks as he turns to watch me make my

throw.

"Yeah. It's nothing."

"Problem with the house?"

"No. The reno is going great."

"Hockey?" He shakes his head. "No, can't be. You just signed a sweet seven-year deal. Mad props."

"Thanks." I chuckle softly.

"That just leaves one thing." His lips twist into a smirk. "You're having girl problems."

"He'd need a girl first," Ash quips, stepping up to join us with Jack at his side.

"Fuck you all very much." I roll my shoulders back to try to ease the tension creeping in. "I'm fine."

"I don't believe you." Jack narrows that captain gaze on me.

Ash's eyes light up as he asks, "Did you finally ask out that flight attendant from Chicago? The one that you hooked up with on the plane."

"No, and I did not hook up with her on the plane." Using two fingers, I rub at my forehead. I don't know why I bother to correct him. He knows exactly what happened, but the guys all like to twist the details to make it more scandalous.

The problem with not having as much drama in your life as your friends is that they latch on to every little thing. I have far fewer outrageous stories than they do, but they remember each one of mine and whip them out every time an opportunity presents itself.

"I think his problem is that none of them are hitting him back," Mav says. "You need a good wingman. Let's see what our options are."

He starts to scan the bar.

"I'm fine. There's no problem," I reassure them. "I got a text from

Crissy, but I ignored it."

Silence falls over the group.

"You're still hooking up with her?" Jack whistles. "I thought you were smarter than that."

"She's messy." Ash nods his agreement.

"I'm not still hooking up with her. She texted. I didn't reply. End of story. Are we going to play some darts, or what?"

No one says another word about it, but I still feel on edge. Crissy is a mistake I made two years ago. She was an intern for the team— something I didn't know until we'd been hooking up for a couple of weeks. I thought it was harmless fun. We'd go out drinking, then back to my place, and the next morning, she'd be gone, and I wouldn't hear from her again until the next time she was going out. I assumed that meant she wanted casual, no strings attached.

That is until I ran into her one night while I was on a date with someone else. She freaked. The next day she posted an old picture of us in bed together on the team's social media account with the caption, CHEATER.

It was impossible to tell it was me and she apologized that day. She took it too far and she knew it. But the damage was done. My teammates hate her for it. Especially Jack. Most people assumed it was him. He's the guy on the team known for hooking up and keeping relationships short and casual. He never once denied it. That's just one of the reasons he's such a good captain. He always has our backs. No matter what.

Anyway, that should have been it for me and Crissy, but I felt bad for the girl, and we did have fun together. So, a month later, we hooked up again. And ever since then, that's how it's gone. We go weeks, sometimes a month, without talking and then she texts me to meet up. The last couple of times we've hooked up, she's guilted me the next morning about not calling her and only wanting her when it's convenient for me. It made me feel like the worst kind of jerk. I've always been honest with her about what I want, but my actions have told another story and that's on me.

The very last time I told her that was it. It isn't healthy for us to keep seeing each other. Not when I have a gnawing suspicion that, deep down, she wants more from me. I refuse to lead the girl on. So even though, yeah, a night of fun together sounds pretty awesome right now, I'm not answering. I can't keep going down that path. It's time for both of us to move on.

"Where are the girls headed tonight?" Jack asks Leo, when we retire from darts and sit back at our table.

"Milwaukee." He glances down at his watch. "They're leaving as soon as Jade gets off work."

My ears perk up at the mention of Jade again. "So, she and Sam are good? I saw her the other day. She showed up at your place looking for Scarlett and said something about cold feet."

"I guess so." Leo shrugs. "Scarlett is all kinds of stressed about it. She's been sure they'd break up for months now, but Sam and Jade always seem to work it out."

He checks his watch again. "Maybe I should call Scarlett to check in."

Ash makes a sound like he's cracking a whip. Leo gives him the middle finger.

"Milwaukee, huh?" Jack nods thoughtfully. "Sounds fun."

"It's a cool city," Leo says.

"Milwaukee definitely has a nice vibe." A slow smile spreads across Maverick's face. "Road trip?"

CHAPTER THREE

Jade

SOMEDAY THIS IS GOING TO BE ME

On Wednesday afternoon, I finally suck it up and go into work. Melody called a dozen times yesterday, but she only left one message, *Tomorrow 3pm.*

I worked from home this morning, perfecting my article on finding the right wedding veil. My personal life might be hanging on by a thread, but my work is still A plus, and if it's the last article I'm ever going to write, then I want it to be the best damn article on wedding veils ever written.

I also spent the morning calling Sam on repeat. He'd already planned to be out of town for a few days, on a pseudo bachelor trip with buddies, since I'm leaving for my bachelorette party tonight, but I didn't expect him to go radio silent after the bomb he dropped on Monday. We need to talk. We have to talk.

"Come in," Melody calls, as I linger in her open doorway.

Her office is large and luxurious. It's creams and pinks, very on-brand for the whole bridal magazine editor-in-chief gig. She has a walking treadmill that she uses every day over lunch. Magazine covers of popular editions from the past twenty years are framed behind her desk. I'm always inspired when I walk into this office. I get that *someday this is going to be me* feeling.

I take a deep breath as I sit in a plush chair in front of her desk and place both trembling hands in my lap. "I'm sorry for the scene Monday during the fitting. That shouldn't have happened there."

"No, it shouldn't have. It was unprofessional and tacky, and if any of the women at that store decided to talk and spill your big secret, your career would be over and mine would be tarnished." Her tone isn't threatening, but I still want to pee my pants.

Panic rises in my chest.

"But it did happen." She sits forward in her chair. "So, let's focus on cleaning up the mess instead of living in it."

"You aren't mad I lied to you?"

"I don't have time to be mad. The magazine is throwing a wedding in three days, and we have no groom."

"Sam will be there."

She arches a perfectly sculpted brow. "Don't make promises to me you can't keep. Have you two made up?"

I consider lying, but what's the point now? "Not yet. He's at his bachelor party."

"He still went. That's a good sign."

I don't share her optimism. Sam wouldn't even call it a bachelor party. It was just a couple days fishing with his buddies that happened to coincide with my bachelorette party.

"What else, Jade?"

"What do you mean?"

"How much of what you told me is true?" She reaches for a bottle of hand lotion, opens it, and rubs it in while she stares me down.

"Our engagement may have started less conventionally than I led on, but Sam and I love each other. That part is true. He wants to get married." Or he wanted to before I screwed everything up.

"I don't like being used. I care for it even less when it impacts my job. The Board of Directors is expecting a wedding. A very decadent and press-filled wedding."

The reminder of the additional media covering the wedding temporarily knocks the air from my lungs. "I know. I'm sorry. I'm going to figure this out. I promise. Worst case scenario, I'll write about being stood up at the altar."

The thought of that makes my entire body scream with humiliation, but I would do it. Better to lose my pride than everything else.

"Absolutely not." Melody swivels in her chair and glances up at the framed magazines on the wall. "We are a *wedding* magazine. We sell love, engagements, *marriage*, and happily ever afters. Do you think hopeful brides and grooms across the world want to read about your failed engagement?" She shakes her head. "We are having a wedding Saturday. One that ends with two people saying, I do. If you can't find a groom, I will."

I chuckle nervously. "You would find me a groom?"

"Yes. Tim in accounting has a crush on you. I overheard him talking in the break room. I'm sure he'd be willing to step in for a promotion."

"Tim, the guy who always has food stains on his tie and smells like garlic?"

She sighs, like I should be way more excited about Tim as a potential prospect. What in the world is happening?

"Or, I'll find another couple to take your place. I'll tell them you were never engaged and that you were only the ghostwriter." She flaps her hand around dismissively, as if it's of no consequence to her, and then rests her elbows on the table. "I will find a way to spin this to protect the magazine's image."

I open and close my mouth, trying to find the words. The magazine's image. Not mine. Nine months of working long hours at the office, giving up time with friends to research wedding invitation etiquette and learn all the shades of white. That's to say nothing of the damage it's all done to my relationship with Sam. It can't have been for nothing.

Who would hire me after Melody inevitably fires me? She'd never write me a letter of recommendation, and people around this city would know. The magazine, and my articles, have been getting a lot of local and national attention. Last week a lady at the grocery store recognized me. For fifteen minutes she fangirled over my articles and told me that I helped her feel less overwhelmed with all the wedding planning.

"It makes sense now why Sam wasn't keen on having his photo taken, and why his groomsmen are your bridesmaids' significant others, instead of his friends or family." Her gaze is narrowed, but her tone is calm. Too calm.

I nod, even though it isn't necessary. She's already put it all together.

Sam had very limited involvement in what I was writing. Early on, when he agreed to get engaged and let me write about it for the magazine, he made a couple of stipulations. He didn't want his name or photo used in the articles, and he didn't want to tell his family (our plan was to go see them in North Dakota after the wedding and honeymoon, maybe have a small reception to celebrate). The first one was no big deal, since the articles I wrote focused on the bridal experience. The second stung, I won't lie, but I've never met Sam's family, and the idea of them stumbling onto my bridal column was such a long shot, I didn't see any harm in it.

Now I'm starting to wonder if he ever wanted to marry me. Maybe his future plans of a wife, two kids, and a golden retriever didn't include me as the woman standing by his side. I know the wedding came in a rush and I've been consumed with getting it all ready, but is it possible I really missed all the signs that my fiancé never planned to walk down the aisle?

"Your call, Jade. Do you want me to find another couple?" she asks.

I stand and find my voice. "No. I'll be there. And so will my groom."

"How'd it go?" Scarlett's waiting for me outside when I get done with my meeting.

"As good as could be expected, I guess." I let out a breath that puffs out my cheeks.

"Wanna talk about it?" she asks.

"No. I need to pack and get ready. What time do we leave?" We're heading to Milwaukee for my bachelorette party. Scarlett wanted to plan a big, beach getaway, but I've never been to the ocean, and I thought it'd be fun to see it the first time with Sam on our honeymoon.

"How about now?" She glances out into the parking lot and I follow her gaze. A pink Hummer is parked along the curb with Piper and Dakota hanging out an open door. Even from this distance, I can see the giant smiles on their faces.

"I don't have my bag and look at me." I glance down at my outfit. The knee-length skirt and button-down shirt will not do for my bachelorette party.

"I've got you covered." My best friend takes my hand and pulls me with her. "I packed you a bag and tossed in all my skimpiest dresses as backups."

As we get closer to the vehicle, I can hear the bass pumping and see the matching pink interior. The first real smile since Sam left tugs at the corners of my lips.

"Hey!" Piper jumps down to hug me. "Happy bachelorette party!"

A sash is thrown over my head and a flute of champagne is thrust in my hand. The hurt and stress of the past two days starts to melt away. Through it all, my friends have been there for me and I know they always will be.

Scarlett and I have been friends since high school. She is the most considerate and reliable person in my life. Piper only came into our lives in the past year, but I feel like I've known her so much longer. And Dakota. She's married to one of the Wildcat players, but because she was finishing college, she only moved to Minnesota a few weeks ago. I'm still getting to know her, but I feel like she's a kindred spirit. I've kept my circle small. Trust isn't easy for me. But these three feel like the sisters I never had.

"Let's party." I lift my glass in the air, and my friends mimic the motion, clinking their flutes against mine.

CHAPTER FOUR

Jade

LIKE HELL YOU WILL

We start with dinner at my favorite local spot. Before this whole thing blew up in my face, I'd already invited a couple of girls from the office and three friends from high school that I've kept in semi-regular contact with since graduation to join us for the first stop on my bachelorette party. None of them know the truth about my engagement or that Sam bowed out. It's fine, though, I don't feel like talking about it tonight anyway.

After dinner, Scarlett, Piper, Dakota and I head for Milwaukee in the ridiculous pink Hummer. We dance and laugh the entire way there, and before I know it, the driver is pulling up to the first bar. I changed into an appropriately skimpy dress for the occasion, and after two glasses of champagne, I'm more than ready to have a good time.

I have done a lot of research on engagement and wedding traditions. I've jumped in feet first to things like attending bridal runway shows and researching ceremony locations everywhere from churches to inside a helicopter. The options are endless and most of the wedding planning seemed like a lot of extra effort in the name of marriage.

But bachelor and bachelorette parties make perfect sense to me. A final hurrah to single life, out on the town with your best friends? Yes, please!

Everywhere we go, heads turn. My friends are hot, but I think it's the bright pink sashes they're wearing, combined with the cheap veil on my head, that is getting us noticed. Everyone loves a bachelorette party.

As with everything else, I did a lot of combing through ideas and Pinterest boards for this weekend. In the end, I told Scarlett I wanted the full-on, tackiest, most epic of bachelorette parties. To say she came through would be an understatement.

Piper holds open the door to the next bar and then hands each of us a piece of paper as we pass by her.

"What is this?" I ask.

"Now that we're all good and tipsy, it's time to start the scavenger hunt." She shakes her cleavage, which is on point in a slinky dress that would make her fiancé, Tyler's eyes pop out of his head.

Scarlett orders a round of shots while Piper goes over the rules. There are fifteen tasks. For each one we complete, we get points, but the points don't really matter. The objective is to embarrass me and get a lot of laughs in the process. Oh, and get photographic evidence. Scarlett is all over that. She's been snapping pics from minute one.

"Which one should we do first?" Dakota asks me.

I glance over the list. It's exactly the kind of stuff I would expect: get a free drink from a stranger, do a blow job shot, make a toast, dance on the bar, etc. I am here for all of it. This is exactly what I need to forget about Sam and work for a few hours. He still hasn't called, and it hurts worse than thinking about walking down the aisle alone.

Lifting my shot glass, I smile at my friends. "A toast to the best friends a girl could ask for and a night I'll never forget."

They each grab a shot and lift it in the air. "Cheers!"

For the next two hours, I focus on the scavenger hunt. I love a good to-do list. I get a condom from a guy, take a picture with a police officer, use a cheesy pick-up line on another random guy, and dance on top of the bar.

I'm living my best life until we stumble into a country bar with sad music blasting on the jukebox and couples dancing. I'm several drinks in, not to mention the shots, and for some reason, it all finally hits me.

I'm at my bachelorette party, and I don't even know if I still have a fiancé. I excuse myself to go to the bathroom. Scarlett eyes me curiously, as if she can feel me spiraling.

The music is quieter in here and somehow that makes more room for all the negative thoughts to crowd back into my mind. I brace my hands on the sink and take a few deep breaths. Scarlett walks in and I stand tall and start to wash my hands.

"Are you okay?" My best friend adjusts the veil on my head.

"Of course. I'm having a great time."

"Don't gaslight me. The second we walked in this bar, something shifted. I felt it."

"Why can't I marry you?" I give her a pouty face. "You see me more than anyone else. Plus, you're smoking hot."

She kisses the air. "Right back at you."

A groan escapes and Scarlett wraps her arms around me.

"I'm sorry." I let my head rest on her shoulder.

"Why are you sorry?" she asks.

"You planned this epic night and I'm hiding in the bathroom."

"Oh please. You think I didn't expect at least one breakdown?" She pulls back, opens her purse, and pulls out a bag of Skittles.

If I were the crying type, I'd be in tears. Also, I think I already used up my quota this week.

"You really do know me better than anyone." I take them from her and clutch them to my chest. Scarlett is my soul sister.

"Still haven't heard from Sam?"

"Not a word, and Melody made it very clear that I'm either getting married this weekend or I'm finding myself a new job."

"Oh, honey." She rubs my shoulder. "What can I do?"

"Agree to marry me so I don't have to beg some guy off the street to be my groom."

"Is that what Melody told you to do?"

"More or less."

"That would be insane. Please tell me you told her no."

"It's not going to come to that. Sam and I are going to work this out. I love him and he loves me." Or he said he did. But if he loved me, why is he not answering my calls so we can talk and make up? I let out a long breath. "Okay, I'm ready. I'm saving these for later."

"Really?" She shakes her purse. "I wasn't expecting it to be this easy. I have other tricks up my sleeve."

"Yes. I will worry about all this tomorrow, when I'm hungover and hating my life decisions. Tonight, let's go boot scoot and boogie!" I shove the candy in my clutch. Those will taste even more delicious later.

"Damn, I'm good," she mutters as I tug her along behind me.

The rest of our group is already on the dance floor. The music has changed to something more upbeat. We dance until sweat trickles down my neck and the smile is back on my face.

"I need water!" Dakota yells over the music and fans her face.

"Me too."

The others stay. We squeeze into an open space at the bar, and while we wait for our drinks, she turns to face me.

"This is fun." She moves her hips to the beat. "I never had a bachelorette party."

"You didn't?"

"No." She chuckles softly. "Maverick and I got married on a drunken whim in Vegas."

"What?!" My jaw drops. "Seriously?"

"Yep."

"That's sort of awesome."

"It actually was, but it did mean I missed things like this."

"Then you absolutely need a turn wearing the veil." I slide the clip out of my hair.

"Oh no." She lifts a hand to stop me.

"You have to. I insist."

Dakota looks like she's going to protest again until I get the veil on her head. Then a big grin takes over her face.

The bartender sets our drinks, two waters and two shots of Fireball, down on the bar. He smiles at Dakota. "Getting married, huh?"

She glances at me before nodding.

"Congrats," he says. "These are on the house, and if you need one last fling…" He trails off and then winks.

"Damn. This thing is magical." She hands me a shot and takes the other.

"Maverick would kill him," I say, in case she's considering it.

"Oh, I know. Besides, it wouldn't compare."

"How do you mean?"

She smiles and seems to consider her words before she speaks. "You know how people always say they can't imagine sleeping with one person for the rest of their life?"

I nod.

"After the first time I had sex with Johnny, I couldn't imagine having sex with anyone else."

"He's that good?"

Her face flushes. "So good. Life changingly good. He completes me in ways I didn't think was possible."

I twist the empty glass around in my hand before setting it on the bar. Sex with Sam is good, but I've never described it as life-changing. And I've absolutely never heard someone say the words "he completes me" and not wanted to gag. But there is something in the way that Dakota says it that is so sincere, I get another one of those twinges of sadness.

"I'm sorry. We're coming up on our one-year anniversary and it has me all sappy." She tips her glass. "Plus, too much alcohol always makes me want to get naked."

"I could help with that." The guy next to her leans in closer.

We both start to laugh, but then a deep voice interrupts, "Like hell you will."

CHAPTER FIVE

Declan

HIS AND HER STRIPPERS

I rest a hand on Maverick's shoulder to keep him from pummeling the guy hitting on Dakota at the bar.

"Johnny!" She screams when she swivels around to see her husband. "What are you doing here?"

"Hey, baby."

Dakota launches herself at him and I move out of the way. Mav gives the guy behind her one last glare before kissing his wife. The two of them don't look like they're coming up for air anytime soon. I slide my gaze to Jade and lift a hand in a wave.

"Hi." An amused smirk twists her lips. I thought maybe she'd be upset about us crashing, but she keeps on smiling as she scans the bar to see the rest of the guys heading to their women.

Jack takes a step from behind me. "Hey, Jade. Happy bachelorette party."

"Thanks," she says with a laugh. "Are you guys the entertainment?"

Jack nods. "If Maverick ever removes his lips from Dakota's, I'd say there is a very good chance that he'll strip. Dude will use any excuse to get naked."

"I am out if that happens," I say. I've already seen Maverick's ass more times than I'd like.

Jack bellies up to the bar and orders a round of Jager Bombs. A few seconds later, everyone else has joined us. We throw back the shots and then the girls decide they're ready to head to the next bar.

I find myself walking next to the bride-to-be. She's in a sexy light-green dress that hugs her curves and stops miles above her knees. A white sash that says, 'BRIDE,' is draped over one shoulder and attached at the opposite hip, and she's wearing a beaded necklace that has little penises dangling from it.

All remnants of the teary-eyed girl I saw two days ago are gone. I want to ask how she's doing, but considering we're at her bachelorette party—celebrating the fact she's planning on walking down the aisle this weekend—it seems sort of tactless and unnecessary.

At the next bar, we grab two tables outside on a patio that overlooks the street traffic. We push them together to make room for everyone and more shots and drinks are downed.

The girls get up to dance in a small area in front of the DJ booth. They're the only ones out there, but they don't seem to care. And they're quite the sight, all of them in their sashes and bead necklaces.

"Damn. This is almost enough to make me want to get married," Ash says, smiling at the girls. Then he points from Tyler to Leo. "When are we having a couple of bachelor parties for you two? I could plan them. I know all the best places."

"He means strip clubs," Jack mutters under his breath.

"Scarlett wants to have a joint bachelor/bachelorette party at the beach somewhere," Leo says. Then adds, "She hasn't set a date yet."

"His and her strippers. I dig," Mav says.

Leo cuts him a look. "No strippers."

"Boo." Ash gives him a thumbs down.

"Joint parties seem like a good idea." Tyler tips the neck of his beer toward the dance floor. "Those guys are creeping."

"What is it about bachelorette parties that makes me want to show the bride a night she'll never forget?" Ash grins. "Not Jade, just, you know, generally speaking."

Tyler's brows lift and then he juts his chin to Leo. "Yeah, I think joint parties are a good call, man." He pushes his chair back and stands. "I'm going in."

"Me too," Leo and Maverick chime in at the same time.

"Ah, what the hell," Ash says with a grin as he dances his way to the group.

"What about you?" I say when it's just me and Jack.

"What about me?" His stare remains on the girls as he takes another sip of the whiskey in front of him.

"Think you'll get married someday?"

Jack huffs a short laugh. He tips his head in the slightest motion and I follow his gaze to find a girl across the room staring at him. She lifts one hand in a wave. I don't know how he does it. The man doesn't even need to speak to pick up girls.

"Someday, maybe." He drains his glass and then sets it on the table as he stands. "But not today."

I don't feel much like dancing, so I stay put, finish my drink, and then order another round for the group.

Leaning back in my chair, I don't have anything to do but people watch. It's a busy bar and our friends have garnered a crowd around them. Everyone's gravitating toward the fun. For some reason, Dakota is wearing a veil, but she takes it off now and puts it on the top of Jade's red hair.

She's something to look at in that little dress and veil falling over her shoulders. Her smile is ear-to-ear. Seems like things worked out between her and Sam. I don't know why, but that doesn't fill me with the relief I expected.

My phone vibrates in my pants. I shift and slide it from my pocket, gaze still locked on the happy bride-to-be. Reluctantly, I look at the screen in my hand and then wish I hadn't. Three texts within minutes of each other. *Where are you?* and *I need to talk to you,* and *I'm standing outside your place.*

Damn. She went to my house? I shouldn't hit her back, but the urgency of her texts has me worried. I stand and move through the bar to a quiet corner as I call her.

Crissy answers almost immediately.

"Hey," she says breathlessly. "Where are you? The lady across the hall is giving me a weird look."

She doesn't know I moved, and I start to tell her, but then think better of it.

"I'm out of town. Is everything okay?"

"No, everything is not okay. I miss you."

Annoyance claws at my chest. "We can't keep doing this. I'm not the guy for you."

"I want you any way I can have you."

Well, that feels…desperate and wrong, and like I'm a giant asshole that has reduced this girl to shucking her pride to give me what she thinks I want.

"I can do casual," she adds when I don't respond.

"We're done, Crissy."

"You don't mean that."

I hate that a tiny part of me suspects she's right. I have enough alcohol in my system that catching a ride back home for a hookup with Crissy sounds almost like a good idea. How long will my attempts to keep her away for her sake last? I can almost see the way it'll happen. A month will go by, she'll hit me up and say all the right things to convince me she can handle it, and then the next day, I'll hate myself again.

Jack would tell me there are too many girls out there to keep going back to Crissy, but I'm not Jack. Girls don't wave me over in a bar. I stay under the radar for the most part. Especially during the season. If she doesn't fall into my lap, it's too much effort. And the girls that fall into a hockey player's lap during the season are usually the kind that earn you a spot in the tabloids. No thanks.

"I do mean it. Don't call me again." I ball my fist at my side, hating myself a little for being such an asshole, but knowing it's necessary. "And stop knocking on my door. I don't live there anymore."

I hang up without waiting for her response, tip my head back, and growl deep in my throat. Fuck me. I stalk back to the table ready to toss back all the liquor I can find.

When I get there, Jade's left the group on the dance floor and sits alone at our table.

"Hey," I say, falling into a chair.

"I think you might need this more than me." She eyes me curiously and hands me the shot glass in her hand.

I don't ask questions, just throw it back. It's sweet, and I cough as it makes my mouth twist up.

"What was that?" I manage to choke out after a sip of water.

"Sex on the beach. Some guy ordered it for me."

My brows lift. "You were going to drink something some random guy handed you?"

"Relax." An amused smile tips up the corners of her mouth. "I watched the bartender make it." She sits back. "Besides, who is going to mess with me when I have half the Wildcats hockey team here to protect me?"

"Guys are assholes, so I doubt that would stop some creep from trying to get you into bed."

Her brows pinch together with a hint of worry. Fuck. I'm really on a roll tonight. I take a long pull of my beer to calm my nerves.

"I'm sorry. Of course, we're looking out for you. Have a good time. We've got you."

She lets out a small laugh. "I can take care of myself, but thanks."

I tip my beer to her in a gesture that I hope says, *sorry I'm an ass and you're welcome.*

"How come you aren't on the dance floor?" she asks me. There's a taunt in her gaze that tells me she knows it isn't my scene, but wants to hear me say it.

"I should be asking you the same thing."

"My feet hurt."

Instinctively, I let my gaze drop to her feet and the strappy sandals that lace around her ankles. They're as sexy as the rest of her.

"Ah," I say, the sound rough in my throat.

"And I was starting to feel like I was in the beginning of an orgy out there."

Some of the weight on my chest eases as I glance out at my teammates and their significant others. Dakota and Maverick are full-on making out, Leo has his hands on Scarlett's ass, and Tyler and

Piper aren't even really dancing—just staring into each other's eyes. And that's to say nothing of the girl humping Ash's leg or Jack, who is sitting at a private table with a girl on his lap. Things escalated quickly.

"Sorry about us all showing up and killing girl time."

"Please, like I didn't expect this," she says, and I'm surprised that there's no irritation in her tone or in her expression. Then she adds, "Leo texted me to make sure it was cool."

"You don't mind?"

"No." She shakes her head and briefly looks over her shoulder at our friends. "I love how in love they all are."

As if she's said more than she's comfortable with, she turns and hangs her head, staring down at the table.

"Are Sam and his friends coming too?"

"No." She still doesn't look up at me. "He went on a fishing trip."

"I'm glad you worked things out."

She pins me with those big dark eyes and smiles in a way that feels more sad than happy. "Thanks."

CHAPTER SIX

Jade

YOU'RE EASY TO READ, BUT HARD TO FIGURE OUT

"There is no sitting down at a bachelorette party." Scarlett pulls me to my feet. "We still have so many more things to cross off the list."

"What list?" Ash asks.

The girl he was dancing with followed him back to our table. Everyone else has returned as well, except Jack.

Piper produces the scavenger hunt list and Ash and Maverick read through my remaining tasks: do a blow job shot, use the men's bathroom, get carried into a bar.

"Bring on the shot," I say. I am almost to that happy drunken state, where I won't care that my fiancé called off the wedding I'm pretending to be celebrating. Almost. My optimism for getting him back is at an all-time low. I'm sure tomorrow I will wake up and find that spark of hope again, but right now, I'm just really sad and frustrated about it all.

Dakota gets me the shot from the bar, and I reach for it.

"Oh no," she says. "A blow job shot can only be taken one way."

"The list does not specify," I say, knowing exactly what she means but not wanting to ask some random guy if I can take a shot from between his legs.

"You know very well that's what it meant," Scarlett insists. She scans the bar. "Want me to find the lucky guy?"

"Is it really necessary?" My question is lost in the excitement of my friends sizing up all the available men.

"What about Dec?" Tyler asks.

Everyone stops and stares at the man sitting across from me. I don't know Declan that well, but something about him seems different tonight. He's always quiet and stays out of the center of attention, but earlier, he almost looked angry. It was a good look on him, not going to lie, but I can't help but wonder what had him all worked up like that. Does he date? I never thought to ask before, but now I really want to know.

He doesn't say anything, and before I know it, I'm being ushered around to him as the shot glass is placed between his massive thighs.

An unexpected rush of heat hits my cheeks as I squat in front of him. He spreads his legs farther, and I rest my palms on his knees for balance. He's warm and hard under my touch. I glance up at him. His eyes are a dark shade of brown with flecks of green I've never noticed before. A small scar above his lip and the short scruff coating his jawline interrupts his otherwise perfect features.

All eyes are on me as I inch closer. My hair falls into my face and one of his big hands comes forward to hold it back for me. Another rush of heat warms my face as our friends cackle. We've just turned this blow job shot scenario into an even more accurate roleplay.

"Sorry." I think I hear him murmur.

I remove one of my hands from his leg and hold my own hair. That'd be more accurate for the BJ scenarios of my life anyway. Wrapping my lips around the small glass, I tip it back, once more making eye contact with Declan. The whipped cream makes it hard for the liquor to trickle out of the glass, but eventually, I swallow it all down.

I hold up the empty glass for everyone to see and wipe my mouth.

"Damn. This is what girls do at bachelorette parties?" Leo asks. He turns to Scarlett. "We're definitely having a joint party."

Declan takes my free hand and helps me to my feet.

"Thanks," I say, meeting his gaze and still blushing. "You're a good sport."

"It's anything but a hardship to have a gorgeous girl kneeling in front of me."

I can't think of what to say to that, but thankfully Declan tips his head and asks, "Can I buy you a real drink?"

"Yes, please."

I follow him to the bar, and he pulls out the only remaining seat for me and orders us two tequilas.

"Tequila is a real drink?" I ask, as the bartender pours it into the shot glasses and adds a lemon to the side.

"It's honest. No frills." He thanks the bartender and pushes one of the glasses toward me.

I pick it up, trying not to smell the strong liquor. He removes the lemon from his and tosses it onto a napkin.

"To you," he says, lifting the glass and nodding at me.

"To me," I mutter. Now that's a cheers I can get behind. The tequila burns. I slam the empty glass down, suck on my lemon, and then steal his. "I think I'm done for the night. Any more and I'm going to have to be carried out of here."

"We can arrange that." He smirks. He asks for a couple of waters and another round of shots, then leans a hip against the bar, staring at me in a way that makes me fidget. When the bartender brings the shots, he pushes one toward me and then takes his without waiting.

I watch as his throat works and then let myself scope out his broad chest and muscular arms. Declan is a sexy guy and easy to talk to; plus, he's a famous hockey player. It brings me back to my earlier thoughts.

"Do you have a girlfriend?"

He fights a grin and shakes his head. "No."

"Why not?"

The smile breaks free.

"You're an attractive guy, with money, and mostly-tolerable friends."

"Those the requirements these days?" Those green flecks in his eyes twinkle with amusement.

"It puts you head and shoulders above ninety-percent of the population, so yes. What gives?"

He doesn't look like he's going to give me anything, so I add, "It's my last night out on the town as a single gal, give me some hot gossip."

"I don't really have time for dating right now," he says, not quite meeting my gaze.

"No."

"No?"

I glance over at our friends. "That might work on other girls, but I've seen it firsthand with Leo and Tyler. If you wanted to make time, you would."

"I don't know." He shifts uncomfortably and then motions with his head to his teammates. "I'm not sure that is in the cards for me."

"Something wrong with you?" I let my gaze drop to his crotch.

He laughs again. A deep, throaty sound I've never heard from him. It's like taking another shot of alcohol, the way it warms my insides and makes me lightheaded.

"No. I'm good. I guess I just haven't found that."

"Something tells me you haven't looked very hard."

His phone buzzes, and he pulls it free from his pocket to look at the screen. When he does, his jaw flexes. He shoves it back in his pocket, then gives me his full attention. "Oh, yeah. Got me all figured out, do you?"

I nod. "I'm getting there. Another hour and I'd have the name of the first girl you had sex with, your social security number, and your blood type."

He laughs again. It's a great laugh and I love being responsible for it.

I meet his stare head on and lean forward. "You're a good teammate and friend. You're handsome, but don't notice when girls try to get your attention. And the way you look right now—like you want to flee from this conversation—tells me you're uncomfortable with praise. You're either not used to getting it, which I would find hard to believe, or you have a hard time believing you're worthy of it. Which I also would find hard to believe. Actually, I take back what I said. You're easy to read, but hard to figure out."

He shifts so his back is against the bar and he stares out at the rest of the space. He flicks his gaze to me and then back around to the people dancing and those sitting at tables. "I think you're full of shit. I don't see any girls trying to get my attention."

Without looking, I say, "Far right corner in the red dress. She glances over every thirty seconds or so. I think she's trying to decide if you're my fiancé."

I count slowly under my breath and true to my words, she looks over in about twenty seconds. I take the tequila shot in front of me as Declan's stuck in a stare off with his admirer.

"I'll be damned," he mutters. I fully expect him to leave me. I'm not great company and he already got the only blow job he's getting from me tonight. He turns and closes out with the bartender. I stand, ready to go back to my friends. I think they might have one more bar in them before they all want to rush back to the hotel and get freaky with their guys. Dakota and Maverick may not even last that long. I smile as I watch them dance. They're so in love. So, so in love.

I open my mouth to thank Declan for the drink. He holds out a hand. "Wanna dance?"

My hesitation only lasts a second. I slip my palm into his, enjoying the rough feel against mine. He doesn't let go until we're in the middle of our friends. The guys are pumped to see him out there. They crowd around and joke about his moves, but he takes it all in stride. He's actually not a bad dancer, and when he grins at me under the terrible bar lighting, I can't help but smile back.

When the music turns to something slower, we decide to leave and go to the bar next door. Jack is still missing, but Ash says not to worry, so we go on without him.

"Wait, wait," Scarlett says before I walk in behind her. "It's your last chance to be carried into a bar."

I glance around at the empty sidewalk. The only guy out here, a security guard, cuts me a look that says, *don't even ask, sweetheart.*

But before I know it, Declan is back outside, sweeping my legs out from underneath me and cradling me to his chest. Gosh, he's strong. He walks in and takes a couple extra steps before setting me on my feet.

"Thanks." I pull at the hem of my dress and adjust my veil. "I'm sorry you keep getting roped into being my random guy."

"I thought we already established I don't mind in the least."

We settle into a couple of pushed-together tables. I find myself next to Declan again. Scarlett makes us all squeeze in for photos. The reminder of work and that I'm going to have to write an article all about this night makes a knot form in my stomach. I excuse myself under the guise of getting drinks. I order a round of rum and Cokes and then pull out my phone.

I can't take the silent treatment any longer. I call Sam for what has to be the hundredth time. I'm reaching stalker status and I don't feel great about it.

"Hello?" Sam's voice is nearly drowned out by the noise of the bar, but it slams into me as if he'd screamed.

"Oh my god, you answered." I hold up a finger to the bartender to let him know I'll be right back and hurry outside. "I have called you like a million times. Is reception crappy at the lake house?"

Before he can answer, I hit the FaceTime button. I want to see him. I *need* to see him.

When his face fills the screen, I breathe a little easier.

"Hi," I say again.

"Hey, Jade."

It's when he says my name that I notice the background and then more closely scrutinize his put-together appearance. He's clean-shaven and wearing his preppy clothes that he usually reserves for special nights out. There's no trace of the guy that walked away from his fiancée earlier this week, and he definitely doesn't look like he's in a fishing cabin with his buddies.

I'm not sure what I expected; it isn't like I've been wearing sweats and eating ice cream out of the tub, but it still hurts to see him look so unaffected.

"Where are you?"

"North Dakota."

I fight back irritation. He left the freaking state without telling me? Has it really gotten to this point?

"North Dakota?! I thought you were fishing with your friends. I've been trying to call you."

"I know. I needed some time."

All things considered, I guess that's fair, but this isn't just about us. There are a lot of things to figure out in a short amount of time.

"The wedding is Saturday."

"I know. That's why I answered. I was going to call tomorrow after your bachelorette party, but I figured if you were calling, then maybe you hadn't gone."

"Of course, I went. Scarlett spent a lot of time putting it together."

He nods but says nothing.

"What are we doing, Sam?"

"I thought about it a lot. I care about you, I do. And I know how much it means to you, but I can't go through with this."

I squeeze my eyes shut. I think I knew this was the outcome the second he answered the phone, but his words still shred my insides.

"You said you loved me," I whisper, voice hoarse. When he doesn't reply, I add, "Please? I will lose everything."

"Jade, it's just a job."

"Not to me." My eyes pop open. He knows what my career means to me. It will give me the stability and independence that I have craved since I was little.

He runs a hand over his perfectly styled hair. "Can't they issue some sort of statement and call it good? Engagements end all the time."

"Is that what's happening?" I swallow the lump in my throat. "Are we really breaking up?"

"Do you even want to be with me? Really?" he asks incredulously, brows raised.

"Of course, I do. I've spent months planning this wedding."

"You didn't answer the question, Jade. Forget the wedding, do you want to be with *me*?" He taps his chest. "We had fun in the beginning and then we moved in together, and…" His sentence trails off. "Let's face it, neither of us saw it going this far."

"That's not true." I cross one arm at my waist, as if I can protect myself from the blow he's dealing.

He lets his hand fall. "It doesn't matter anyway. I'm not just in North Dakota visiting. I've decided to move back home."

"To North Dakota?" In all the time we've dated, not once has he mentioned wanting to go back to his home state to live.

"Yeah. I applied for a job a few weeks ago and they flew me out for an interview yesterday."

"Weeks ago?" Anger makes my voice shrill. "When were you going to tell me?"

He sighs. "It gives us a clean break. We can both figure out what it is we really want."

"A clean break? Maybe for you. What am I supposed to tell people? My boss is expecting us to get married. Married!"

"I don't know." He waves his hand dismissively. "Tell them whatever you want. That's what you've been doing all along, right?"

I'm fuming and stunned. Hot tears prick the back of my eyes. I will absolutely not let him see me cry. "That's not fair. You agreed to this and now you're making it out like you never wanted this."

Like he never wanted me.

"I did. You're right. But at least I stopped it before we made a huge mistake."

I bite the inside of my cheek to stop the tears. It hurts worse than I'd like to admit, hearing him call our almost marriage a huge mistake.

He walks through what I assume is his parents' house. Pictures in ornate frames hang on a wall behind him. "The apartment is paid for through the end of the month. You can have any of the furniture you want. I took everything I wanted with me."

Great. I'll be homeless, but at least I'll have a used couch that reminds me of him every time I sit on it. How can he be so callous about all of this? Twelve months and it's like it meant nothing.

When I still don't speak, he adds, "I'm sure you're going to write about this, but if you could leave my name out of it, I would appreciate it."

I huff a laugh.

"You owe me that much," he says.

I swipe at a tear the second it defies me and slides out the corner of my eye. Like I'd want anyone to know about this. It shows how little he really knows me.

"I'm sorry it had to end like this."

"Yeah, I bet," I mutter.

"Bye, Jade."

When he ends the call, I finally let myself cry. It's over. I can't believe it.

What the hell am I going to do now?

CHAPTER SEVEN

Jade

MATCHMAKER

"**A**re you okay?"

I glance over to see Declan, standing a step outside of the bar. I'm not even surprised he followed me. One thing I know for sure about Declan, he notices things other people don't.

"Yeah." I nod and pull myself together.

"No, you're not." His jaw hardens and he looks around like he's hoping to find some jerk who made me cry so that he can kick their ass. I wish he could. "What happened?"

I clear my throat and squeeze my phone in my hand. "That was Sam. It's over."

"Shit. I'm sorry. I thought…"

Shaking my head, I speak before he can finish the sentence. "That was the first time I've talked to him since I saw you Monday. I hoped we could still work things out."

He studies me silently.

"I'm having my bachelorette party for a wedding that isn't happening. God, how pathetic am I?"

"You're not pathetic."

"No?"

"Never." He steps forward and runs his thumb underneath my left eye to remove the smudged makeup. "Drink? Dance? What do you need?"

"A drink sounds good." More like a dozen of them.

He stares at me a beat longer, before stepping back toward the bar and holding the door open for me.

The rum and Cokes I ordered are waiting for me. I take a long drink of one, then ask the bartender for two tequilas for Declan and me.

Declan lifts a brow in surprise. I wave a hand toward the veil and sash, reminding him I'm a jilted bride-to-be. "I should have yelled at him. Think I should call him back and tell him he's lousy in bed?"

He isn't, but it might feel good to yell it in his face.

I pull out my phone and Declan promptly grabs it. "Definitely not."

"I'm so mad," I say, but I'm sad too. Part of me knows I pushed Sam too far, but I can't find it in me to regret getting engaged.

"I'm holding onto this," he says and slides my phone into his front jeans pocket. "If he's truly bad in bed then I think you're better off."

A small laugh escapes me. Declan offers me a crooked smile. "It still sucks to have to call off the wedding, though. I'm sorry."

"I'm not calling off the wedding," I say and drain the rest of the rum and Coke. Declan is quick to order me another.

"I don't understand," he says.

"My boss told me that the wedding is happening with or

without me."

"She could just replace you? How's that work?"

"She would spin it to say that I was writing the articles for another bride. A million girls would kill to have the kind of wedding I planned. I'm sure she'd have no problem finding one to take my place."

"Damn. That's cold."

"She's ruthless."

"Almost sounds like you admire her for it." He grins.

"Oh, I do. She gets shit done for sure. Plus, I did sort of do this to myself."

He takes one of the tequila shots as soon as the bartender puts them in front of us. "What are you going to do?"

"I'm not going down like this." I don't blame Declan for looking unconvinced. "If Sam won't marry me, then I guess I'll let Melody play matchmaker and find me a groom."

His brows shoot up toward his dark, messy hair. "Find you a groom?"

I tell him everything Melody said earlier today and all the ways this could play out as well as the repercussions. I expected at least a little judgment from him, but if he thinks I've lost my mind, he doesn't show it.

"Please don't tell anyone else. If this got out—"

He lifts a hand. "I would never. Your secret is safe with me."

"Thank you."

"You'd really let your boss bully you into marrying some guy of her choosing?"

"As opposed to what?" I throw up my hands. How could I expect him to understand? He's a successful hockey player, loved and adored by his teammates and fans. I'm a girl still fighting to show my worth and earn respect. "I can't exactly call up every guy I know and ask if they want to marry me, so I can keep my job. I need this job."

"What about your family? Can they help you out while you find something else?"

I shake my head. "My mom is the only family I have, and we're not close. I don't have family like that. The kind that swoops in to save the day. Except Scarlett. She's not blood, but she's the only person in my life that's always had my back when I needed it."

When I dare to look at him, his face holds more understanding than I expected.

"And what happens after you marry this random guy?"

"I'm not sure," I admit. "I imagine we'd have to stay married for a few months to make it all look legit, but since I never used Sam's name or photo in the magazine, I don't think it would be that hard to convince people. No one besides my friends and his would know the truth. And Melody, of course, but she's the last person who would out me."

I turn and find our friends dancing again. Seeing them happy actually brightens my mood a little. Were Sam and I ever like that?

"I'm sure once the wedding is over, all the interest in my articles will die off and I can get divorced and move on to writing about something else, without anyone noticing or caring." Except that's another fear of mine. There is no better feeling than having people read and connect with my words. I don't want to keep lying, but I also don't want to lose everything I've worked for. It's all I have left now.

"You think I'm crazy, don't you?"

"No, actually."

"That makes one of us." I blow out a breath. "I thought this was going to be my break. Melody is a big name in publishing, and *I Do* is one of the few magazines around that still has a print presence. I always dreamed of seeing my words in a magazine you could pick up in a grocery store."

His smile puts me at ease and even though I doubt he wanted to hear my life story tonight, I keep rambling, "I know it's gauche to say, but I want the kind of success that means I never have to rely on someone else."

"Yeah, I get that. I think I felt the same way when I signed my first NHL contract."

"Really?" I try to picture a younger version of the man in front of me. I've always looked at him as someone who had it easy, but it's so much simpler to look at the success and not consider the road he had to take to get there.

"Really. I didn't have a lot of people I could count on when I was starting out either. It took me a long time to spend the money I was making. I drove this old Honda that broke down every other day. Jack gave me so much shit about it."

"Saving it in case it all blew up?"

"Exactly." He lets out a little chuckle. Even after the sound falls away, his smile remains. "I think we're more alike than I thought."

I want to ask him what he thought I was like, but I'm not brave enough. I can't take another ego hit tonight.

I take the last tequila shot. *Oh, I'm going to regret that one tomorrow.* "Thanks for making this night suck a lot less. For a few minutes, the prospect of figuring out how I'm going to pull off a wedding without a groom didn't seem so bad."

"I'd do it. I'd marry you, if you wanted."

Too many seconds pass before his words sink in. My head snaps up and a small giggle escapes my lips. I wait for him to tell me he's kidding or to laugh, something, anything to acknowledge the hilarity of his words.

"Why?" I finally ask, when it's still unclear if he's joking or not.

The girls yell for me to join them on a little makeshift dance floor in front of the jukebox as "Single Ladies" starts playing.

"Does it matter why?" He lifts one shoulder in a shrug and pays for our drinks.

My head spins. Piper and Dakota come over and drag me out to dance with them before I can think of what else to say. Declan follows, standing with the guys off to the side and watching us dance our hearts out to Beyonce.

I meet his gaze as my friends scream the lyrics around me. I'm still waiting for him to crack a smile or do something to indicate it's all some elaborate joke. Why in the world would Declan want to marry me?

And why do I not totally hate the idea of taking him up on it?

I don't get any more alone time with Declan Wednesday night. We hit one more bar and then crash at the hotel. Thursday morning, we all have breakfast together before we head back, but all I can do is focus on not throwing up.

Scarlett drops me at my apartment with a smile and a squeeze. I didn't have it in me to tell anyone else about my conversation with Sam. I will, just not today.

"See you tomorrow," she calls as I walk up to my apartment building.

It's strange being back in the small apartment I share with Sam.

Shared, I guess. I keep thinking he'll show up any minute and tell me he changed his mind and can't live without me. He doesn't, of course, so I throw myself into work. There are a million last minute things to do before the wedding. I'm writing two articles that will run while I'm on my honeymoon. One on gifts for the wedding party and another on the rehearsal dinner.

The actual wedding article is going to be written by Melody herself and will be the feature story of the summer print issue. I get to do a follow-up in the fall issue, a short piece on the honeymoon and life as a newlywed. It could very well be the break I've been waiting for since I penned that first blog post on wedding cake.

I have my eye on a Features Editor position. Rumor has it that there's going to be an opening soon and I want it. I want it badly. The pay is better and it's one step closer to my goal. But do I want it bad enough that I'll marry someone besides Sam? Ugh.

On Friday, I still don't have my answer, but everyone else is carrying on like this wedding is happening, so I do too. Scarlett is hosting a brunch at her house with just us girls, and I show up, hoping an afternoon with my friends will provide some sort of clarity.

I know the sensible solution is to suck it up, tell Melody the wedding is off, and face the consequences, but I just can't seem to make myself do it.

She has connections all over. Plus, the exposure of the articles has been more than I ever could have dreamed (that was a positive until now). There is no way I'm going to get another job in this city if I mess this up. I'll be the girl that faked an engagement or the bride expert whose fiancé dumped her the week of her wedding. I'll have to move, change my name, and start all over. New York City has too many people for me and California is too blonde. And dammit, I don't want to go down like this.

Piper, Dakota, and Scarlett stare at me intently as I tell them about my conversation with Sam.

"It's really over?" Piper asks, a hint of hope still present in her tone.

"Yeah. He's gone." I set my mimosa on the table in front of me. "If I can't find somewhere cheap to live in the next week, I'm going to be homeless on top of everything else."

I can't afford our apartment on just my salary. My paycheck as a staff writer for the magazine is barely enough to cover half the rent.

"You can move in here," Scarlett says so matter-of-factly that my heart squeezes in my chest at the offer. I really hope I don't have to take her up on it. She and Leo just moved in together a few months ago. They don't want a third wheel around.

"How are you going to tell everyone about the wedding?" Dakota asks.

"I'm not." I stuff a cracker stacked with three kinds of cheese into my mouth.

"Good. Make Melody deal with all that," Scarlett says.

We're sitting outside on the patio. The house has a great outdoor space and today is the perfect day to use it—warm, sunny, with a light breeze. The doors from the dining room are pushed open, and I can faintly hear Leo, Tyler, and Ash inside playing video games.

Piper nods her agreement, and my palms start to sweat as I reach for the courage to tell my friends I'm still going through with the wedding regardless of Sam backing out.

I love my friends. I value their thoughts and know they always want what is best for me, but my mind is made up and they aren't going to like my decision.

"No, I meant I'm not going to call off the wedding."

Silence hangs around us.

"I don't understand," Piper finally says. "You just said Sam is gone."

"He is."

Dakota gives me a small smile. "I think people will notice if your groom is missing."

"No one knows who my groom is. Well, no one but you guys. He didn't want his name or photo included in the articles."

Scarlett's face pales. "Jade, no."

"What?" Dakota glances around, trying to piece together my plan.

"I don't see any other way." My voice climbs defensively. "If I don't go through with the wedding, I'll lose my job."

"Then get another job." Scarlett leans forward and her eyes widen as she stares at me like she doesn't recognize me, or maybe who I've become. She doesn't get it. She grew up with two loving parents, who provided everything she could want. She's worked hard at her photography, don't get me wrong, but she doesn't know what it's like to have nothing and no family to depend on if everything falls apart.

I hang tight to my resolve. "I love my job and I've worked too hard to quit now."

"Wait a minute." Piper raises both hands. "Did I miss something? Who are you going to marry?"

Twisting my fingers in my lap, I keep my gaze locked on my chipped pink nail polish as I open my mouth to speak.

A deep, confident voice answers before I work up the courage. "Me."

My friends' heads snap to the doorway where Declan stands, but his stare is locked on me.

I open my mouth to speak, but nothing comes out. Piper's eyes are the size of saucers and Scarlett squeaks but can't seem to make her voice work either.

I stand quickly and walk toward Declan, grabbing him and pulling him inside.

"What are you doing?" I whisper, or at least I try to whisper. My heart is beating so loudly it's hard to tell if I manage it.

"I didn't have your number, but Leo mentioned you were coming over today."

"No." I shake my head. "I mean, why did you just tell them that we're getting married?"

"I told you the other night I would do it."

"I appreciate how sweet you were that night. I was drunk. You were drunk. We both said things we might not have with a clearer mind."

"I wasn't that drunk, and I meant it. I'll marry you."

"You can't just say that."

"Why not?"

"I don't know." I cross my arms over my chest, then immediately drop them. "Everyone thinks I've lost my mind. Now they are going to think you have too."

He shrugs. "It's none of their business."

With a roll of my eyes, I say, "Have you met our friends?"

"Look, if you don't want me to be the guy, fine, but I stand by my offer."

Is he serious? Of course, I'd rather marry Declan, a cute and nice hockey player, than resorting to Tim or any of the other options Melody might have found. But can I really let him do this?

I feel my gaze narrow and some unfamiliar emotion swirls in my stomach. "Why?"

He's dressed in black jeans and a white T-shirt. So casual and chill as he offers himself up like it's no big deal to marry a girl you barely know.

"I understand your situation. I've been there. Talking to you the other night reminded me what it was like."

"But this is huge. I can't let you do this."

"Sure, you can. Everyone should have people that will show up for them. Let me be one of those people for you."

"I still don't understand."

"Call it me paying it forward if you want." His fingers brush against mine, and a little jolt shoots up my arm. "I see you. You work hard, you have big dreams, and you just need a little help right now."

I finally place the emotion still swirling through me. It's relief at finally having a solution that doesn't totally suck.

"Thank you." My heart is racing as I start to let the idea really sink in.

"We're doing this?"

I swallow the lump in my throat. "If you're sure."

"I'm sure."

"Thank you. Really. It doesn't seem like nearly enough words to express my gratitude."

"It's more than I need." He smiles. "What now?"

CHAPTER EIGHT

Declan

YOU JUST UPPED THE ANTE

We're interrupted before Jade can respond to my question. Scarlett steps in from outside, glancing between us. She holds out a phone to Jade. "Sorry to interrupt. Your mom has called twice."

She takes the phone and stares at it with a look of shock or disbelief on her beautiful features. "My mom. Crap. I forgot she's going to the resort today. She wants to help decorate even though I told her that was already being handled. I need to go make sure she doesn't cause a scene."

"Do you want me to go?" Scarlett asks. "I can manage Momma Davis."

"No, I've got her." Jade's mouth pulls into a tight line, while she continues to stare at her phone, then she looks up at me through thick, dark lashes. "Can you come with me?"

As soon as she's asked, she seems more nervous and unsure. She adds, "It'll give us time to talk."

"Yeah." Suddenly my nerves amp up too.

"Jade, wait," Scarlett calls as we start for the door.

The two women share a look that I can't decipher, then Jade goes to Scarlett and hugs her hard. I glance away to give them a moment of privacy, and then a few seconds later, Jade is back by my side.

"Ready?"

As she drives to the resort, Jade lays out the plan. "If we're going to do this, we need to get our story straight and establish some rules. A few people have met Sam, but most haven't, and I've never mentioned him in the articles, so you should be easy enough to explain. Your middle name doesn't happen to be Sam, does it?" She briefly removes her stare from the road to look at me.

"No." I shake my head.

"It's fine. I'll tell them you didn't want your real name to get out before the wedding since you're a local celebrity."

An involuntary groan escapes.

"No?" She makes a turn into the hotel parking lot.

"It makes me sound like a diva."

She parks and kills the engine. "No, not a diva. Someone who values privacy in his personal life. Do you have an agent or PR person we need to work with for an official statement?"

My throat tightens, and this small car starts to close in on me.

"Look. It's a lot. If you're having second thoughts, say the word."

"And then what would you do?"

"I haven't a clue." She blows out a breath that lifts the short, red bangs off her forehead.

"I'll call my agent this afternoon." I have no idea how I'm going to word that conversation.

"Okay." She rests both hands on top of the steering wheel. "What about your mom? Has she not met Sam before?"

"Definitely not," she says. Then sinks back into the seat. "My mom and I don't have a great relationship."

I nod slowly. I assumed as much from what little she said at the bachelorette party.

Jade must feel like she needs to tell me more, or maybe she's just stalling, because she continues, "My dad walked out when I was a baby, and the next eighteen years of my life, she dated one loser after another. I'm sure she'd say it was all in the name of love, but we moved around a lot, and it was hard and frustrating. She always seemed to care about them more than me, you know? Sounds petty and childish saying it now. Anyway, I left as soon as I graduated high school."

"I'm sorry."

She shakes her head. "I just thought you should understand the situation."

"Okay."

Angling her body toward mine, she asks, "Do you have family we need to…"

"No, no family."

"Well, that's lucky," she mutters, then curses. "I'm sorry. I didn't mean it like that."

"It's fine," I say. "Is your boss going to be cool with this? With me?"

"Are you kidding? She's going to be thrilled. You just upped the ante."

I stare at her with confusion, and she lets out a little laugh.

"You may not like being referred to as a local celebrity, but you are. She's going to eat this up. Trust me. We will probably have to keep up the story for six months or so, until we can go our separate ways, without causing a big stir. By then, hopefully, I'll be writing about ring insurance or beauty trends instead of the life of a bride. Does six months work for you?"

I incline my head as I think. Six months doesn't seem like such a big deal. Once the season starts, I'll be so busy that the days always pass in a blur. "That puts us in late December. I'd want to wait until after the season to make a big announcement, so it doesn't take focus away from the team."

"Of course. That shouldn't be a problem." She rubs her lips together as she studies me. "I swear I'll stop asking this, but are you sure? We barely know each other, and even in the best-case scenario, we're going to have to spend a lot of time together in the next six months."

Something in the panic of her voice, combined with her ability to worry about me instead of herself in a time when it's her life on the verge of blowing up, has me reaching across the console and taking her hand, interlacing our fingers. Her skin is soft and her long nails scrape against my knuckles as she squeezes my hand back.

"I'm sure."

"O-kay. I guess we're doing this then," she says quietly. "Ready to meet my mom?"

I drop her hand, and she reaches for the door handle.

"Eric," I say before we get out, "my middle name is Eric."

A relieved smile lights up her face. "Nice to meet you, Declan Eric Sato."

CHAPTER NINE

Jade

IF YOU TRIP, I'LL CATCH YOU

Later that night, Declan and I show up at the rehearsal prepared to face Melody. As I predicted, she's tickled to find out my new groom is a Wildcat hockey player.

"Do you have some sort of legal agreement on this?" She taps away on her phone like she's taking notes. "A prenup, for example?"

"Oh." I glance at Declan.

"My lawyer sent one over. I was going to talk to you about it later."

"Of course." My face flushes with embarrassment. "I'll sign whatever you want. I don't want your money. Six months of your life is more than enough payment."

Melody lowers her phone. "Six months?"

Before either of us can respond, she shakes her head. "No. That isn't long enough. One year minimum. I'm not throwing a wedding that doesn't make it to year one. I'll be laughed out of a job."

Declan doesn't speak, but a muscle in his jaw ticks.

"It'll be great for both of you," Melody insists. "Jade can continue writing, focusing now on the first year of marriage. People will be begging for behind-the-scenes content about what it's like to be married to an NHL player. And, Declan, this is the kind of press that will skyrocket you from a quiet, pro athlete to someone getting national endorsements and attention."

He doesn't look completely on board, but doesn't say no.

"We'll talk about it tonight," I say. "Can I let you know?"

She sighs loudly and shoves her phone into her Prada bag. "Tonight. Before midnight. But, Jade, this kind of opportunity won't fall into your lap again."

I hate that she's right. Hate even more that it puts Declan in this position.

"I'll see you two in the morning," she says, then casts one more smile at Declan before she leaves.

I blow out a long breath and resist asking him if he's really, *really* sure he wants to do this.

"That went well," he says.

"Yeah." A little laugh with no joy behind it slips from my lips.

"They're waiting for us." He nods his head toward the barn, where the ceremony and reception are both happening tomorrow.

"Go ahead. I'll be right there."

I go in after him, but only to find the bathroom, so I can splash water on my face. "I hope you know what you're doing," I whisper to my reflection.

The door creaks open and Scarlett and Piper step inside.

"Hey," they say in unison.

"Hi." The word comes out on a near-sob. I have got to get it together.

"Oh, honey. You don't need to do this," Scarlett says, rushing to my side. "Whatever happens, we will figure it out together. You can live with me and Leo. I asked him, he said it was fine. And I bet Mike would hire you at the bar until you could find something else."

"No," I say, my resolve firming under their scrutiny, "I'm doing this. I know it isn't the perfect love story you both have, but I'm not you. I never wanted to get married anyway, so what does it matter if it's Sam or Declan?" It isn't that simple, but maybe it should be. "You can either support me or not, but I've made up my mind. I'm going to get married tomorrow."

Piper squeezes my arm. "We're just worried. This is a big deal."

"I know."

They share a worried look, but then Scarlett nods. "Okay. I think you're making a mistake, but I love you."

I get hugged from both sides. If I weren't keeping myself together by burying every emotion threatening to bubble up to the surface, I'd be teary at their willingness to love me through all the chaos. They're good friends. The best. I know they don't get it, but I *have* to do this.

"But if at any point you change your mind, I'll have a car on standby," Scarlett says.

The actual rehearsal goes by in a whirlwind. I feel like I'm in someone else's body as I walk down the aisle toward Declan. He has Leo and Tyler standing up with him, and Scarlett and Piper are on my side. My mother watches from a chair in the front row with a tissue in her hand, dabbing at her eyes as we recite our vows. How she can still feel emotional about weddings after three of her own is beyond me.

If my stand-in groom is nervous, he has the coolest poker face I've ever seen. As he holds my hands in front of the officiant, his confidence slowly steadies the shake of my fingers and the racing of my heart. It's all over in minutes and then the guys are loosening their ties and heading for the door.

Declan lingers with me at the front of the room under the floral archway. "I know it's traditional to have a rehearsal dinner, but the guys want to take me out, and I overheard that Scarlett is hosting a girls-only sleepover."

I can't imagine eating right now. I also wonder if his friends wanting to take him out is an intervention like the one Scarlett and Piper obviously had planned for me earlier. "It's fine. I didn't expect you to put one together."

"All right. So, I'll see you tomorrow?"

"What about Melody and the prenup and everything?"

"I'll drop it by Leo's before we go out, so you can look it over. Have your lawyer read it and if you have any issues with it, just note them and I'll get it updated."

I love that he thinks I'm the kind of person who has a lawyer on standby.

He must read my hesitation.

"It's a pretty standard prenup."

"And what about Melody's condition of one year instead of six months?"

"One year is fine. My agent actually suggested the same thing. That puts us in the off-season and the marriage will have lasted long enough that there won't be any speculation on why it ended so quickly."

"Oh." I bite the inside of my cheek as I nod.

He steps forward until I can feel the warmth radiating off him. "You keep asking me, but are you sure that *you* want to do this?"

I stare up at him, leaning into him the tiniest bit, just to feel how strong and steady he is. I need a little of that to make it through the next twenty-four hours. "Yeah. One year isn't that long, right?"

He chuckles. "What time do you want me to pick you up tomorrow?"

"I'll get a ride with Scarlett. You aren't supposed to see me until I walk down the aisle."

"Right. Okay, then. I guess I'll see you tomorrow at the wedding."

"I'll be the one in white, trying not to trip up the aisle."

"If you trip, I'll catch you." One side of his mouth quirks up as he walks off.

CHAPTER TEN

Declan

TRUTH SERUM

After repeated attempts to get me to the strip club, we end up at Wild's at our usual table.

"Trying to get me drunk?" I ask, as Jack sets down three pitchers of beer and Maverick follows with a dozen shots.

"A little truth serum," Leo states, resting both elbows on the table.

"I already told you guys everything." Or everything I'm going to tell them.

"What I don't understand is why she would ask you instead of me?" Ash asks, sounding genuinely miffed.

Laughing, I grab one of the shots and toss it back.

"I think it's dope," Maverick says. "I can see you two together."

"Sure, Jade's great," Jack says. "But you don't need to marry her. Date, talk, hook up, whatever. Marriage is forever, or at least the paperwork is."

"How's this going to work when you two part ways?" Tyler asks.

"Piper and Scarlett are tight with Jade. You're my teammate. It's a tangled web."

"I appreciate the concern, but it's misguided. I'm helping her out, that's all."

The guys stare at me in disbelief.

I don't owe them an explanation, but I give them one anyway. "I understand her and the situation. I've been where she is. When I was playing in the minor league, I worked two side jobs to keep myself afloat, all while busting my ass to get the call up. Times were tough, and like Jade, I didn't have family that could help me out if things went sideways."

Silence falls over the table.

"Fuck, man. I'm sorry," Leo says.

"I understand her, and it feels good to help someone now that everything is solid in my life." I finally feel like I'm getting some acceptance and understanding out of them.

A grin takes over Ash's face. "Okay, but what about sex?"

"Oh yeah. How's that gonna work? Are you going to consummate the marriage or work out some other system?" Mav's eyes light up. "Or do you put a sock on the front door when you bring a chick back?"

In truth, I hadn't thought about sex, or the possible lack thereof, with this arrangement. So I say, "It's just one year."

The next day, I get up early, go for a run, and then decide to rip out the vanity in the upstairs guest bathroom. I already took out the huge jet-tub that was taking up a huge section of the room. It's a big space but the setup is awkward and all the finishings are seriously dated.

I carry everything out to the construction dumpster in the driveway. The neighborhood is quiet. I stare over at Leo and Scarlett's house, but can't detect any movement. The girls are probably already at the resort.

Back inside, I glance at the time and then curse under my breath. Showing up late today would be very bad.

After a shower, I pack and hit the road. The wedding is at a resort about twenty minutes away on the lake. As I drive up, there's a big wooden sign with the word WEDDING and an arrow pointing off to the right.

I park my car and watch as two women carry floral arrangements into the barn, where we're holding the ceremony and reception. The nerves finally hit. I'm getting married today. Never really thought it'd happen for me. And even as unconventional as this situation is, it's not all unease I feel as I step out of my car.

The guys are waiting for me in the dressing room, which is really just a suite in the resort. Leo and Tyler are standing up with me today, but Jack and Ash are here too.

"The man of the day," Ash says, and claps me on the shoulder.

Someone pops champagne, and while I get dressed in the tux Jade sent over, it's all smiles and laughs. They may not completely understand my reasons for going through with this, but they're here and that means more than they know.

Thirty minutes before the ceremony is supposed to start, a blonde with a headset comes by to tell us it's time to head down to the barn.

For the first time since I volunteered for this, I have a moment of indecision. A million what-ifs race through my mind. What if we're both miserable? What if it impacts my career somehow? What if, what if, what if.

The guys file out of the room. Leo is the last one, and he holds the door open for me. "Ready?"

When I hesitate, his expression almost seems relieved that I may not go through with this.

"Do you know where the girls are? I want to talk to Jade before we head down."

"Fifth floor, suite at the end of the hall, but you can't see her before the wedding. It's bad luck."

Laughing quietly, I push past him. "I'll see you down there."

I take the stairs up two floors, and as soon as I step into the hallway, I can hear them. I knock twice, but no one answers. I lift my hand to knock again, and I start to say, "Hello?" but the word gets caught in my throat as the door opens and I spot Jade.

Her profile is to me. Red hair hangs in curls over her shoulder and a white veil, kind of like the one she had on at the bachelorette party, sits on the crown of her head. Her mom is teary-eyed as Piper zips up the back of the white dress.

Jade turns at my voice, and it's like a punch to the gut. Simple diamond stud earrings catch the light. Her gaze drops to take me in and a slow smile spreads across her face.

Scarlett gasps and steps in front of me, blocking Jade from view and shutting the door on me.

"You can't see her in the dress. It's bad luck," she screeches.

"I just need a minute with Jade," I say through the door.

A second later, it opens again, and my soon-to-be wife appears.

"Hi. Is everything okay?" She looks past me, then steps out into the hall. The shoes she's wearing put her almost at eye level and her red mouth is close and tempting. "I sent over the signed prenup this morning."

"Yeah. I got it. Everything is good."

"Oh." She glances over her shoulder at her mom and friends, then lowers her voice. "Then, why are you here? You're dooming this marriage."

I get an eye roll out of her that breaks loose the knot in my stomach.

Sliding my hand into my pants pocket, I wrap my fingers around the velvet box and pull it out.

"What is this?" she asks, when I hold it out to her.

"I heard, I mean, I read that it's tradition for the groom to get the bride a gift on their wedding day."

She stares at me wide-eyed. "You didn't need to do that."

"I know. I wanted to."

Hesitantly, she opens the box and then squeaks her surprise. "Oh my god, Declan. Is this real?"

"I hope so." I chuckle as she stares at the diamond necklace.

"Is it a rental?"

I can't decide if she's kidding or not. "No."

"You bought this for me?"

"Umm… yes."

"Declan, it's stunning, but I can't accept this. You've already done so much."

"I want you to have it. Do you like it?"

Her eyes widen. "Are you kidding? I love it. It's the nicest gift anyone has ever given me. Thank you."

"You're welcome."

"Help me put it on?" She lifts it from the box, unclasps the hook, and drapes it around her slender neck.

I close the distance between us and clasp the necklace in place.

She rests a hand over the diamonds and steps back.

"No kissing until after the vows," her mom yells from the other side of the door.

"I better get back in there."

"Yeah." I put my hands back in my pockets.

She grabs the doorknob and pauses before going inside. "Last chance to back out of this."

It's a final out. Maybe one I should take.

But instead, I say, "You look beautiful. I'll see you down there."

CHAPTER ELEVEN

Jade

PLANNING FOR THE FUTURE IS A LUXURY

The ceremony is over in a blink of an eye. Which is good because I felt like I was going to pass out the entire time.

I was like freaking Sleeping Beauty up there, totally out of it at my own wedding because anxiety and nerves had me in a chokehold, and then the officiant must have said it was time to kiss the bride because Declan leaned forward and put his lips on mine and I woke right the hell up.

While our guests enjoy cocktail hour, the wedding party goes outside for pictures.

"You look beautiful, baby." My mother has tears in her eyes as she hugs me and then Declan. "Welcome to the family."

"Thank you," he says. It's the first time he's looked uncomfortable at our fake wedding. I don't blame him. I'm biting back irritation and a million catty things on the tip of my tongue. Our family? What freaking family? This is the first time we've seen each other in over a year. Since she started dating Kenny. He seems okay, but there's no use in getting to know him.

Still, it has been nice to have her here. I love her and I miss her. Or at least the idea of her. We don't even spend holidays together anymore. I tried the first couple of years after I left, but it's too hard to watch her with these terrible men, who treat her shitty and are exactly like the twenty others that came before them. She'll never learn.

I save Declan by telling my mom the photographer is ready for us. The photos are endless. We take about a million with the entire wedding party and then it's just me and Declan being posed this way and that.

When the photographer finally frees us, my face hurts from smiling, but the nerves from earlier are gone.

Declan hooks a finger under his collar and tugs gently. "Are we serving food at this thing?"

I giggle. "This thing? You mean our wedding reception?"

He smiles sheepishly.

"Yeah. You ordered the chicken, or well, technically, Sam did."

Rubbing his hands together, he grins. "I don't care what it is. I'm starving."

"First, I have to change. I have a whole second outfit and then we make our grand entrance as a married couple."

"All right. Wardrobe change, entrance, food," he recites like a to-do list. How weird must have today been for him? I've been so consumed with my own nerves that I haven't had a lot of time to wonder what must have been going through his head as we said vows in front of our friends.

I take his hand and squeeze. It's rough and warm and steadying. Somehow, he's always steady. "I'll be right back."

Scarlett is waiting for me near the barn entrance with the dress bag. I snag two glasses of champagne from a server on the way to the bathroom. She helps me out of the long, white gown, and while I get into the reception dress, she carefully hangs the first one on the hanger and puts it into the bag.

"Well?" I ask, holding my hands out to my sides, "as good as you remember?"

"I love it," she says in a quiet voice that tells me something is wrong.

"What is it?" I ask.

"It's beautiful. You're beautiful. The ceremony was like a dream."

"O-kay. And that's bad because?"

She looks away before meeting my gaze. "Aren't you worried that when you do find the right guy, you're going to regret all this?"

I doubt she'd believe me if I told her it hadn't even crossed my mind. One of the many differences between growing up with a support system and not—I'm trying to survive the day, the week, the month. Planning for the future is a luxury.

"No," I tell her, "and you shouldn't worry about that for me. I'm okay. Really. Today brought me one step closer to my goals."

Picking up the champagne flutes, I hand her one. "If you can't celebrate my fake wedding, then celebrate that."

A smile pulls at her lips and she cocks a brow. "It wasn't fake. You're really married."

"I know. Weird, right?"

She nods, then lifts her glass. "I will always celebrate you."

"Ditto." I start to clink my glass to hers, but she pulls it back.

"But promise me there isn't a fake baby coming next? I've started grinding my teeth at night from the anxiety." She works her jaw back and forth.

"I promise," I say with a laugh.

The reception is a blast. Tables are decorated like something right out of a magazine (my magazine) and because the guest list was small, it feels intimate and fun. Scarlett and Piper even managed to put together a photo display with pictures of me and Declan from various events we both attended. They even found one from my engagement party, where we're standing in the same circle, and Sam is out of the frame. How someone managed to get a pic of us that night is beyond me. He showed up with Ash for less than twenty minutes. I remember, though I don't know why I recall that detail.

The DJ plays all my favorite songs, and Scarlett, Piper, Dakota, and I dance our hearts out for hours. Declan is the best sport about all of the couple stuff. The only time he seems to sweat is when Scarlett's dad, the head coach of the Wildcats, stops by. I've known Coach Miller since I was a kid, and because Scarlett is my best friend, he's in on the whole Sam bailing at the last-minute thing, but he's a true gentleman and doesn't say a word as he hugs me and offers his congratulations.

We skip toasts, but have our first dance and cut the cake, and the next thing I know, it's time for the garter toss.

Up until this moment, I hadn't worried about looking like a regular couple. Most of the guests are our friends and are 'in the know,' and we've been having such a fun time hanging with them, I'm sure that to anyone who doesn't know, we look like a couple having a blast with their friends.

But as I take a seat on a chair in the middle of the dance floor and Declan squats in front of me, my pulse races. His dark eyes lock on mine as one hand closes around my ankle. He seems to wait for some signal from me.

I manage a slight nod, and his warm, calloused palm slowly drags up my calf. The single guys are crowded around, clapping and yelling.

Warmth spreads up my body as Declan's fingers graze my knee. He pauses again and a throb starts deep in my core. Suddenly I'm all too aware of how long it's been since a guy had his hands on me. A month? Two? I try to remember to distract myself. Sam and I had grown apart, that much is obvious with all the reflection I've been forced to do in the past week.

Declan's hand disappears under my dress and a shiver rolls down my spine.

I hear Maverick yell from a table nearby, "Use your teeth!"

My eyes widen. I swear if his mouth gets near my pussy, I might combust right here in front of everyone. Is it possible to get off from this? I would have said no, but my body is betraying me. *Back down, girl, you're not getting it on with your fake husband.*

Luckily, Declan keeps it PG. He finds the lacy garter on my thigh and tugs it down at a much faster speed than his ascent to the promised land. Standing, he slingshots it into the crowd. Ash catches it and holds it up high to more cheers.

While everyone's attention is on Ash, Declan turns to me and holds out a hand to help me up.

"Thanks." My voice is breathy as I accept his hand and he pulls me to my feet.

His arm wraps around my waist and keeps me at his side.

"How'd I do?" he asks quietly.

"Perfect. Just the bouquet toss left, and our official duties are done."

"All right. Where do you want me for that?"

I motion my head toward the guys. "Hang with them. I'll find you after."

He pulls away, taking his warmth with him. I head to the table to grab my bouquet. A lot of women keep their real bouquet and have a second for this tradition, but I didn't see the point in having a memento from this day. It's beautiful—one of the few things I picked out just for me. It isn't made up of all the trending flowers of the year or even the colors.

I've always liked flowers and never really had a reason to keep them around, so for one day, I wanted all the flowers I like. Muted pinks and yellows, whites. A softer, more elegant mixture than anyone would expect from me but that ended up pairing well with the whole barn and lake setting. I don't even know the names of a lot of the flowers. I flipped through a book the florist had and pointed to all the ones I wanted. Melody insisted on some tulips in the ceremony archway (tulips are going to be big next season—her words), but I'm happy I was able to pick the rest of the flowers.

"Congratulations." Melody steps in my path on the way to the DJ booth to let him know I'm ready for the bouquet toss. "You really pulled it off. Everything was beautiful."

"Thank you."

Her gaze leaves mine and travels over the party, stopping on my friends dancing in one big circle. I glance over to find Declan looking this way, with a hint of concern over his handsome features. I look away from him back to Melody. A pleased smile is plastered on her face when she meets my stare.

"And if I didn't know better, I'd think your new husband is smitten. The way he looked at you all night is going to sell *a lot* of magazines."

I fidget uncomfortably and manage a smile back at her.

"Enjoy the honeymoon. Take lots of pictures and notes in case we decide to feature it with the wedding article. And as soon as you're back, I want you in my office, so we can discuss the best way to continue your articles, while bringing in Declan and your new life together."

Our life together. My stomach flutters, and my mouth goes dry. "Yes, ma'am."

With a small wave, she turns on her heel and heads for the door. *Holy crap.* We did it. I threw the wedding of the season, got married, and I did it without anyone realizing I switched grooms at the last minute.

My mom stops me next.

"I'm so proud of you." She wraps her arms around me and guilt washes over me. When I told her that Sam and I had broken up and I was marrying Declan instead, she didn't bat an eye. I might have fibbed about the length of time between the switcheroo. A few days, a few months—we don't talk often enough for it to make much of a difference. And I guess because she jumps into serious relationships just that fast, it was believable to her that I did too.

"Thanks, Mom." I squeeze her with one arm. "I am going to do the bouquet toss and then I think we'll make our exit."

"Kenny and I are going to head out now before everyone else does," she says. "Beat the crowd."

"Oh, okay. Yeah. You're staying at the hotel tonight though, right? I'll see you in the morning before you leave. Let's grab breakfast in the restaurant."

She tilts her head to the side and smiles in a way that makes me dread her next words. "We're not staying. Kenny wants to drive up to Duluth tonight and go to the casino tomorrow." She reaches over and takes my hand, then glides her thumb over my knuckles. "You don't need your mother. You never have, but definitely not on your wedding night. I love you. You two come see us sometime, yeah?"

Is she serious? I shouldn't be surprised that she's choosing Kenny over being here with me, but somehow, I am. It's my wedding. My fake wedding, sure, but she doesn't know that. I've never felt like I needed her more. I hate that feeling.

"Sure, Mom," I say. "We'd love that."

And just like that, I realize I'm part of a "we" now.

CHAPTER TWELVE

Declan

DID YOU BEDAZZLE THAT JUST FOR TONIGHT?

After the reception is over, Jade and I go to the outdoor bar at the resort with our friends. We crowd around two tables. Funny how a night watching two people get married has all the couples snuggled up and looking even cozier than usual.

Scarlett sits on Leo's lap and his head is buried in her neck. Piper and Tyler are in separate chairs, but his hands are all over her. And Mav and Dakota? Let's just say, I walked into the men's room during the reception and saw more than I wanted.

The only other single guys are Jack and Ash. I guess I'm not technically single anymore. Weird.

Jack is kicked back smoking a cigar, and Ash is wearing Jade's garter like a bracelet.

My wife—holy shit, I have a wife—sits in the chair next to me. She's been distant, quieter, since we left the reception. Then again, it's been a long ass day, and she's had to be *on* for most of it.

At last call, only Jack and Ash order another round. The couples stand and start to say their goodnights.

I get to my feet to hug Leo, Tyler, and then Maverick.

"Congrats. Marriage is amazing. Welcome to the club." Mav slaps my back and pulls me in for a second hug, before turning with Dakota and heading to their room.

When I begin to take my seat, Jade stands. "Are you ready?"

I stare at her, unblinking.

For a man who thinks about sex an average amount of time per day (read: a lot), it's just now hitting me that we're going to be sharing a hotel room. Should I have booked my own room?

Nah.

Maybe?

Nah.

I clear my throat before attempting to speak. "Yeah."

Ash snickers as I wave to him and Jack, then fall into step behind Jade. We ride the elevator up to the fifth floor in silence.

I start to sweat and the top button of my shirt feels like it's trying to strangle me as I follow her down the hall. She pulls a keycard from her purse and swipes it in front of the pad, before pushing the door open.

Pausing in the doorway, I watch as she sets her purse on a table and then sits on the couch and unbuckles the clasp on one shoe, then the other.

"Should I…" My words trail off and I hitch a thumb toward the hallway.

"Relax." She laughs lightly, then pads barefoot to the middle of the room and opens a door. "It's a suite. Separate bedroom and the couch folds out."

"Right." I walk in and shut the door. My fingers fumble to undo the top two buttons of my shirt, so I can breathe.

Noise next door stops us both in our tracks. It takes a second for me to realize what I'm hearing. Maverick. Maverick talking dirty and making sex noises that have me wanting to pull a pillow over my head.

"Is that...?" Jade asks, taking a step closer to the wall and listening intently.

Dakota lets out a high-pitched squeal that makes Jade's eyes widen.

I move straight to the mini fridge. Of-fucking-course Maverick would be in the room next door. Grabbing all the liquor bottles in one hand, I hold them up. "Drink?"

An hour later, I've figured out how to make this night less awkward. Alcohol. Lots of it. We went through the mini bar in record time and then popped the champagne that apparently came as part of the whole newlywed suite. The newlywed suite! There are freaking rose petals on the bed.

"Oh my gosh. Again?" Jade laughs as Mav and Dakota start up again next door. We're sitting on the floor in the living room area of the suite. I don't know why. This is where she sat, and it felt weird to be on the couch or chair with her down here.

She stands and gets the champagne bottle, walking back with it in one hand, her flute in the other. "I don't know whether to be impressed or worried. Is Dakota going to be able to walk tomorrow?"

"I walked in on them at the reception," I tell her.

"Really?" Her eyes light up with something like admiration. She stops in front of me and leans down to refill my glass. The movement puts me eye level with her cleavage. I'm too drunk to do the polite thing and look away. Besides, her boobs are really nice.

"I think they're making up for lost time after the two of them lived apart for a year."

She nods and sits down in front of me, then crosses one leg over the other. Her toenails are painted a light shade of pink that matches her fingers. She's still in her dress, but the veil came out and her hair is now loose and hanging over her shoulders.

"Did you know that most couples don't even have sex on their wedding night?"

"Why not?" I ask, then swallow down another long drink of the sweet, bubbly liquid.

"Most brides said they were too tired or the groom got too drunk." She eyes the near-empty glass in my hand.

I set it down on the floor next to me. My jacket is long gone and my shirt is untucked. I'd like to kick off these shoes, but that feels…I don't know, more intimate somehow. This whole thing is a trip.

"Speaking of sex, I know you don't have an official girlfriend, but are you dating anyone?" she asks, watching me closely for the answer.

Crissy flashes through my mind for the briefest of seconds. "If I were, this probably would have scared them off."

"Probably," she says, but keeps staring at me like she's waiting for more details.

"I don't really date much. Nothing serious, anyway."

"Well, that's good. I don't have to worry about some chick showing up to kick my ass."

"What about you and Sam? No chance of reconciliation there?"

"No. That's definitely over."

"I'm sorry."

"He was probably right to bail. We're so different. I don't think there's any scenario that doesn't have him running out the door eventually. Better that it happened now."

We fall quiet for a minute, and then I'm the first to speak.

"We should probably talk about how this is going to work. Do we live together? Are we allowed to see other people?"

"Minor details most couples have probably figured out before they walk down the aisle," she says dryly with a grin, then takes another sip.

"Yeah, probably."

She laughs lightly and then shrugs. "I have an apartment near Whittaker College that I shared with Sam."

Damn. That has to suck, living in a place she used to share with her ex.

"You can stay with me. I have three extra bedrooms."

She nods. "I can pay you for the room and chip in for utilities."

Another thing we didn't discuss—finances. And I can tell this is a touchy topic for her. I remember those days all too well.

"Whatever you want," I say. "But it isn't necessary."

Her shoulders sag with what I assume is relief to have that conversation out of the way.

"And other people?" I ask.

She looks apologetic as she says, "I think it could get tricky and they'd have to be someone we trust not to out us."

"So, no dating other people."

"Sorry." She scrunches up her nose.

"It's fine."

"Who has time for dating anymore?" she asks and wiggles her pretty pink toes.

I huff a sound of agreement.

Mav and Dakota reach the finale again. The alcohol is flowing through my system and I feel an ease around Jade which might be a result of that or maybe just that we're getting to know each other better.

"Now that I'm going to miss."

"Sex?" She arches a brow in question.

"Yep." I nod and reach over to get the champagne bottle and fill up my glass again. I should have let the guys take me to the strip club last night, or picked up someone at the bar. One last hurrah before I'm confined to porn and my right hand.

She sighs dreamily. "I can't even remember the last time I had sex. How sad is that?"

"Uh...didn't your dude just leave town last week?"

"Yeah, but we hadn't had sex in..." She pauses and thinks. "I still can't remember."

How's a guy live with someone like Jade and not try to get in her pants every freaking day?

"What?" she asks, gathering her hair and pulling it over one shoulder.

"I'm just surprised."

"What about you? When's the last time you had sex?"

"Three months ago."

"That seems like a long time."

"You're telling me." I chuckle and then finish unbuttoning my dress shirt and toss it onto the nearby chair.

Jade's gaze roams over the snug white T-shirt I wore underneath. "Oh, god. We just signed up for twelve months without sex."

"Fifteen if you count the last three months." I swallow the final drop of champagne, then reach for the bottle again, only to find it empty. "And we're officially out of booze."

"Now what?" she asks.

"Sleep, I guess."

Her gaze goes to the wall we share with Mav and Dakota's room. "They finally passed out, so at least we won't need ear plugs."

"Don't fool yourself. They're probably just catching their breath." I get to my feet and then hold out a hand to help her up.

One, or both of us, is unsteady on our feet and she catches herself by placing a hand on my chest.

"Woah. Sorry. Too much champagne."

"Yeah. Definitely time for bed." I rest a hand over hers, the ring on my left ring finger rubbing against the diamond on hers. She smells like the sweet alcohol we've been downing, and her skin is so soft.

My fingers have a mind of their own, gliding up to her wrist and then to her elbow. Jade's chest rises and falls quicker as her breathing picks up, but she doesn't say a word until it's clear I'm not going to take any more liberties.

"The guys asked me if we were going to consummate the marriage." I meant it to be funny, but the air is thick with tension.

Her tongue darts out to wet her lips. "A year is a long time, and technically, we are married."

"True, but it could make things more complicated."

"Is that even possible?" she asks.

My brain says yes, but my dick says no. I shrug.

"Are you even attracted to me?"

I laugh. Is she for real?

"Seriously." She does her own exploring, gliding a hand up my arm and squeezing my bicep. "Forget that I'm the only candidate for sex for the next twelve months. Forget you know anything about me. You see me at a bar sitting by myself, are you attracted to me?"

"The first time I saw you *was* at a bar," I say. "And yes, of course."

"You remember the first time we met?"

"We didn't officially meet that night, but yeah."

Surprise dances over her face.

"Your hair was a darker shade of red." I twist a finger around a strand of her strawberry-blonde hair. It had been a bright, Ariel the mermaid, red then. "And you had on a pink skirt and a white top with these tiny little straps."

"How do you remember all that?" The question comes out just above a whisper.

"I remember because you were the hottest girl in that bar." She's the hottest girl in most rooms she walks into. The fact that she doesn't seem to know it, makes me question the jerk she was engaged to. If I had a girl like Jade, really had her, I'd make sure she knew it.

I don't know if she lunges first or if I do. My mouth covers hers in a rough kiss and she grabs a fistful of my T-shirt.

I back her up against the nearest wall and press into her. My dick is so hard, I see spots.

"Are you sure you want to do this?" I ask, hoping like hell the answer is yes.

"Positive." She pulls my shirt up and I lean back and lift my arms to help her. Pleasure zaps through me as she stares at my bare chest. "But we're only doing this once."

"Definitely." I know there are a million really smart reasons why we shouldn't, but right now, I can't make my brain work to come up with any.

"Help me out of the dress?" She turns and moves her hair out of the way. About a million little buttons run down her back.

My fingers are too big and my adrenaline is too high. After a minute of me struggling, she says, "Rip it."

"What?" I ask, certain I didn't hear her right.

"Rip it off. I'm never going to wear it again anyway."

"Oh, thank fuck." Using both hands, I tear the material, and it pools at her feet. Her back is still to me. She's bare up top and only a pair of lacy, white panties, that I'm going to remember until the day I die, cover her perfect skin.

She glances over her shoulder, but before she can turn around, I place a hand in the middle of her back. She's warm and soft and my fingers tingle as I let them travel over her lean figure.

"Do you have condoms?"

"Yes," I answer. "But we're not going to need them for a while."

"Why no—"

Her question is cut off as I lightly cup her pussy through the lacy material. She leans against the wall and I drop to my knees. Her body quivers as I kiss the back of her thighs and move my hand from her center to push her legs farther apart.

Jade makes the sexiest noises I've ever heard as I place soft kisses on her calves, behind her knees, and just below her ass. I'm torn between wanting to take it slow and drive her wild, and the overwhelming desire to taste her and feel her orgasm on my tongue.

I hook my fingers into the sides of her panties and slide them down. Fuck, she's perfect.

She steps out of them, and I don't wait a second more to cover her with my mouth. The moan that comes out of her makes my balls tighten. I hook an arm around one of her legs and shoulder my way closer.

Clinging to the wall for support, she finds her first orgasm so quickly, I haven't had near enough of her, so I keep going. She whimpers and moans and mutters things I can't make out.

I need more.

Standing, I spin her around and crash my mouth down onto hers. Her arms wrap around my neck tightly, and she rubs those amazing boobs against me.

"Bed," I say, scooping her legs up and carrying her into the suite. I lay her on top of the covers and then get rid of my pants and boxers.

She watches me, perched up on her elbows. Her gaze travels over my arms, chest, abs, and then freezes when she sees my dick.

"Did you bedazzle that thing just for tonight?" She sits up and moves closer to where I'm still standing at the end of the bed. I can feel her breath on my skin.

A rough chuckle scrapes up my throat, but the second her delicate fingers runs along the piercing, I suck in a breath through my teeth.

"You are full of surprises," she says, hand still stroking me. She scoots closer and wraps her lips around the head of my cock.

Blood roars in my ears and then she looks up at me. Fuck me, this girl.

My wife.

CHAPTER THIRTEEN

Jade

THREE HUNDRED AND SIXTY-FOUR DAYS TO GO

My eyes fly open the next morning and I sit straight up in bed with a gasp. I wince at the way the sudden movement makes my head ache, and then look to the spot next to me.

It's empty, but I know I didn't dream it. Declan and I had sex last night. A lot of it.

I get up, taking the sheet from the bed with me and wrapping it around my body. The comforter and pillows are tossed around the room. I pick up a lamp from the floor and then have to step over an overturned chair. This room is a wreck.

Quietly, I walk out of the bedroom and peer into the main part of the suite. There's no sign of Declan, and I relax. I'm not ready to face him. Last night...holy crap.

I pass by my panties and shoes, then laugh when I see my torn dress. My head is fuzzy from the alcohol, so I sit on the couch. A delicious soreness jolts through me and I stand back up.

Maybe having sex all night after my hiatus wasn't the smartest idea. No regrets. That's the closest to life-changing sex I've ever had.

The door to the suite clicks open and I clutch the sheet tighter as Declan walks in. He's in his dress pants from last night and a white T-shirt that stretches across his broad chest.

"Hey." His voice is deep and quiet, a hint of uncertainty that amplifies the awkwardness of the situation.

"Hi." I'm frozen in place, watching him move farther into the room.

"I wasn't sure what you liked." He lifts the drink carrier in his hand and then sets it on the TV stand. "There's coffee, tea, water, and Gatorade."

As he says the last thing, he pulls a red Gatorade bottle from his pocket and sets it next to the other drinks.

"Coffee is great," I say.

He pulls one of the to-go cups free and hands it to me.

"Thanks." I wrap my hands around the warm cup.

I note that he takes the Gatorade and unscrews the cap.

"Listen, about last night," he starts, then rubs at the back of his neck like he's struggling for the right words.

The awkwardness between us eases, and I laugh lightly. "Yeah. Pretty crazy night, huh?"

"Yeah." He takes a drink of Gatorade and scans the room like he's remembering all that we did in here. I can't read his expression. Does he regret the sex, the marriage, all of it?

"We probably shouldn't…again." I struggle to get the words out. God knows why I'm embarrassed now. The man has seen, touched, and kissed, every inch of my body. A shiver rolls through me at the hazy memory.

"Yeah." His smile is regretful…or maybe I'm projecting. "Probably not."

"Then it's good we got it out of our system last night, right? Only three hundred and sixty-four days to go."

"Right." He caps the Gatorade and shifts his weight from one foot to the other.

"What time is it?" I ask as I search for my purse.

"Just after ten."

"Oh my gosh. Are you serious?"

"Yeah," he says slowly. "I think we have a couple of hours until checkout."

In a panic, I set the coffee down, without taking a drink, and rush to my overnight bag by the door. "We need to be at the airport like now."

"The airport?"

I shove my dress and panties in the bag, then pull out clean clothes. "Our flight leaves in an hour."

"Our flight?"

Why does he keep repeating me?

"Yes." I drop the sheet and his gaze sweeps over my naked body. "We need to get to the airport to catch a flight to our honeymoon."

"Honeymoon." This time when he repeats me, it clicks in place. Add the honeymoon plans to the embarrassingly long list of details I did not run by my groom.

"Oh shit. I didn't tell you." I'm still naked, and his eyes seem to be locked in on my boobs. I pull on a tank top and he blinks then finally looks up at my face.

"It's in St. Lucia. Six days, all-inclusive. The magazine is paying for it." I don't know why I add in that last part. I guess so he understands that not going is giving up a vacation I could never afford on my own. Not to mention, Melody is expecting me to write about the experience and take photos of the two of us on the beach, looking happy and in love.

His mouth pulls down at the corners. "I have contractors coming to the house all week."

"Right. I understand."

"I can drop you off at the airport."

I can only nod. "Sure."

I spin around and finish getting ready. After all he's done to help me out, I shouldn't feel disappointed that he is holding back on this one small thing, but I still do. The honeymoon was all me. Yes, the magazine approved it, but I've been dreaming of finally seeing the ocean for months. Longer, really. And I guess the vulnerable truth is, I don't want to go alone. I want to be with someone else when I walk into the water for the first time.

We rush to pack all our things and then head down to Declan's car. It's a shiny, black Ferrari, and when he starts the engine, it hums with power that reminds me of his strong, sculpted body.

I cannot think about sex with him right now. I will do that alone in St. Lucia, with an endless supply of pina coladas.

He pulls up to the curb at the American Airlines departure sign. "Do you have everything?"

"Yeah. I'm good. Thanks for the ride."

"Of course." He hops out and helps me with my suitcase. "When do you get back?"

"Friday."

"Text me your flight info and I'll pick you up."

"Sure." We pause awkwardly, and then I lift a hand in a wave and start for the check-in line.

Some of my disappointment eases after I'm through security with ten minutes to spare. I go to the bathroom and wash my face, then stop by a store near my gate for water and Twizzlers. I even decide to splurge and get one of those neck pillows.

I'm in the last boarding group, so I take my time walking back to the gate and avoiding the mass of people anxious to get on the plane. I open my candy and tear off a string of red licorice.

They call the final boarding group, and I step forward and hold my phone over the device to scan my ticket.

"Thanks." I take one step into the tunnel that leads to the plane and then hear my name.

I glance over my shoulder in time to see Declan jogging toward me with his bag slung over one shoulder. I move back next to the lady at the podium as she stops him.

"What are you doing?"

He's breathless and his dark hair sticks up all over. I've never been more attracted to another person than I am now.

His lips pull into a crooked grin. "Ash rushed to bring me my passport. I only have a change of clothes, but fuck it. I can get whatever I need there."

CHAPTER FOURTEEN

Declan

I AM IN HELL

We arrive at the resort in St. Lucia at sunset. I am in desperate need of a shower and a change of clothes, but Jade is practically vibrating with anticipation to get to the beach.

Tossing our bags in the room, we walk straight out from our patio to the water.

It's quite a view, I gotta admit.

Jade kicks out of her sandals and her eyes light up as her toes dig into the sand. She jogs the rest of the way, pausing when she gets to where the water comes in and then pulls back away from the shore. Cautiously, she takes one step into the ocean and then that grin gets bigger.

"It's so warm," she says.

"Your first time in St. Lucia?" I ask, hanging back so my dress shoes don't get soaked.

"My first time at the beach." She raises her arms at her sides and turns in a circle.

I stumble on her words. "Wait, like, any beach?"

"Yes. Any beach." Her laughter gets lost in the sound of the waves.

Woah. I can't fathom that. My job has taken me all over the world and given me the funds to visit places on my bucket list.

Jade wades in until her legs disappear in the blue-green water and then squeals when a wave pushes her back. She has no regard for the jean shorts and tank top she's wearing. I try to think back to my first time seeing the ocean in person. Was I this excited? I was sixteen and traveled with some high school hockey teammates for spring break. Even if I was excited, I was probably too cool to show it.

"Can you swim?" I ask, as she wades out far enough that I might need to be concerned about her being pulled out over her head.

Her lips part to reply and she takes in a mouthful of ocean water.

I'm seconds from stomping in, dress shoes and all, when she starts to swim back. She reaches land again, smiling so big it's impossible not to smile back at her.

Her white tank is see-through and stuck to her body, showing off her curves. She starts giggling and does a scan of my outfit, staring specifically at my polished dress shoes. "You look ridiculous."

"This is all I had." I brought a change of clothes, jeans and a T-shirt, but forgot to pack extra shoes for what I thought was one night at the hotel for the wedding.

She walks backward into the water, not taking her eyes off me, and kicks water at me, spraying my shirt.

My lips twitch with amusement. "Whatcha doing?"

"Nothing." She sends another spray of water my way, then another.

I charge her without warning, taking her legs out and putting her over my shoulder as I run farther into the water.

She clings to me, squealing and giggling all at once. I hold her tightly as the ocean swallows us up. Stopping when it's at my shoulders, I let Jade slide down my front, and she wraps her legs around me. The position is familiar, and I can feel her hard nipples through the thin fabric of her tank top. My dick reacts as memories of last night assault me.

She seems to have the same realization because in a flash her legs fall away, and she lets go of me. "Sorry."

"It's fine." I let my head fall back into the water.

"It's easy to lose control with you."

"Is that a good or bad thing?"

Instead of answering, she says, "I don't think it's a good idea to go there again. A year is a long time and we're going to be spending a lot of time together."

I'd be lying if I said I wasn't disappointed. Last night was phenomenal. But she has a point. It could get awkward if we keep hooking up. "All right. Friends then?"

I'm not sure I've ever been balls deep in a friend before, but this situation is anything but ordinary.

"Sure. Friends." She looks relieved. "Thank you for this."

"For agreeing to be your friend?"

"No, for this." She motions toward the horizon. "For helping me, for being here now. All of it. It means a lot. I can never repay you."

"I'm glad I'm here," I say honestly.

Her chin dips.

Clearing my throat, I ask, "What's the plan for this week?"

"We didn't book much." The 'we' she mentions is her and Sam. I wonder if she's sad about him not being here. It has to be a little weird, even if she is as convinced as she claims that things wouldn't have worked between them.

"That's cool. A few days of lying on the beach sounds pretty nice."

"I cannot picture you lying on the beach," she says, a little of that playfulness returning.

"Oh, I look fantastic lying on the beach." I wink. "Just you wait."

I wake up the next morning on the small pull-out couch in our room. Unlike our suite the night of the wedding, our honeymoon digs are much more intimate. The end of my feet hit the side of the king-sized bed Jade is still sleeping in. The springs creak as I get up, but as quietly as I can, I grab my bag and go into the bathroom.

After a shower, I put back on my wrinkled wedding pants and white undershirt (my jeans and T-shirt from yesterday are still damp) and head down to the gift shop to get swim trunks, some shorts and shirts, and even some boxers and socks. The shoe selection is basically crocs or flip flops, so I grab a pair of the latter.

When I get back to the room, Jade is sitting up in bed, her laptop open in front of her.

"Hey," she says, briefly looking up at me. When she sees the bags in my hand, she smiles. "New shoes?"

"Yeah. Thank god. These are wet and filled with sand." I toss them in the trash and dump the contents of my shopping spree on my bed. Without thinking too much about it, I pull the shirt I'm wearing over my head and replace it with one of the new ones. Then, hold up the two pair of trunks. "Which ones?"

"Hot pink for sure."

With a grin, I take the hot pink trunks into the bathroom and change.

"Do you want to grab breakfast or head right to the beach?" I ask when I get back out to the room.

She gives me a brief smile and then refocuses on her computer. "I need an hour or two. Melody emailed over some ideas for my new column, and I got edits back. Go ahead without me."

"All right." I glance out the window to the beach, but hesitate to leave her. She was so excited last night and now she's working?

"I'll meet you for lunch," she promises.

I walk around the resort, grabbing breakfast and then scoping out all the activities. They really have it all. Options for everyone from kids to retirees. If I were with the guys or by myself, I'd golf and maybe scuba, but I have no idea what Jade likes to do.

In the end, I grab a lounge chair on the beach and order a couple of drinks—one for me and one for Jade. But by the time I've finished mine, she still hasn't shown up. I order another round and then finish off hers.

Four drinks later, I decide to close my eyes for a few minutes. I didn't get a lot of sleep last night, despite being exhausted from not sleeping at all the night before, thanks to Jade lying a foot away. I'm attracted to her. I've always been attracted to her, but now that we broke the barrier, it's harder not to act on that attraction.

I wake with a start. A shadow falls over me then Jade peers down at me with a humored expression.

Sitting up, I take her in. My mouth goes dry. A red bikini covers only enough of her body to keep the important bits hidden. Her boobs are trying to bust free from the top and the bottoms sit low on her hips. She takes the chair next to mine.

"I see you got the party started without me." She takes one of the drinks and slurps up the melted ice and what's left of the fruity drink.

"Finished working?"

"For today." She takes out sunscreen and starts rubbing it all over her skin.

"Does your boss really expect you to work while you're on your honeymoon?"

"I don't mind. Work is the only thing keeping me going. I'm good at work."

"Yeah." I mull that over. I've definitely put work first for most of my adult life.

"Missing Sam?"

"I don't know if I'm missing him or just mourning the relationship I thought we had. Work is the only thing that distracts me." Her gaze briefly scans my naked torso. "The only productive thing."

"You're in paradise. You don't need to be productive. Enjoy it."

A smile that tells me I'm going to eat my words spreads across her face. "Don't you worry. I plan to."

As expected, I eat my words over the next twenty-four hours. Enjoy it, she does. In bikinis of every color and pattern. The only thing that they all have in common is how little of her they cover.

I am in hell.

We've skipped structured activities, but spent lots of time at the pool with a swim-up bar, and eaten at different restaurants around the resort. We're together nonstop, but carefully avoid touching or any topics of substance. Almost as if we both know that getting too intimate in conversation and letting our guards down, could lead to a repeat of our all-night bang fest.

But I'm already tired of surface conversations. There are only so many times you can talk about how beautiful it is here. Or ponder what our friends are doing back in Minnesota.

Tuesday, we split up after breakfast. While she works for a few hours, I sit on the beach and call my contractor, Rick. He's been able to continue most of my renovation plans while I'm gone, thankfully.

On my way back to the room, I spot a couple just arriving. They can't keep their hands off each other—or their lips. They ask the concierge for a restaurant recommendation somewhere off the resort. Something romantic and quiet. I pause long enough to hear his answer. A night out sounds nice. Maybe I'll suggest it.

Just because it's romantic and quiet doesn't mean Jade and I can't go and have a good time. It'll be fun, maybe we can reach a level of comfort with each other that makes my attraction take a back seat to friendship.

A guy can hope.

By the time I get back to the room mid-afternoon, I'm hopeful Jade's done working because I'm eager to spend some time with her. I like being around her. Under almost any other scenario, a trip like this with her would be amazing. I've let the weirdness of the situation drive a wedge between us for the past couple of days, but I'm done with that. Maybe we can grab lunch and then go snorkeling or something before taking her to dinner off the resort. But when I get to the room, there's no sign of Jade.

I wait, but after thirty minutes, I'm too antsy to sit in the room by myself. She doesn't reply to a text. I check the restaurant downstairs and even the quieter lounge area, thinking maybe she wanted to work someplace other than the room.

I can't find her anywhere. I've all but given up on locating her, when a flash of long, red hair grabs my attention at the outdoor bar. Fun, upbeat music pumps louder with each step closer. A crowd has gathered, mostly guys, and Jade is standing on top of the bar, holding a drink the size of her head, and swaying in rhythm to the music.

She's a damn sight in a little pink bikini that pushes up her boobs and cuts low on her slender hips. And I am not the only one that's noticing.

I shove through a group of dudes to get to her. When she spots me, her brown eyes light up. She lifts both arms in the air, spilling her drink in the process. "Declan!"

People sitting at the bar make room for me.

The closer I get, the drunker I realize she is. I tip my head back toward the hotel. "Wanna come down from there and we can grab lunch?"

She shakes her head. "I want to drink until I can't remember anything."

"All right. We can do that, but let's go sit by the water or in the pool."

After taking a long slurp of her drink, she finally nods. "Okay, but you need to put a shirt on."

I don't have time to ask why I need a shirt before she's attempting to step down on her own. There are some cheers and some boos as I grab her hips and help. When she's standing in front of me, she leans against my chest and peers up at me.

My pulse quickens as she glides a hand along my bicep. "You still don't have a shirt on."

"We can stop by the room and change."

"No, that's okay. I'll just look and not touch."

She lets me lead her to a lounge chair, where I flag down a waitress and ask for water.

"You have a nice body," she says, gaze roaming over me.

"Thanks." I keep the, *So do you*, to myself.

"I keep replaying it over and over. You are a surprising guy."

My stare drops to her pouty mouth.

"Do you think if I drink enough, you'll start to look not as hot? Like reverse beer goggles?"

My throat is thick as I swallow. Her fingers find mine. My heart is racing impossibly fast. If I leaned in just a couple of inches, I could kiss her. I can't though. I know I can't. But fuck do I want to.

Sprints on the ice sound like fun compared to sitting here and doing the decent thing, which sadly is *not* kissing her until she sobers up and then kissing her everywhere else. I know that isn't what she truly wants, despite her drunken rambling. We agreed, only the one time.

"It was all my fault."

"What was all your fault?" I brush her hair out of her face.

"Sam."

The mention of her ex has me pulling back. She isn't over him. I need to remember that. Whatever attraction she has to me is a balm to her broken heart.

"It's his loss. Trust me."

"I'm not the kind of girl guys want to marry." Her chin wobbles with the admission.

"I married you, didn't I?"

"It isn't the same thing."

"No, I guess it isn't, but I think you're pretty great."

Her stare locks on me. "I think you're pretty great, too."

CHAPTER FIFTEEN

Jade

HENCE MY CURRENT STATE

This trip has been full of amazing, unforgettable memories. It's also been full of awkward moments. Like yesterday, when I woke up in the middle of the night with a pounding headache and brief memories of Declan pulling me off a bar top earlier that afternoon.

And like right now, as the restaurant host gushes over us, asking how our honeymoon is going, while he leads us to a small table outside with a breathtaking view of the ocean.

I've lost track of how many times we've been asked if we're on our honeymoon. I mean, we are, but being reminded of it ten times a day is giving me an ulcer.

I flash the host what I hope is a smile, and not a grimace, as I take my seat. Declan thanks him and grins out at the water. "This is nice."

It's more than nice. This is the top recommendation for a romantic dinner off the resort. The pictures from my research didn't do it justice. The lighting is low and, like everything else this week, super romantic.

Our server fawns over us, too, referring to me and Declan as 'the happy couple' and even winking at Declan as he asks if we've been getting any sleep. Cringe. I stare hard at the menu as he takes our drink order and tells us the specials.

I'm thankful when he's gone, but the tension doesn't go with him.

"What looks good?" Declan asks, looking at his own menu.

It takes me too long to answer. I'm staring at the hint of tan chest peeking out of his V-neck and the way his shirt sleeves hug his biceps. Declan's brown eyes finally peer at me over his menu and I flush.

"Excuse me," I say, standing and motioning my head toward the restroom. Once inside, I check to make sure I'm alone and then pull out my phone.

"Freaking finally." Scarlett answers on the second ring. "I was ready to book a flight and come check on you."

"I wish you had," I say. "I'm losing my mind over here. He's all tan and sexy and he keeps looking at me with those eyes!"

I sent her the bullet points the day we got here: Arrived safely, saw the ocean, and oh, by the way, I had sex with my husband and his big, pierced dick.

She didn't see that one coming either.

My best friend laughs freely and loudly. "You're still thinking about him naked then?"

I sigh. "Yes. He's so hot. He even looks hot when he sleeps." An image of him this morning, bare chested, lying on his back, hair ruffled, flickers through my mind.

"Maybe you should just keep banging him then."

"Oh yeah, that's a great idea." I roll my eyes, not that she can see it. "And since when did you become Team Declan? You didn't even want me to go through with this."

"But you did." She laughs. "You married him, so I guess you might as well enjoy yourself."

"We're going to be living together for a year. Sex makes things awkward. Hence my current state."

"Hence? Oh man, you are stressed if you're pulling out the big words."

Looking in the mirror, I adjust the straps of my dress and push up my cleavage. Oh yeah, I wore my sexiest dress tonight. It seemed only fair since he constantly looks like sex on a stick. Except, he seems way less affected than I am. He checks me out when he thinks I'm not looking, but true to our friendship pact he hasn't so much as let his hand graze mine since that first day in the ocean.

Also, he ordered garlic knots. Nobody orders garlic knots if they expect to be going to pound town later.

"Maybe I should just pretend to be sick or tell him something came up for work and spend the rest of the trip in the hotel room."

"No." Scarlett's voice takes on a hard edge. "You will absolutely not do that, young lady. You have been dreaming of this trip since the second you proposed to yourself."

A small laugh escapes at her phrasing because, yes, that's exactly what happened. Aaaand look how great that turned out.

"Enjoy the eye candy that is your new husband and sleep with him again or don't, but you absolutely need to do all the things you wanted when you booked that trip. I know it's probably hard being there when you planned it for you and Sam, but screw him."

"It's a little weird," I agree. I don't miss being with him as much as I thought I would, but it's still an adjustment not talking to him every day.

"He's missing out. He doesn't even know how lucky he was to be with you. You're amazing, you're on a freaking island, have fun!"

I squeeze my eyes closed and nod as she speaks. She's right. I've been dreaming of this for almost a year, and now I'm here, and not fully appreciating it, because I'm too distracted by the chaos of this new relationship and how to navigate it.

When the truth is, I have no idea how we're going to get through it, and I could spend every second of this trip trying to figure it out and still not know. We're in unchartered territory. I should be writing a book on how to survive a year pretending to be married to a guy I barely know but had the hottest sex of my life with.

Can we really go back to a time when we're not picturing the other one naked and establish a friendship to make the next year bearable?

"Thank you. I love you."

"Love you too," Scarlett pipes back in a cheery tone. "I gotta go. Text me later and let me know how dinner goes."

After we hang up, I take a cleansing breath and vow to have fun and get to know my new husband, while trying not to ogle him. There are still so many things I don't know about him. I'm going to focus on that. Maybe he has some deep secrets that will make him less attractive.

When I get back to our table, Declan has ordered two rum and Cokes.

"Thanks." I take a sip and then push it away and grab my water instead. Alcohol probably won't make this easier. "How was paddleboarding today?"

"Good," he says, nodding.

Okay, this is going to be harder than I thought. Declan is succinct in his answers, something I already knew, and understand. I don't open up to people that easily either.

"Have you gone before?" I ask.

"Paddleboarding?"

"I've never been," I share, in hopes it encourages him to say more.

"Yeah. A couple of times. It's fun. You should try it tomorrow."

"Maybe. If there's time. I booked an excursion for our last day. Dune buggies. It sounded fun."

His face lights up with his smile. "Really? I looked at a pamphlet for that today. It looks awesome."

"You'll come then?"

"Of course," he says, like he's up for anything I want. And I guess he has been. Some of my tension releases at that reminder.

"Is there anything else you want to do on our last day?"

He thinks for a moment. "Dune buggies and paddleboarding."

"Determined to watch me make an ass of myself, huh?"

"Something tells me you'll master paddleboarding like you do everything else."

I hardly master everything, but I take the compliment and let the words warm my insides.

"Have you ever been here before with a girl?"

"No." He takes a drink and then leans back in his chair. "I've only been to St. Lucia once and that was with Jack and a buddy that got traded after my first year with the Wildcats."

"But you've gone on beach vacations with girls before?"

"Sure," he says, holding my gaze. "What exactly are you trying to discern about me?"

The question doesn't come with any irritation or hostility, but he seems to understand that I'm trying to learn what kind of a guy he is.

I decide to just ask the thing I really want to know. "How are you still single?"

He lets out a rough, hearty laugh.

"I'm serious. I know you said you don't have time and it isn't in the cards for you, but why?" I meant to get to this topic gently, ease into it. Instead, I dove right in, but I'm just so curious. Some morbid part of me wants to know all his deepest secrets, in hopes that he's as messed up as I am. He feels like a kindred spirit, like he's experienced things his teammates haven't.

"I guess what it really comes down to is I haven't made it a priority. Being a hockey player was my dream for so long. I've seen guys let their personal lives derail all their hard work in a blink of an eye."

He's right, of course. When Scarlett and Leo first started dating, the media around a player dating the coach's daughter impacted his game. But it's what Declan doesn't say that makes me understand him better. Hockey is his dream, and when you've worked that hard for something you've wanted so long and you finally achieve it, there are two choices—let up or cling to it with everything you have. Declan holds tight to it, like it's the only thing worth living for.

"What was your childhood like?"

His expression tightens immediately, and I know I've found a delicate topic. I guess I should have assumed that when he said he didn't have family.

"It was…not always great, but it could have been a hell of a lot worse."

"I get that." I won't push on this one. I don't want to share my pain, so I'll respect his. "And here we are on this beautiful island. All week it's felt surreal."

"Like you won the lottery and don't really belong?" he asks with a hint of a smile.

"Exactly. Which, I kind of did. I never could have afforded this kind of honeymoon on my own."

"Money doesn't change that feeling," he says.

Our food comes, halting the conversation. I consider his words during dinner, though. After we get back to the resort, Declan tips his head to the lobby bar. "Wanna grab another drink?"

I do want to spend more time with him, but I'm not really getting anywhere on discovering his deep, dark secrets and getting drunk together seems like a potentially bad idea for our friendship. I shake my head. "I think I'm going to call it a night."

I can't be sure, but I think disappointment crosses his face. Though he covers it with a smile. "Okay. Night, Jade."

"Night."

The next morning, I wake up with a fresh burst of excitement. It's our last full day here and I want to make the most of it. I get up and head to the shower, while Declan is still sleeping. I didn't hear him come in last night, but I laid awake for hours, thinking about our conversation at dinner and everything else I've learned about him.

It may take me the entire year of marriage to fully understand my husband. He has a white knight complex, always swooping in to save the day, but he's guarded in a way that makes it difficult to spot because he pulls back with no desire for thanks or recognition for his help. What does helping people give him if not love and respect?

When I get out of the shower, he's sitting up in bed with his feet hanging off the edge. He runs a hand through his messy, dark hair.

"Morning," I say, averting my gaze.

"Hey." His deep voice sets off a swarm of butterflies in my stomach.

"The bus to take us to the excursion leaves at nine."

"All right." He stands. White boxer briefs are the only stitch of clothing covering him. His chest and arms never seem to get less impressive, no matter how many times I stare at them. I can't bring myself to look lower, but a peripheral glance is enough to make my body tingle. The only good thing about leaving this island will be that I won't have to wake up every morning assaulted with images of Declan half-naked. Unless he walks around his house like this. In which case, I am seriously screwed. And not in the fun way.

CHAPTER SIXTEEN

Jade

BECAUSE I WANT HIM

I haven't stopped smiling since Declan and I got on the dune buggy. I forgot to read the fine print, which required a driver with manual transmission experience, but thankfully, Declan had us covered. We drove on roads, dirt paths, and on the beach—which was my favorite. We went up hills and down valleys, cruised local streets, and stopped to take in breathtaking views.

My hair is windblown and I'm wet and covered in dirt, but it was worth it. Declan pulls to a stop with the rest of the group. I get out and remove my helmet. My legs feel shaky from the long ride. Declan's grin is just as wide as he pulls off his own helmet. There are two other couples and two friends, a pair of teen guys with us. It's our last stop, a quiet stretch of beach off the beaten path.

Everyone heads for the water. I kick off my shoes and strip down to my bikini. Declan is still pulling off his T-shirt when I wade into the water. It feels so good to wash off some of the dirt.

I'm staring out at the endless green-blue water when Declan swims out to me.

I turn to him while treading water. His dark gaze is warmer, softer somehow after this morning.

He brings his hands together in front of him and squirts water at me.

"Hey." I send a splash back at him, and soon, we're in an all-out war.

With no other clear path to victory, I move behind him and grab hold of his shoulders, essentially using him as a shield.

"Oh, I see how it is." He holds onto my legs and then falls back, dunking us both underwater.

When he comes up, we're both laughing.

"The water is pretty, but it doesn't taste very good." I remove one hand to wipe my eyes, then hold onto him again. He's so strong and steady, and I'm tired from tensing my muscles throughout the bumpy drive.

"I think you enjoyed the dune buggy more than me," I say. "I thought the guide was going to lose his shit when you took off past him along the water."

"I'll probably be blacklisted." He keeps right on smiling. "Worth it."

"Not gonna lie, I spent a majority of the ride holding on for dear life. You're a crazy driver."

"What?" His brows tug together. "No way. I'm a great driver. I'd never put you in any danger."

"I didn't mean it like that. I never felt unsafe, just a little scared."

His expression eases. "I've been driving four wheelers and dirt bikes since I was little. I know when I can push it and when to back off."

"Where did you grow up?"

"Mostly Illinois, outside of Chicago."

"Mostly?"

He looks away from me, but I note the tensing of his muscles underneath my touch. "When I was seven, I went to live with my grandparents. Before that, my mom and I moved all over. Missouri, Kansas, two months in Arkansas. She was an addict," he clarifies, his voice lowering. "She did her best to stay clean after she had me, but it never lasted that long. She'd burn one bridge and we'd pack up and move somewhere new, where she'd have a clean slate."

I barely breathe as he speaks, too afraid any noise or movement will stop him from confiding in me.

He clears his throat. "My grandparents had a lot of land, and my granddad was always buying and fixing up old dirt bikes and stuff."

"And you tested them out?" I want to know so much more, but that feels like the safest question.

"Oh yeah." A small laugh lifts his chest.

I try to picture a younger Declan racing around on a dirt bike, probably going too fast and driving a little too recklessly. Is that how he dealt with the turmoil in his life? I locked myself away in my room and journaled or escaped to a friend's house.

"I have a motorcycle and a four-wheeler; we'll have to go sometime when we get back."

"I'd like that."

I'm ready for a nap when we get back to the resort, but Declan insists we paddleboard first. I do not master it, but I'm able to stand up after a couple of tries.

The day has been amazing, but as the afternoon comes to a close, I realize it's almost over. Tomorrow morning, we'll head back to Minnesota, and while some part of me is looking forward to that (no more half-naked Declan in the mornings, thank goodness), another part of me is sad (no more half-naked Declan in the mornings, bummer).

As we walk back to our room, we pass by the outdoor restaurant. They're setting up for the night. They do this cheesy, romantic dinner with live entertainment. We have carefully avoided it all week and instead gone to more private restaurants, where we can eat without prying eyes or feeling like we need to act a certain way.

"We should have dinner here at the resort tonight," I say. It's so not our scene, but I'm feeling some sort of way about this trip ending and maybe a little cheesy fun is the perfect send-off.

His brows rise in surprise, but he nods. "All right. Sure."

When we get back to the room, Declan decides to go to the driving range, and I jump in the shower, eager to wash off the day. After, I text with Scarlett and then decide to spend a little extra time getting ready. I saved my favorite dress for tonight. It's short and flowy and the white material makes my tan seem darker. I put on makeup and curl my hair. I even watch an episode of *The Kardashians*. Declan still isn't back.

Instead of waiting for him, I decide to text him that I'll meet him at the restaurant, and I go downstairs to the gift shop to buy a few souvenirs for my friends.

When I get to the lobby, my gaze halts on a familiar dark head. Declan is sitting at the bar. The bartender, a woman, leans on her elbows in front of him. She's wearing the resort polo and smiling at him. Jealousy hits me so hard it's difficult to breathe.

He's just talking to her; there's absolutely no reason for me to be jealous, but I can see it in the way she looks at him. She's attracted to him. She wants him.

I fight every instinct in me to go over and claim him, because that's not fair. He's already done so much for me. And even if he is flirting, so what? I've shackled him to twelve months without sex. Maybe I should tell him to sleep with her. It'd be the best gift I could give him, but even so, rage at the idea has me balling my fists.

Turning away, I find the gift shop, but I can't stop seeing the bartender and that look on her face. It's the same one I know was on mine today when I looked at him. Because I want him. Bad.

CHAPTER SEVENTEEN

Declan

THIS CONVERSATION MAY ACTUALLY KILL ME

Something is wrong.

I haven't quite figured out what, but from the second Jade and I sat down at dinner, she's been acting strange. The vibe of the restaurant is fun and playful, which makes her behavior stand out that much more.

A live band plays at the front of the restaurant. The meal is buffet-style, and the drinks are bottomless. The tables are pushed close together, making the place feel like a big party. It's not what I would have chosen for our last night here. Slowly, I've been finding out more about Jade, but here, it's impossible to talk, without couples nearby hearing our every word.

The band switches to a slower song and several people around us stand and make their way to the dance floor. Jade watches them almost wistfully.

Downing the rest of my drink, I stand and offer her my hand.

She hesitates, but slips her hand in mine. That familiar heat at her touch has my chest tightening. I've been careful not to let my gaze linger too long and to keep my hands to myself this week. She said that she didn't want to go there again, and I respect that. Doesn't make it any easier, though. Jade is smoking hot and the chemistry between us is unreal, but more than that, I just like being with her.

I pull her close and we move to the music. I keep my tone playful as I say, "You look beautiful tonight."

"Thanks. I figured I might as well go all out for our final night." She moves one hand from my shoulder to my neck. "You look nice too. Then again, you always do."

"I do?" The question is out before I can think better of it.

"Don't play like you don't know. The bartender earlier was ready to jump over the bar and eat you alive."

"The bartender?" I ask. It hits me as soon as she starts speaking again.

"I saw you on my way to the gift shop. She likes you."

I tense a little, hoping she didn't get the wrong idea. The bartender was cute and nice, but I'd never do something like that to anyone. Let alone Jade. "We were just talking."

"I know," Jade says. "I trust you."

"Good."

"But I think maybe you should sleep with her." The words tumble out quickly and then she peers up at me.

"You want me to sleep with someone else on our honeymoon?"

"No one really knows us here and it might be your last chance."

I don't say anything. I'm angry and frustrated, and I don't entirely know why.

"Twelve months is a long time," she adds.

"And you? Are you going to sleep with someone else too? Maybe that server that keeps checking you out every time he walks by." My jaw tightens while I wait for her answer.

"What server?" She looks around but then shakes her head. "No. I'm not...I don't want to sleep with some random person."

"And you think I do?"

"I'm responsible for getting you into this mess. I owe you this at least."

"You owe me the chance at a quick fuck with some chick I don't know?"

Her eyes squeeze shut, and when she opens them again, she looks flustered. "I don't know how to navigate this. The gravity of what I've gotten us into is sinking in and I don't know how we move forward, but I don't want you to hate me when this is all over."

Her chin drops and I use a finger to lift it, so I can look in her eyes when I say, "I could never hate you."

"You say that now." Her voice is raw and filled with pain.

"I promise it." I take her hand and place both of our palms over my heart. "I vow it. Whatever happens, at the end of this, we stay friends."

"Friends," she whispers, and her stare drops to my lips.

Adrenaline makes my limbs feel jittery. I'd like to kiss her and say damn the consequences. Not that it'd do either of us a lick of good. But, hell, if it wouldn't feel amazing.

We dance through the song and then stay for the next.

Slowly, the pained look on her face has abated.

"I feel like I still don't know that much about you," she says.

"What do you want to know?" I ask, hoping the topic doesn't go back to my mom. I've told very few people as much as I told her today.

Her face flushes and an almost embarrassed smile pulls at her lips before she asks, "When did you get the piercing?"

"I was nineteen or twenty and drunk off my ass. I lost a bet."

"A bet?"

"Yeah, it was dumb."

"But you kept it."

"Should I not have?"

Her face flushes again. "No. I like it. I was just surprised."

I remember how much she liked it and the thought sends all my blood rushing south.

"What else do you want to know?" I ask, hoping to change the subject.

"Have you slept with a lot of people?" she asks. Then says, "No wait. Don't answer that. What I really want to know is if it's always like that for you?"

"Like what?" I ask, knowing damn well what she means, but wanting to hear her say it. That night was…unbelievable.

"I know we were drunk, but I've never gotten off that many times in one night."

This conversation may actually kill me. My dick is inflating fast.

"No, it's not usually like that for me either."

She lets out a breath. "Maybe we should have spent the week banging it out of our system. It's going to be a long year without sex after that."

She's right about that and if she'd said it on day one, I probably would have jumped at the opportunity. But tomorrow we're going home, and we have to figure out how to be around each other and stay friends. Plus, I don't think she's over Sam, and I don't want to be his stand-in when it comes to sex.

I press a soft kiss to her lips, letting myself linger there only a second before pulling back. Her pupils are blown wide, and I can feel her heart hammering in rhythm with mine. "Maybe, but I doubt I'd ever work you out of my system. I'd just want you more and more."

CHAPTER EIGHTEEN

Jade

SOME CHANGES

Declan and I arrive back in Minnesota late Friday evening. We've almost been married for one whole week. One down, fifty-two to go.

My nerves ramp up as he pulls into the garage at his house. I only have the bags I had for the wedding and honeymoon with me. I packed up everything I wanted in my apartment the day before the wedding, and had it sent to Scarlett's house while we were gone. It felt like a safe plan at the time, in case Declan hadn't shown up to the wedding, or any other myriad of possible issues that could have arisen, but now it feels like a pain. I am so tired and the last thing I want to do is go get my stuff, but I want the comfort of having my belongings around me.

Declan carries our bags into the house. I follow behind him, feeling like a stray animal he's taking in for a while. Something shifted between us last night. An acceptance that no matter our attraction, nothing else is going to happen.

The house is big and open. Tools and construction materials line the kitchen counter, and his living room holds a really big couch that takes up most of the large area. The only other furniture is a dark wood coffee table and a Declan-size recliner.

It's hard to see beyond the many projects going, but he points out the new flooring and windows on our way up the stairs to the bedrooms.

"My office is downstairs," he says. "It's mostly filled with weights and workout machines now. Eventually, all that will move to the garage, I think."

"The garage?" I question because when he pulled into the four-car garage, I didn't see a lot of room for anything else. Besides his Ferrari, he has the motorcycle and four-wheeler he told me about, plus a Mercedes SUV. Not to mention, the many tools that are also taking up a decent amount of the space.

"I'm thinking of selling the Mercedes. That'll give you room to park in the garage."

"That's not necessary," I say.

He doesn't respond; instead, he heads down a long hallway and flicks on a light in a room at the end of it. "This is the only room that doesn't have shit stacked up in it right now or wallpaper I need to remove. It's also the second biggest room in the house. Mine is at the other end."

He walks in just far enough to let me pass.

"This is the *second* biggest?" I mutter, mostly to myself. I think mine and Sam's apartment could fit inside the space.

He chuckles softly. "I wasn't sure what furniture you had. Anything you don't want, just let me know and I'll move it out tomorrow."

The bed looks heavenly. It's upholstered in a beige tone, that feels too feminine to believe Declan picked it out, and has lots of white fluffy blankets stacked on top. I pick up a cherry red throw pillow.

"It's gorgeous. I was going to shop for a new bed this week. Most of the furniture I had at the apartment belonged to Sam. The rest of my stuff is in Leo's garage. I don't have much."

"Do you want me to grab it all now?" He takes a step back into the hall.

"No." I stop him. He's already done too much. I can get it all tomorrow after a good night's sleep. "I'm good tonight. All I want to do is shower and crash."

"Let me show you where that is."

"Great." I toss the pillow and give the bed one last longing look. I cannot wait to get clean and climb under the covers. Just the thought of stepping under the warm spray has my muscles relaxing.

Declan heads back down the hall. I look closer at the other rooms we pass this time. They're empty, except for boxes and a few pieces of furniture, like he hasn't decided what to make of the spaces yet.

I'm staring into a room with an ugly rose and hunter green border around the top of the walls and nearly collide into the back of him.

"Oh, shit," he says, just loud enough for me to make out the words.

"What's wrong?" I ask.

He turns the handle of the door in front of him and it swings open. I follow his gaze inside the bathroom. He moves forward a step and flips on the light, then lets out another string of curses.

"Woah," I say, staying behind him but peering inside.

The entire bathroom is wrecked. An old toilet has been pulled from where it was once located near the sink (or what's left of the sink) and is in the middle of the room. The walls are the only thing still intact, and they're covered in an ugly striped wallpaper that has yellowed with age.

Declan rubs two fingers between his eyes. "I forgot I demo'ed this right before we left."

"You did this?" Carefully, I step farther into the room.

"I like to hit things with a sledgehammer occasionally." A boyish grin takes over his face and then it drops. "I'm sorry. There's another full bath downstairs, or you can use mine until I get this put back together."

"It's a great space."

"Too big really. The master has everything I need—a huge shower and dual vanities."

"No tub?"

He shakes his head.

"You need a tub." I walk over to where I think the tub or shower was before. "Not here though, over there." I point under the window. "One of those clawfoot tubs."

"I don't take baths."

"You're missing out."

He aims that easy smile of his at me again. "Twenty minutes in my shower and you'll never want to take a bath again."

"Oh yeah?" I ask, arching a brow. I don't know what it says about me that my mind is always ready to take a leap to sexual innuendos when it comes to Declan, but I can't stop the flashes of memories of our night together.

He chuckles softly. "Not what I meant, but yes. Follow me. This shower is the solution to all the world's problems."

Declan walks me into his room and waves a hand toward an open door leading to his bathroom. "Straight through there. Towels are in the cabinet. If you need anything, just holler. I'll be downstairs."

"Thanks."

He lingers for a second longer and then leaves me, closing the door behind him. Before heading into shower, I take in his bedroom. The room is painted a light gray and his bed and nightstands have a dark wood finish. It's simple and masculine, no real personal touches, except a framed jersey, from what I guess is his high school or minor league team, hanging on one wall.

I walk by the dresser, pick up a watch and set it back down. Loose change and a receipt are the only other things in view. No photos or anything that gives me any more insight into my new husband.

In the bathroom, I gasp. It's stunning. The same wood tones and gray walls carry through into this room. The shower is giant with clear walls and what look like a million jet sprays. Eagerly, I strip down and get inside. While the water soothes my tired muscles, I squirt a glop of soap into my hand and the scent I've only ever thought of as Declan fills the room.

Damn. He might have been right. All my problems feel very small in here. Except the one where I wish Declan would take off all his clothes and join me.

On Monday morning, I wake up early and get ready for work. After that first night, I've started using the bathroom downstairs. It's easier, and I don't have to worry about asking Declan if it's okay first. He assured me I could use it whenever, but while living together, the only real respite is our individual bedrooms, and I don't want to invade his space. Also, I need to get a grip. I can't walk around imagining him naked and pushing me into walls to kiss me for an entire year. A little time and distance will hopefully help.

I know Declan is up because coffee is made and it smells faintly of bacon in the kitchen, but there's no sight of him as I pour myself a small cup and then head out the back door. There's a fence around the property, but someone put in a gate that opens into Leo's backyard. Scarlett is sitting on the patio with her own coffee.

"'Morning," she says.

"Morning." I take a seat across from her, taking in her shorts and tank. "Are you heading into the office today?"

"No. Melody has me covering a shoot on location." She smiles at me. "Today is the day!"

My stomach flips twice and I set my mug down. Today the newest issue of *I Do* hits shelves.

"Have you seen it yet?" my best friend asks.

"No. You?"

"No. Not yet." She cocks her head to the side and her smile grows. "It's going to be great. The wedding was beautiful and the reception was a blast."

"Somehow, this all makes it so much more real."

"Oh, it's real, honey." She leans forward and picks up my left hand. I've gotten used to wearing the wedding ring and forget it's on most of the time. It's hard to explain because I know how much a ring like this means to most women, but it's just a ring. Maybe it feels different when someone gets down on one knee and vows to love you forever, offering the ring as a symbol of that bond.

But for me, it's just a piece of really nice jewelry to convince other people I'm someone I'm not. Although, I guess I am now married. My head spins at the mess I've created. I breathe through my nose. *It's all going to work out, somehow.*

"How are things going over there?" she asks, taking another sip of her coffee.

"We mostly avoided each other this weekend. Thanks for bringing my stuff, by the way. I was hiding out in my room, binge-watching *Bachelor in Paradise.*"

"I didn't bring it by. Declan came by at the crack of dawn, knocking until Leo opened the garage for him."

"Oh." My cheeks warm. I just assumed, which was dumb. I should have known it was Declan. He's always more considerate than I expect. I don't know how I'm going to repay him for that. I wonder if you ever get to a point with a partner, where their expression of love or consideration feels normal and not like you owe them something. Sam and I had a system where we split everything—bills, cleaning, cooking.

"I better go." I stand with my mug. "See you tonight?"

She nods. "I'll come by when I get home. I want to see your new place and read the article with you."

"It isn't really mine, but sure. We can hang in my room and flip through magazines like we're teenagers again. My bed is big enough for the both of us, plus a few friends."

A mischievous grin lifts the corners of her mouth. "Or you and one big, hunky hockey player."

The office of *I Do* magazine is buzzing with excitement. I can feel it the second I step off the elevator. The usual quiet, low murmuring of voices and tired eyes first thing on a Monday morning is replaced with enthusiastic chatter and wide smiles as people hold copies of the latest issue. My fingers itch to grab one and see exactly what Melody wrote.

As I walk to my desk, I get more than the usual hellos and good morning greetings. I have a few coworkers I talk with in the break room, or go to an occasional lunch or happy hour, but this is different. It's almost like I'm being seen by people who have never given me a second glance before now. It doesn't make any sense to me. My articles were already one of the most popular on the site, so why the sudden friendliness, just because my wedding landed in a feature story? They all knew this was happening. We've been planning the issue for months. Ever since BuzzFeed picked up one of my articles.

A copy of the magazine rests on my desk, a large Post-it stuck to the front with my name scrawled in Melody's handwriting. Before I can reach for it, the woman herself appears in front of me, wearing her sunglasses and carrying her purse.

"Let's go for a little walk," she says, like that's something we do on the regular.

"Umm…" I glance back at the magazine.

"Come on then. It won't take long."

"All right." I fall into step behind her. Now all eyes really are on me. I muster a smile and pretend like all is well.

Melody says nothing as we get into the elevator and she hits the button for the lobby. Is she firing me? A cool sweat breaks out at the nape of my neck. I swallow around the lump forming in my throat, while my mind spins with reasons she might be angry. Is she upset about how the wedding went? I didn't think so, but maybe she changed her mind.

Is she angry that I didn't work more while on my honeymoon? I did the few things I'd promised, but ultimately decided to actually enjoy the time off, since I wasn't getting paid, and I was on a once-in-a-lifetime trip. She *is* all work, so maybe that's it?

Her heels click on the lobby floor in a quick rhythm. She still doesn't speak.

"I'm sorry that I haven't been available the past week, but I did take a lot of notes and I started an article on the honeymoon, focusing on different options based on a couple's vacation preferences. The best places to go and things to do for adventurous couples versus couples who want to relax and unwind."

She holds the door open for me and we step outside. The office building sets on a busy downtown street, so she heads for the crosswalk and we go across. A coffee shop and a bagel place are just a couple of the nearby shops. Is she buying me a farewell latte?

Instead of stopping at either of those stores, she goes to a small convenience store and again holds the door open for me to go first.

"What are we doing here?" I finally ask.

She removes her sunglasses and holds them in one hand in front of her. "We made some changes to this month's issue of the magazine while you were gone."

"Oh." My mouth forms the word, but it's barely audible. It all clicks into place. "You decided not to feature the wedding."

It doesn't come out as a question. It's a statement. Of course, that's what she decided. It was a sham wedding. Can I really blame her? I put on a white dress and said vows to a man I barely know. Somehow her firing me feels like the universe giving me the finger for trying to fake happily ever after.

Her lips purse and then she waves a hand to a display near the register. "We decided to do a double feature and put you on the cover."

I can't make sense of the words, but I let my gaze slide to where she's motioning. I inhale sharply, letting out a little gasp. On the cover of *I Do* is me and Declan, looking like the quintessential bride and groom.

CHAPTER NINETEEN

Declan

YOU'RE THE UGLIER HALF OF AMERICA'S NEW FAVORITE COUPLE

I'm tossing the last bits of trash from the bathroom demo into the dumpster, when a familiar voice calls, "Hey, stranger."

I turn to see Everly crossing the street to me. Tyler's little sister just graduated high school and spent the past month travelling with some friends. France, London, Amsterdam, and a few other stops.

Tyler's been worried sick. Not that he said that out loud, but I heard from Ash that Ty was texting Everly twice a day and scoping out international news on the hour.

"Hey, Little Sharpie."

"I leave for a month and you get married?!" Her eyes widen in surprise and, I think, excitement before Everly lifts up onto her toes to hug me around the neck. She pulls back and searches my face. "Why didn't you tell me? I would have come back for something like a wedding."

I search for the right words. Everly is eighteen, young and a little naïve. She's had a hard life growing up with parents who didn't care for her like they should have. They kicked her out after one too many screw ups and she was forced to live with her brother. She then fell into a shitty relationship with an older boyfriend who freaking hit her. But, somehow, she still has this innocence about love and relationships that I don't have it in me to squash it by telling her the wedding wasn't real.

"Ty told me you were doing Jade a favor," she says, reading my mind, but I don't see any surprise or judgment on her face at that added bit of news.

Well, shit.

"Actually, Ash let it slip, but Ty and Piper confirmed it. What's been going on?"

I give her the brief version, ending with, "Please don't say anything."

"I would never." She looks appalled at the suggestion otherwise. "I was really curious why you randomly wanted help picking out a guest bedroom set. Did she like it?"

"Yeah. You have expensive taste, by the way."

Totally worth it when I saw the look on Jade's face.

"I figured you were good for it after signing that seven-year contract." She punches my arm lightly. "Congratulations, again."

She texted me from a café in Paris when she heard the news. Ev and I are tight. When she came to live with Tyler, I recognized something in her. She was angry and acting out, which is why her mom tossed her out. I knew that feeling though, like your whole life was in front of you but held nothing good.

I was young when I went to live with my grandparents, so my acting out was different, but it stayed a constant in my life until I was about seventeen. My granddad passed suddenly, a heart attack in his sleep, and it shifted things for me. I was still angry, but I realized that I could either hold on to that anger or decide to let it go and see what else there was out there for me.

In some ways, being angry was easier. Living life, that's hard. If you let people in, they can disappoint and hurt you. I already knew that lesson, but what I learned when my granddad passed was that sometimes people slip past your defenses anyway. I was angry, but I still loved him, and it hurt worse knowing I hadn't been the kind of grandson I should have been to him. He gave me a chance, and I repaid him by being a shithead.

I shake the thoughts and smile at Everly. "Thanks. Want to see how the place is coming?"

"Definitely."

I show Everly around the house. She loses interest about five seconds in, and I give up the tour, grab her a Monster energy drink from the fridge, and ask her about the trip. She is animated and excited as she tells me stories and shows me pictures.

She looks different. Her hair is straight and shiny, and she has on a preppy skirt and midriff shirt with spotless white shoes. She's a far cry from the girl I met almost a year ago in scuffed boots and dark eyeliner. She's figuring out who she is, finding her place in the world, and it makes me smile. She deserves it.

When she's done telling me about her trip, she hops down off the counter in my kitchen and says she has to go. As I walk her out, Jack is pulling up.

He gets out of his car and comes up short when he sees me and Ev.

"Hey, Jack," she says.

He has sunglasses on, hiding his eyes, but a muscle in his cheek flexes at the sight of her. "You're back."

"Yeah, late last night," she says.

He just stares at her.

"It's good to see you too," she quips. She rolls her eyes and then waves at me one last time, before jogging across the street to Ash's house.

Jack watches her go and then turns his attention back to me.

"What's up?" I ask. Jack and I are old friends, teammates for eight years now, but he's the kind of guy that shows up with a purpose.

"I've been trying to get ahold of you. Have you been online this morning?"

"No. Why?"

"Dude, you and Jade are everywhere."

"What do you mean?" I ask.

"The magazine came out today," he says, and looks at me like I'm supposed to know what that means.

"So? It's just an article with some pictures from the wedding." Unease prickles up my spine. "Right?"

"Not exactly." He pulls something up on his phone and then hands it to me.

"Holy shit," I mutter as I look down at the picture of me and Jade on the cover of *I Do* magazine.

She looks gorgeous. Of course, she does. She's always stunning. But she looks up at me with a look of pure happiness, and even crazier, I'm staring down at her like she completes me. Something was definitely in the air that night.

"There are a bunch more inside the magazine. Like a bunch. And local news reports are picking it up. I even saw one of those Instagram WAGS accounts tagging her and referring to her as the new queen."

He claps me on the shoulder. "Congrats, buddy. You're the uglier half of America's new favorite couple."

"I better go." I hand his phone back to him. "Thanks for letting me know."

"Call me if you need anything." He whistles under his breath as he walks backward to his car. "One week of wedded bliss and already making national news. You should have held out longer on your contract."

He waits to give me time to respond. I don't. Then he adds, "Maybe I should get married."

I flip him off and he finally gets into his car. I pull out my phone and my gut churns seeing fifty notifications. Oh, hell.

When Jade gets home from work, I'm three beers in and still not sure how I feel about everything. Leo and Ash wandered over after they heard the news, but they make their excuses when my wife walks through the door.

"Hey," Jade says, coming into the living room.

She's avoided me since we got back from the honeymoon, mostly staying in the guest room. Her room.

"You saw?" she asks, sitting on the edge of the couch.

"Yeah." I tip back the bottle and drain the rest of my beer.

"I had no idea," she says, and pulls the magazine from her purse. "Melody made a last-minute decision to swap out the cover and delay another feature to give us double the page space."

She twists her fingers together in her lap. "Are you pissed? I can't read you."

"No." I sit forward. "I'm…not sure how I feel. I wasn't expecting this to blow up like this. I had to turn off my phone today." I have so many interview requests, they could fill my schedule for the next two months. "It'll blow over though, right?"

Jade's expression makes my pulse pick up speed. "Melody wants us to…lean in."

"Lean in?"

I sit quietly, while Jade explains that her boss has given her a spot in the print issue for the next twelve months to cover our first year as newlyweds. I can tell by the excited glint in her eyes that Jade is all in. This is probably a good opportunity for her, but it's a lie. Does she really want to keep perpetuating that?

Melody also wants us to attend a few functions, ritzy things that I get invited to all the time for hockey, but rarely attend. Local PR fluff. James, my agent, would be thrilled, but I just signed a contract, and I don't care about additional endorsements. Though, maybe I should. That feeling of not knowing what's next still sits just below the surface at all times, reminding me that I don't have anything except hockey.

When she's finished, she asks, "What do you think?"

I run a hand through my hair and then rub at the back of my neck. "I don't love the idea of putting myself out there like this."

A flicker of disappointment flashes in her eyes. "Okay. Yeah, I understand."

"If you're going to do this," I pause and restart, "if we're going to do this, we need some boundaries. I don't want personal details of my life out there as cheap fodder to sell a life that isn't real."

Some of that disappointment lingers, but she nods. "Of course. I will run my articles by you first, and I'll choose only the top events for us to attend."

She waits for my agreement. I'm still uneasy, but she looks so damn excited, and I know how much it means to her. In for a penny, in for a pound, I suppose. "I'll get you a copy of my schedule."

I barely get the words out before she lunges for me, hugging me tight around the neck. "Thank you. It's going to be good for both of us. You'll see."

CHAPTER TWENTY

Declan

I REALLY HATE BEING BAD AT THINGS

Two weeks after Jade's big promotion, Scarlett invites everyone over to celebrate. The girls are in the living room, talking and laughing.

The guys are standing in the kitchen with the food.

"How's married life?" Ash asks.

"Good. Fine." Annoyance hums under my skin at the question. It's hard, and I feel like I suck at it, and I really hate being bad at things.

The guys all stare at me with expressions that range from calling bullshit to feeling sorry for me.

"Her stuff is everywhere," I say on an exhale. I'm surprised how good it feels to say it out loud.

My friends chuckle.

"She didn't even have that much stuff." Leo raises one brow in question.

"I know," I say. He's right. It seemed like nothing when I brought it over. "Somehow, it's multiplied. And she uses like three different mugs every day."

"Mugs?" Jack asks. "Like coffee mugs?"

I nod adamantly. "She gets one, has her coffee, puts it in the sink, and then five minutes later, she decides she wants more and grabs another mug. Why can't she use the same mug?"

Ash is holding back his laughter. "You've never lived with anyone, have you?"

"Not since I was eighteen."

"Ask her to put them in the dishwasher when she's done?" Leo offers the suggestion.

"No. It isn't about them sitting in the sink. By the time I get in from my morning workout, there aren't any of *my* clean mugs."

"So buy more mugs, man." Ash shakes his head with a small laugh.

"Oh, no. We have so many mugs, they're coming out my ears. Mugs of every shape, size, and color. Did you know they make a coffee cup for every holiday? She has all these mugs, but she only ever uses mine. Then I have to drink my coffee using a Lisa Frank unicorn mug."

Mav bumps me with an elbow. "Forget the mugs. What we really want to know is are you still sleeping with your wife?"

"Dude," Leo says, "none of our business."

I'd bet my new contract that he knows. Jade and Scarlett are tight. I can't imagine any world in which she didn't share what went down between us on our wedding night.

"Wait *still?*" Jack asks.

"None of our business?" Mav huffs a laugh. "You weren't sleeping in the room next to theirs after the wedding."

All eyes are on me, but I stay silent. I love these guys, but I'm a steel trap on this topic.

"I think you knocked your head against the headboard one too many times that night," I say to Maverick.

"Oh no. I know what I heard, bro, but if you don't want to talk about it, all right. Mums the word." He pretends to zip his lips and throw away the key. With Maverick, that's highly unlikely.

Jade and I walk home together a few hours later. Besides the presence of her stuff, I haven't actually seen that much of her. She spends a lot of hours at the office, and even when she's at the house, she has her laptop open in front of her.

"How's work going?" I ask, holding open the back door for her.

"Really good." She beams at me, and I get a reminder of why I'm doing this. For her. To give her the opportunity to prove herself and have the job and life she wants. "Are we still on for the charity event next week?"

Shoving my hands in my pockets, I nod. She's stayed true to her word and runs events and articles by me. To be honest, the whole thing died down pretty quick for me. A few people in the Wildcats' front office commented on the magazine, but otherwise, the people in my life don't really care.

Last week, I went with her to a company picnic and those people were far more excited about all of it than anyone I've come into contact with have been.

Inside the house, she kicks off her shoes immediately and leans down to pick them up, giving me a view of her ass. The skirts and dresses she wears to work every day are driving me crazy.

"Well, goodnight," she says, standing straight and starting for the stairs.

I watch her walk away and that familiar feeling of disappointment at the space between us tugs at me. It's only midnight on a Friday night, and she's running off to bed, where I know she'll stay up for another two or three hours. Jade is a night owl. Actually, I think she only sleeps for about five hours every night.

"Do you want to watch a movie or something?" The question is out before I can think better of it. This situation is tricky. We have no real relationship. Even the friendship we'd been adamant about keeping by not sleeping together has turned into something more like an acquaintanceship. As if both of us knows that a real friendship is highly unlikely, given our history and the length of time we're committed to this lie.

But I want to spend more time with her, even if it means going to bed with blue balls every night for the next eleven months.

"Umm…" She pauses three stairs up. "I was going to work a little more."

I nod my understanding and resolve myself to a night flipping through the channels and trying to forget Jade is in my house, wearing her little skirts and looking so sexy.

"I could bring my laptop down here and hang out while I work, though."

"Sure. If you want."

"Okay." There's a hint of excitement in her smile before she jogs up the rest of the stairs.

While she's grabbing her stuff, I pick out a movie. Even though she said she's going to work, I settle on a comedy that I think she'll like.

I hear her footsteps on the stairs as I'm grabbing a beer from the fridge. "Do you want something to drink?"

"Yeah. Will you get me a seltzer, if there are any left?"

"You got it," I say, holding both drinks in one hand as I shut the fridge. When I turn, Jade is standing in the space between the living room and kitchen. My eyes do a slow scan of her, from her bare legs to her red hair piled up on top of her head. The tight skirt might have been safer because the little white shorts she has on make my mouth go dry. She has on a light pink tank top with Strawberry Shortcake on the front and she's clutching her laptop to her stomach.

"Here you go." I walk closer and hand her the seltzer. My voice is rough and tight, and I move past her to sit on the couch. I hit play and wonder if there's some sort of shock therapy to help prevent lusting after someone you know you can't have.

"What are you watching?" she asks, as she sits on the opposite end of the couch and pulls her legs up underneath her.

"*Deadpool*. Have you seen it?"

"Of course. I *love* Ryan Reynolds."

Perfect. I'm lusting after her and she's lusting after the dude on TV. Fuck my life.

About halfway through, Jade abandons her work to drool over Ryan Reynolds.

"He's so funny," she says, setting her laptop on the table in front of us.

"He's all right," I bite out.

She glances at me briefly, confusion knitting her brows together, but then refocuses on the TV.

Great. Now I'm acting like a jealous asshole.

I set my beer on the coffee table, my attention pulling to her laptop in the process.

"What are you working on?"

"Hmmm?" she asks, and then follows my stare to her computer. "Oh. Nothing, really."

Now, I am even more curious. Jade doesn't strike me as someone who passes up an opportunity to share her work.

"Tell me," I push gently.

Angling slightly toward me, she says, "I have this idea. Instead of writing articles about us or what it's like to be married, I want to interview people who have been married for a long time. Couples at the five-year mark, ten, and so on, then write about what I learn."

"Is that an article?"

"No." Her shoulders slump forward. "It isn't. Or maybe it could be, but it isn't something I could churn out monthly. I want to really dig in and figure out what it is about two people that makes them compatible and happy for that long. How did they know that they'd found the right person? Is it fate, or do you just reach a point in your life where you're tired of being alone and settle down with the next person that seems nice?"

"Just because two people get married, doesn't mean they're happy."

"That's true." She laughs lightly. "Look at us."

"I'm not unhappy." And it's true. I'm not. Just...frustrated.

She doesn't give me the words back and I wonder if she regrets marrying me.

"I'm just so curious why some people seem to find their person and make it work for thirty years, while others spend a lifetime searching and come up empty."

"That's a lot."

"I know, and I'm not looking to write some big, scientific study, but I want to hear what other people think and share it as inspiration or something. That sounds far more compelling than twelve articles about newlyweds. What the hell do we know about how to be married?" Jade picks up her seltzer and sips it, then turns the can in her hands.

"Maybe it's a book. I'd read that."

"You would?"

"If you wrote it, absolutely."

Her smile widens. "What do you think makes two people right for each other?"

"Respect, understanding, love."

"And what about fate?"

"Accepting fate as the reason for good things, means you have to accept that it's responsible for the shitty things too. I think that lets people off the hook too easily for screwing up. I'm not saying bad shit doesn't happen to good people, but believing it's all part of some cosmic plan feels disingenuous."

"Yeah, I guess you're right, but the idea of a magical intervention transforming you into the right person at the right time sounds pretty appealing too."

Would I want that even if it were possible? Maybe. I don't know.

"Do you think you'll ever get married? Like for real, once this is all over."

"Do you?" I ask, without replying.

"No. I don't want to be like my mom, hopping from one great love to another."

"It doesn't have to be like that."

She looks down at her seltzer as she speaks. "My mom said something once when I was a teenager. Another guy had left us and taken our rent for the next two months with him. She said, 'Jade, honey, there are women out there that get the happily ever after and then there's us. We're too much for any one man long-term.'"

My jaw clenches. What a shitty thing to say to someone, let alone your teenage daughter.

"You don't really believe that, do you? That you're too much? What does that even mean?"

She shrugs. "I am kind of a lot." She lets out a brittle laugh. "I know that. I mean, look at the mess I got us into. We're *married*."

"Everyone makes mistakes and finds themselves in tough situations."

"Have you?" she asks. And then adds, "aside from this one."

"This wasn't a mistake," I say. I believe that, even if it's gotten messy. "And to answer your question, definitely."

Crissy crosses my mind for the first time in weeks. I haven't heard from her, though I hadn't expected to. I was an ass. Maybe rightfully so, but it still doesn't feel good. That situation, that was a mistake. This is…something else.

"You never really answer questions, you know that?"

"What do you want to know?"

"Anything. Everything. I still feel like I barely know you."

When I don't offer up anything, she asks, "What happened that sent you to live with your grandparents? What are you like as a boyfriend? Where do you see yourself in five years? What's your favorite color?"

I chuckle at the last question. "Green."

"Figures that's the one you answer."

"I'm not good at sharing."

She turns fully toward me, legs still crossed. "You like games though, right?"

"Yeah."

"I'll play you for answers."

I feel the surprise of her statement lift my brows.

"Do you have any cards?" she asks.

"In the drawer in front of you."

She leans forward, opening the drawer of the coffee table, and pulls out a deck.

"How about war? Every turn, winner gets to ask a question."

"That's a lot of questions."

She rolls her eyes playfully. "Some of them will be ones you get to ask. Come on, it'll be fun."

I'm hesitant, but she looks so damn excited.

"I'm shuffling," I say, motioning for the cards.

"Afraid I'll cheat?" she asks, pretending to be offended.

I shuffle, then let her cut the deck, before I deal out all the cards.

"Ready?" Her voice is eager, and she scoots another inch closer to me. So close, I can see the outline of her black bra under the pink shirt.

"Ready."

We flip our cards. She has a two of hearts and I pull a five of diamonds. The thrill of competition and victory lights through me.

"Your question," she says.

I was so worried about not answering her questions, I didn't think about what I wanted to ask her. I decide to start out easy. "What's your favorite color?"

"Red," she says automatically.

"I knew that," I mutter.

"You did?" She sounds surprised.

"Your car, your hair, your laptop cover."

"Right." She grins and moves to flip another card.

I win again. It's harder to come up with questions than I expected. "Who was your first kiss?"

"My mom was dating this guy. I can't even remember his name."

My muscles tense.

"He didn't." She assures me, picking up on my body language. "He had a nephew that he'd bring over occasionally. His name was Justin and he rode a skateboard. I was smitten."

"Did he kiss you or the other way around?"

"He kissed me. Although I all but put a neon sign in front of my face before he did. I remember I had this Dr. Pepper flavored ChapStick and I kept putting it on my lips. He loved Dr. Pepper."

"That's funny," I say as I laugh.

We go back to the cards, and this time, she wins.

"Same question. Tell me about your first kiss."

"She didn't wear soda-pop flavored ChapStick, sadly. A little grape-flavored ChapStick would have really done it for me back then."

I earn a soft giggle.

"I was in junior high and a buddy had a pool party on the last day of school. I'm pretty sure her friends dared her to do it."

"She kissed you?!" The idea seems to catch her off guard.

"Hell yeah. I was terrified of girls back then. She marched right up to me, laid one on me, and left me standing there with my jaw hanging open."

Jade's head tips back and a big, hearty laugh erupts out of her. She looks so happy and carefree.

We keep playing, asking questions about our childhoods and past relationships. Fun, safe topics.

When we near the end of the deck, Jade flips the winning card and stares at me a beat before asking, "What was your last relationship like?"

"Messy."

"How so?"

"We wanted different things."

She doesn't pry, but I guess she'll ask me more on that later. I don't like the idea of laying out my shit with Crissy for her, but I won't lie about it either.

On my next win, I ask, "How'd you and Sam get together?"

"We met at a frat party my senior year."

"You approach him or the other way around?"

"He approached me. He gave me some line about how I was the hottest girl at the party and he just had to come over and get my name."

"A line for sure, but it was probably true."

We flip the cards again. My muscles are starting to tense. I know the question is coming about my mom and how I went to live with my grandparents. It isn't something I've shared with many people.

When she wins again, I don't wait for her to ask.

"My mom died of an overdose."

The smile on her face is gone in an instant.

"Sorry. I just know it's what you want to know and figured I'd tell you instead of drawing it out." I tap my finger on the side of my beer.

"I'm so sorry," she says. "I wasn't going to ask. I did want to know, but I decided about five cards ago that it wasn't really my business."

"Oh."

"Do you want to tell me about her?"

I guess I do because the next words out of my mouth are, "I was at school. I'd won some stupid math competition and couldn't wait to tell her about it. When I got off the bus, cop cars and an ambulance were outside the apartment. I just knew. I think maybe I always knew, even as a real little kid, that it wasn't a cycle she was going to stop. She wanted to for me, but not for herself. I think you have to want things like that for yourself. My dad, whoever he is, was never part of my life, so I spent a night with a family friend until my grandparents could get to me, then they packed me up and took me with them. That was it."

"That had to have been awful." She reaches forward and squeezes my forearm.

"Worse on my grandparents. I think they blamed themselves for not coming to get me sooner, but I don't. I was what kept her alive that long. In the end though, I wasn't enough." My voice breaks on the last word. I couldn't save her, even though that's all I wanted to do.

"Declan," Jade whispers, and then comes to me, crushing the cards between us, wrapping her arms around my neck and basically sitting in my lap. "I'm so sorry. So sorry."

She leans back and places her palms on either side of my face. "It wasn't your fault. You know that, right?"

I nod because my throat is on fire. I do know it, but I can't help but play the what-if game.

Her stare moves from my eyes to my lips. Heat swirls in my chest. I close the distance between us, kissing her like I've wanted to do for weeks. She gives back just as well, like maybe she's been consumed with the same desire.

I gather her into my lap with an arm behind her back. Our tongues tangle together in a frantic exploration of the other. She feels so good. Tastes so good.

One of her hands drops to my chest and she uses it to push back.

"Wait. Wait. We can't."

"I'm sorry." Guilt washes over me. She's trying to console me, and I'm taking advantage of her kindness. I lift her from my lap and stand. "Fuck, I'm sorry."

"No, it's okay. It's just—"

"I know." I run a hand through my hair. "My brain knows, but the rest of me doesn't give a shit. I like you. I think you like me. We're attracted to one another. We're married."

"What if we give in and then you stop liking me? This isn't a normal situation, where we can just walk away."

Jesus, she's already thinking about the end, and we haven't even had a real beginning.

"I'm not walking away. No matter what. I already told you that."

She bites the corner of her lip, and I can tell by her expression that there's no convincing her that this ends any way but with us causing more of a mess. Maybe she's right.

"I'm gonna go to bed," I say.

"I'm sorry," she whispers.

"No. I get it. I don't like it, but I get it." I take a step out of the room, then turn to face her. "Night, Jade. I'll see you in the morning."

CHAPTER TWENTY-ONE

Jade

I KNOW EXACTLY WHAT KIND OF WOMAN YOU ARE

A couple of weeks later, post the kiss that I can't stop thinking about, I go over to Scarlett's house with the girls to hang by the pool and catch up.

"It's been two weeks," I say. "He's definitely avoiding me."

"Leo's barely been home either. I don't think he's avoiding you."

The guys have started meeting up at the arena to skate and workout together, so I know it's not all about me, but even when he is home, I barely get a grunt out of him. He doesn't sit in the living room and watch TV or ask me to hang out. He fills his few hours at home working on one house project or another.

"Tell me again, why you two can't be a real couple?" Piper asks. "I love him for you. You two are cute together. He's all tough and quiet, and you're vibrant and fun. I think it could work."

"I'm rarely the sane one, okay, but I feel like I owe it to him to make the right decision for us. I got him into this mess and I don't want it to get worse. I owe him too much."

Kissing him again was everything I thought I wanted until it happened. Knowing what he's been through and how he's made so much of himself, I don't want to drag him down. I respect him too much for that.

"No." Dakota shakes her head and lifts her sunglasses to rest on the top of her head. "You can't take the decision out of his hands and claim it's for his own benefit."

I usually appreciate Dakota's bluntness, but today, I scowl at her. "He doesn't see how bad this could be."

"I think Dakota's right," Scarlett says, glancing quickly at her. "Declan's a smart guy. Maybe he jumped in without thinking it through, but he's had plenty of time now to consider all possible outcomes. He wants you, and he doesn't care if it makes it messier."

He might not, but I do. "I'm living in his house, writing about how happy and in love we are. If it goes south—"

"Stop focusing on the negative," Piper says, cutting me off. "What about if it goes right?"

"You've all lost your minds," I say, but her words fill me with more hope than I'd like to admit. Is it possible we could make some sort of relationship work amidst all this?

"Are you still hung up on Sam at all?" Scarlett asks softly.

"Definitely not." I've barely thought of him since the honeymoon. I feel some guilt for how it all ended, but I think he probably made the right decision. "I like Declan, but I don't think it's a great idea for us to start something right now."

"Has he dated anyone since Crissy?" Dakota asks, pulling her shades down and lying back on the lounge chair.

"Who's Crissy?" Piper asks.

They all look at me.

"I have no idea."

Dakota hesitates, then says, "She was an intern a couple summers back."

"I've never heard anyone mention her." Scarlett sits up. "They dated?"

"I figured one of you had the details." She lets out a breath before continuing, "All I know is that she is the reason that they put a 'no dating players' rule into the handbook for interns. They hooked up or dated, not sure on the specifics, while she was interning one summer. Then, something must have happened because she posted a photo of them together in bed on the team page with the caption, CHEATER. It was a whole thing."

Piper lets out a little gasp. "Wait. Really? Declan?"

Dakota nods.

"Actually, you know, something Leo said makes sense now. I asked him if Declan had dated much, you know, getting the basic background check since this one decided to marry him." She points to me.

"What did he say?" I ask.

"That he didn't really know of many women Declan had dated, but that he tended to go after the wrong kind of girls. He must have meant her. What kind of person do you have to be to post something like that?"

"Maybe he really cheated on her?" Piper suggests.

A knot forms in my stomach. Not because I think he cheated. I'm still stuck on the idea that he goes after *the wrong kind of girls* because, isn't that what I am?

I'm still mulling over this new information about Declan when I get back to the house. I slide open the back door and the air conditioning sends goosebumps over my skin. My bikini is still a touch damp from my last dip in the pool.

My steps falter when I spot Declan in the kitchen. His hair is wet, like he just got out of the shower, and he's only wearing a pair of black workout shorts, leaving his broad chest and amazing arms in full view.

"Hey, I didn't think you were back yet."

His stare lowers to my boobs and my nipples harden at the brief look in his dark gaze.

"Short workout today." He looks away from me and turns to grab a Gatorade from the fridge.

"I was at Scarlett's," I say. "Pool day."

He nods, but still won't look at me.

"All right, well, I'm going to change and probably work for a couple of hours."

"Sounds good." He takes his Gatorade and heads upstairs.

I wait a minute before going up after him and shutting myself in my room. I can hear him in the room next door, moving furniture from the sounds of it. He's been working on it all week, stripping the wallpaper and painting. Between that and getting the new vanity in the hall bathroom, plus hockey, I don't know when he manages to rest. The house is coming along nicely, though.

Sitting on the bed, I wonder how we're going to get through the next year. I've made him a prisoner in his own house. Hockey season starts soon, so maybe him being gone more will be good? Except the thought of him being gone all the time just makes me sad.

A knock at the door catches me off guard, and I'm not sure if I'm just hearing things. I wait for the sound again. This time, it's followed by Declan's deep voice, "Jade?"

I stand quickly and pull the door open.

"Hey." He shuffles uncomfortably. He's put on a T-shirt, since our encounter downstairs, and that seems like a damn shame. "Can I show you something?"

"Yeah," I say a little too eagerly.

He steps back and motions for me to go in front of him.

I brush past him and then pause, looking over my shoulder. "Where am I going?"

"Right." He points to the room next door to mine and I walk in without a lot of thought to what we're doing. I'm just glad he's speaking to me.

It smells like fresh paint and my gaze automatically goes to the walls, which are a light yellow. It's the first non-gray room in the entire house. A desk is set up in front of the window and there's a bookcase along one entire wall.

"It looks great, but I thought you already had an office." It's also not at all like the style of his downstairs office. This is lighter and brighter. I'm having a hard time imagining his hockey jerseys and awards in here.

"I do. This one is yours."

I spin around to look at him. "Mine?"

Nodding, his gaze scans the room. "I thought you could use this as an office when you work from home, or it'll give you another room to hide from me."

"I'm not hiding from you."

He meets my gaze. "It's all right. I've been avoiding you too. It's easier."

"And lonelier," I admit.

I walk to the desk and let my fingers run along the smooth surface. The window looks out into the backyard. It's perfect.

"Thank you. I don't know how to repay you for all the nice things you've done for me."

"You don't need to repay me. I like doing things that make you smile."

"Why?" The question is out before I can take it back.

"You know why." He takes two steps closer. "I like you. I admire so many things about you. And I know that you want to keep things between us purely platonic. I'll respect that, but we're not going to keep tallies on every nice thing we do for each other."

He takes another step. "I'd win. I plan on doing a lot of nice things for you over the next year."

I swallow thickly. "It isn't that I don't like you."

His dark eyes blaze into mine, with an intensity that has me leaning against the desk for support. "I'm just not the kind of woman you're looking for. At least not now. My life is a mess."

"I know exactly what kind of woman you are, Jade." With one more step, he's so close I can feel his warmth and smell the faintest hint of his body wash. "You're determined and stubborn, guarded and independent."

I'm not sounding that impressive, but he's right about all of it.

"You're also incredibly kind and generous, empathetic, loyal, and beautiful—inside and out. The most beautiful woman I've ever known."

I can't speak, can barely breathe. When he moves away from me, my entire body protests the distance.

"I'm going out for a run. If there's anything else you want or need for the room, let me know."

And then he's gone, leaving me all alone again.

CHAPTER TWENTY-TWO

Declan

I NEED TO STUDY HIS MOVES

After the night I showed Jade her new office, things shifted between us. We no longer avoid each other, or at least not quite as much.

Development camp is next week. Rookies and future Wildcat prospects spend a week going through workouts and drills, a few scrimmages. It's one of my favorite weeks of the year. I'm not required to go, but I like working with the younger guys, giving them a taste of the pro league, while offering whatever advice I can.

After that, the countdown to the start of the season is on. I look forward to it all summer long, but never more than this year. The Stanley Cup was so close, I could taste it. I can't wait to get back. The guys and I have been working out and skating most days, but there's nothing like having the entire team back together.

Tonight, Jade and I are going to an event—the details I've already forgotten. She ran a list of parties and promotional work events by me, and this one didn't conflict with anything. Also, Leo and Scarlett are going, so at least I'll have another guy to talk to, while the girls socialize with people from the magazine.

Jade looks stunning. She always does, but tonight's hot pink dress and gold shoes are something else. We walk in behind Leo and Scarlett, mirroring their body language. He has her hand tucked close to his body, so I do the same.

Jade peers over at me with a nervous smile before we step into the party.

It's only the second one of these I've had to go to and the last one was not nearly this fancy, just a small company picnic at a local park. They had games and food trucks, all real casual.

But this place tonight is packed, and there are servers walking around in stark white shirts, carrying trays with hors d'oeuvres and champagne.

"Remind me what tonight's event is for?" I ask as I take two flutes from a nearby tray and hand one to Jade.

"It's a dinner and silent auction for a local charity. One of the magazine's board members is the co-founder."

"Nice."

"There's Melody," Scarlett says, glancing back at us. "Should we say hello?"

Jade takes a sip before nodding. "Yeah, let's get it out of the way first."

I squeeze her hand for reassurance, and then we weave through people, heading toward a table with some of the execs I recognize from the picnic and a few others that have that air about them, like they think they're more important than the rest of us.

Melody is the first to spot us. The corners of her lips lift with a small smile, and she steps forward. "Jade, Scarlett." Then she nods to me and Leo. "I'm glad you all could make it."

"Of course," Scarlett says.

Melody angles her body to the people behind her and introduces us to each one. The last woman, Olivia something-or-other, moves to Jade after all the introductions are made.

"Congratulations," she says. "I have been following since the beginning. I'm a huge fan. It's like reality television meets bridal handbook. I can't get enough."

"Thank you." Jade looks a little taken aback by the compliment. "That means so much coming from you."

The woman continues to beam at Jade. "What are you writing about now?"

Warm brown eyes seek me out first before she answers. I wrap an arm around her waist and peer down at her as she begins to talk.

"It's about cohabitating. All the new, fun things about living together, like slumber parties and lazy Sunday mornings cuddled up on the couch, as well as the tricky things like fighting over dirty dishes and deciding who's going to take the trash out."

"You two didn't live together before the wedding?"

"Nope."

We share a secret smile that Olivia seems to take as a sign of how happy and in love we are because she says, "Ugh. You two, I can't take it. I miss those first years of marriage. Enjoy this time together before kids and hot flashes." She waves a hand in front of her face.

"We will," Jade says, still with a smile, but I don't miss the tension that's made her body go rigid under my touch.

"I can't wait to read your article and everything that comes next. I won't keep you. Go enjoy the party. The lobster tails are to die for."

With a polite nod, she moves along, probably to a food tray.

Jade keeps her perfectly-composed smile in place until I pull her away from the group. Scarlett and Leo are stuck talking to other people, but I don't wait for them.

"Are you all right?" I ask, once we're out of earshot.

"Yeah." She lets out a shaky breath. "I just hate lying to all of them."

"We are technically married and cohabitating. And you do leave like twelve mugs a day in the sink."

"I drink a lot of coffee." A real smile finally breaks free.

"Where'd you get the other stuff? Slumber parties and Sunday snuggles?" I cock a brow. We have definitely not done either of those things.

"Scarlett. She and Leo are my inspiration." Her gaze moves back to them. "They're so happy together."

"Yeah. Seems so," I say.

The next words come out quieter. "I know it's probably my imagination running wild, but it feels like everyone is watching us tonight."

I do a quick scan of the party. She's not wrong. "Must be me looking all slick in this suit."

She rests a palm on my chest, smoothing out the starched fabric. "You do look nice."

"Back at you."

"But that's not it. I feel like," she starts and then reconsiders her words. "I feel like they can all see right through me. I'm a liar and a phony. I hate that I'm tricking people. Before, with Sam, it never felt so malicious, but I just keep getting deeper into the lie. And now, if this blows up, I'll lose everything."

My hand finds her hip. "It's not just you in this. If this gets out, it won't look good for me either."

Her expression becomes even more broken.

"All I mean to say is we're in this together. For better or worse and all that." I brush a strand of hair behind one ear. "You look beautiful. We've already established that I'm looking great. How hard can it be to convince a few people that we're in love?"

"A few?"

I step forward and place a kiss to her forehead. She smells so damn good. It's a struggle to pull away, but I do. "We've got this."

I lace my fingers through hers again. "Now, let's go find Leo and Scarlett. I need to study his moves."

A carefree laugh finally slips from her lips and the happy sound makes the air around us lighter. "I thought you were mimicking him earlier."

"You said it yourself, they're good inspiration."

She leans into me and we walk slowly toward our friends, taking our time and stopping to see what kind of food they're serving.

Jade takes a canape from a tray and stops. "They're not us, though. We wouldn't be like them if we were a real couple."

Leo can hardly keep his hands to himself and Scarlett isn't any better. Doesn't seem so bad.

"How would we act?"

She studies me for a beat. "At a party like this?"

I nod.

"We'd show up late, probably because we spent too much time kissing in the car or at the house before we left. And once we got to the party, we'd spend time together, of course, but we'd be confident in what we had, so we could each go our separate ways to chat with people, too. You don't strike me as the kind of guy who wants to hang around and talk about magazine business or one who needs to show his affection constantly."

In the past, maybe she'd be right, but I'm not so sure when it comes to Jade.

"But every few minutes, we'd find each other's gaze across the room, a sort of reassuring smile and reminder that we were thinking of each other. And when you'd had enough socializing or I was itching to get home, so I could work, you'd give me a look and we'd sneak out early, without saying our goodbyes to anyone."

I'm stuck in a trance, imagining all that. Sounds nice. Too nice.

"Or something like that," she adds, a hint of embarrassment pinking her cheeks. "I don't know much about being a great couple in public. Sam and I rarely went anywhere together."

"Why?" I ask.

"We didn't share a lot of friends, and aside from the occasional party with his frat brothers, he wasn't a fan of going out after he quit his job with the karaoke company. I think all those late nights at bars and parties got old for him."

I stay quiet because nothing I have to say about her ex-fiancé is nice. We reach Leo and Scarlett, who have finally escaped the group of people they got stuck talking with and are looking over the auction items along three tables on one side of the party.

"Anything good?" Jade asks her friend.

"I've got my eye on the spa package. Thinking I might hide the clipboard."

Leo chuckles. "Let's not resort to stealing from charity."

Scarlett makes a face at him but sets the clipboard back down.

Jade and I do our own slow perusal of everything up for bid. It's a lot of local businesses, offering everything from dog grooming services to a thirty-foot boat.

"What should we bid on?" I ask my date.

She arches a brow, but grins. "A year of house cleaning so you don't divorce me over coffee mugs?"

"Eh." I shake my head slowly.

"Signed baseball?"

"There's a lot of baseball stuff here. I'm feeling really underrepresented."

"Maybe the Twins are just more generous."

Laughing softly, I pick up a clipboard and write my name down. Jade leans over to see what item I picked, and her eyes widen in surprise. "If you win that, I may be down one best friend."

"Nah. I'm sure Leo won't let me off that easy. Just driving the price up a bit."

Looping her arm through mine, Jade's laughter hangs in the air around us.

"Now what?" I ask.

"Well, dinner isn't for a while yet, so I guess we hang around and mimic Scarlett and Leo for a bit."

We glance at them at the same time and just in time to see Leo grab a handful of Scarlett's ass. We both laugh.

"Not really my style," I say.

"No? I seem to remember you being pretty fond of my ass."

"Oh, I'm fond of it, all right, but I have a little restraint."

"Hmmm." She turns on her heel and sticks out her ass toward me, as if testing said restraint.

Eventually, we find our way to a table for dinner. Scarlett and Leo are with us, as well as two other couples. When Leo puts his arm around the back of his date's chair, I wink at Jade and do the same. It becomes a sort of game between us.

Scarlett leans toward Leo and nuzzles into his shoulder, and thirty seconds later, Jade does the same to me.

It's little brushes of hands and looking adoringly at one another, simple stuff, but it still has heat rushing through my body each time.

They start announcing the auction winners and our friends go from a little flirty to thinking about going at it right at the table.

When Leo, very obviously, scoots his chair closer and drops a hand to Scarlett's lap, I do the same. I keep my palm firmly in place on Jade's knee, but it still has her sucking in a breath.

It's a dangerous game we're playing, but I can't seem to stop.

I don't hear a lot of what's happening around us. My every sense is locked in on Jade.

At some point, they announce Leo as the winner of the spa day package. Real shocker. I knew he'd make sure Scarlett got it.

Jade and I share a knowing look, and then watch as Scarlett hugs him and presses her mouth to his. What looks like it might be a quick kiss turns into much more when Leo cups the back of her head, keeping her close and deepening the kiss.

My mind isn't even on imitating them anymore, I'm just watching them thinking how easy their love seems. But then Jade's linking an arm around my neck and looking at me in a way that has my pulse racing.

Her expression bounces between emotions, like she's trying to decide just how far she's willing to go to keep everyone around us believing we're a real couple.

I open my mouth to say something dumb like, 'we don't need to do this,' but then she closes the distance.

CHAPTER TWENTY-THREE

Jade

THIS IS US

Declan stills as my lips press into his. I linger there, letting all the sensations wash over me. I could so easily get lost in him. I start to pull back, but then his palm comes up and caresses the back of my head, just the way Leo had done with Scarlett.

I smile against his mouth as a shiver rolls down my spine. Pulling back, I look at him. His features are hard, his expression almost pained. What I told him earlier, how I thought it could be with us, I feel that deep in my bones. I think we could be great together, but will it last or will we burn hot and fast, then spend the rest of our time together miserable and uncomfortable? Though, isn't tiptoeing around this thing between us already miserable?

Dragging my nails lightly over his dark stubble, I bring my lips back to his. This time, it's not me pretending to be anyone but myself. And the way he reacts, sliding his hand down around the back of my neck and sliding his tongue into my mouth, I know he isn't imitating anyone else either. This is us.

I don't know how long we get lost in the kiss, but when we break apart, we're both breathless.

"What was that for?" he asks, voice quiet and gruff.

"I guess I just wanted to kiss you. Is that all right?"

One side of his mouth lifts. "Yeah. More than all right."

Applause starts up for the next auction winner, and I turn my attention back to the table. I catch Scarlett's gaze. Her eyes are wide and her mouth hangs open in a shocked smile. Declan's arm goes around the back of my chair, and he pulls me closer, while giving his focus back to the event. I sip my champagne and try to calm the flurry of warring emotions inside me.

We say our goodbyes as soon as the last auction winner is announced. At the car, he walks me to the passenger side, but instead of opening it, he presses me against the door and kisses me again.

Reaching up, I lace my fingers together behind his neck and press into him. He doesn't make any move to take it further, but I can feel how his body reacts to the kiss.

"I think we should take things slow," I say, pulling back an inch and looking up at him. "And if either of us isn't feeling it, we say so right away, and we go back to just being friends."

His hands glide up and down my back. "Whatever you want."

I want to get lost in him, but I know I owe it to him to make sure we both survive this year. "Well, what do you want?"

"I want you," he says. "But if taking it slow is what you need, then that's fine by me."

He reaches down and opens the car door for me. I sink into the plush leather seat, and he closes me in and then walks around and gets in to drive us home.

Once he starts the engine and puts it in drive, he looks over at me. "Home?"

"Yeah," I say. "Let's go home."

He holds my hand the entire way back, but otherwise, we're silent until he pulls into the garage. Inside the house, we both linger in the kitchen. Declan reaches up and undoes the top two buttons of his shirt, watching me. "Heading to bed?"

"Yeah. I have to go into the office tomorrow."

He nods. Slowly. We're taking this slow, I remind myself.

"I'll see you tomorrow night, then?" he asks. He's usually gone in the mornings by the time I wake up, but the thought of going so long without seeing him suddenly feels like an eternity.

"Yeah." I hesitate, but he seems to have this transition between friends and more already dialed in because he steps forward and brushes his lips against mine again.

He moves back far sooner than I'd like. "Night, Jade."

"Night." I head upstairs in a trance, still feeling his lips on mine. I get ready for bed and pull out my laptop to check on work.

Fifteen minutes later, I hear Declan coming upstairs. I pause, listening as he walks in the opposite direction to his room. He usually shuts himself in, but I don't hear the click of the door tonight.

When the house finally goes totally silent, I get up and pad quietly down the hall. I stop, then start again. Is this too much too fast? I pause again and squeeze my eyes shut. It might be too fast, but I don't want this night to end. At the realization, I continue down the hallway in long, confident strides. When I get to the doorway, he's lying in bed, holding his phone in one hand in front of his face. It illuminates his features enough that I catch the surprise when he spots me.

"Hey." He drops the phone and leans forward. "Everything okay?"

"Yeah. I'm fine, but I was thinking." I fidget with the hem of my long T-shirt. It hangs just above thigh-level. "I do want to take this slow, but maybe we could try a slumber party?"

Smiling, he picks up a pillow and tosses it to me. I catch it and hurry over to the other side of his bed. It's just as big and comfy as the one in my room, and bonus, because the sheets and pillows smell of him.

"What do you think couples do at slumber parties?" I ask, climbing under the covers.

"I don't give a shit what other people do, what do you want to do?"

"I want to kiss you until my lips hurt," I admit.

He sets his phone on the nightstand and turns to me, bringing me flush against him and then he does just that.

Saturday morning, I wake up in Declan's bed for the third morning in a row. He's already up, as he has been every morning. The faint sound of a saw tells me he's working on the house. After he finished the room he turned into my office, he went back to working on the bathroom. The sink and showerhead he wants are on backorder, but are supposed to be here tomorrow.

It's all coming together. The longer I'm here, the more it's feeling like home. And today, I'm going to pitch in. Maybe it's not my forever home, but I am living here, basically for free, so the least I can do is help with some of the renovations. Seriously, how hard can it be?

I take a quick shower and get dressed in shorts and a tank top, then pull my hair back and slide into a pair of old tennis shoes.

I find Declan outside in the driveway. The gray T-shirt he's wearing stretches across his back as he uses a miter saw to cut baseboards. When he sees me, he stops and lifts the safety glasses to the top of his head.

"Morning." His gaze scans my outfit. "Where are you headed?"

"Nowhere. I thought I'd help you today."

A flash of surprise crosses his face. "You don't need to do that."

"I want to. You look seriously hot in these." I step forward and take the safety glasses, then slide them on. They're sweaty. It's already hot out here and who knows how long he's been at it. "How do I look?"

He grins. "Like I might not get a lot of work done."

He wraps an arm around me and pulls me against his even sweatier chest to kiss me. I wonder if I'll ever get used to the thrill that runs through me with each kiss.

The next weekend, Jack has a pool party at his house since some of the new rookies are in town for development camp. Declan has been gone a lot more this week, staying at the arena later to help out with the camp and to get to know the young guys.

As for taking thing slow, we've managed to keep things very PG. Maybe, TV-14 is more accurate. Most nights, I end up falling asleep in his bed after kissing for hours, but he hasn't tried to take things any further, and I'm so giddy with how good things feel that I'm nervous to push for more.

"I don't think I've ever seen Declan like this," Dakota says, watching him and Maverick in the pool. They're playing volleyball against Ash and Leo. Declan is grinning big and trash-talking as he and Maverick win their second game in a row.

"Like what?" I ask, not taking my eyes off him.

"Like you screwed him into a happy-go-lucky man instead of the broody, serious guy he's been as long as we've all known him," Piper says.

Scarlett nearly spits out the seltzer she's drinking.

The four of us are sitting on the edge of the pool, feet dangling in the deep end, as we watch the guys.

"I didn't do anything."

"She means she still hasn't slept with him again," Scarlett clarifies for me.

"I don't want to rush him. I'm giving him lots of time to make sure this is what he really wants."

"What about you?"

"I'm having fun with him. Besides, I got us into this. I owe it to him to find the least complicated way forward."

"Jade, honey, you're dating your husband. It's already complicated." Scarlett reaches over and squeezes my hand.

"I don't think sex is the thing that has you worried," Piper says. "You like him. *You're* different, too. Don't think we haven't noticed the dreamy look in your eyes."

A glance at Scarlett and Dakota tells me they're in agreement. Am I holding back sex because I feel too invested emotionally? That sounds so unlike me, but this whole thing is completely outside my comfort level.

"I am exactly the same," I insist, sliding into the pool. I paddle over to Declan, while the guys are still trash-talking about the last game.

I wrap an arm around his neck to keep myself afloat. One of his big hands finds the back of my thigh under the water.

"Another game?" Leo asks.

"I'm done," Declan says.

"Gonna hang with the wifey, eh?" Mav asks, with a knowing grin.

Declan doesn't respond, just smiles as he scoops me up and heads toward the stairs. He doesn't let go as he walks out of the water.

"Where are we going?" I ask, a laugh breaking through.

"I'm starving."

"I already ate," I say wriggling, so he'll put me down.

"Oh no." He tightens his grip. "You're coming with me. I haven't seen you all day."

"You want me to watch you eat?" I quirk a brow. "That sounds entertaining for me."

He sets me on the floor as we get into the kitchen, then dips his head to claim my mouth. He smells like sunscreen and chlorine and his skin is wet but warm from the sun. And man, can he kiss.

When he pulls back, I feel a little dazed. He's made a plate with a hot dog and chips before I fully find my bearings again. Leaning one hip against the counter, he stares at me. "Having fun?"

"You're shirtless and kicking the other guys' asses at every game you play, of course, I am."

He lets out a hearty laugh. "I guess I better not start losing then."

"As long as you do it shirtless," I say, and steal a chip from his plate.

He holds the plate out to me, and I take a few more.

When he's done, we head back outside. He grabs my hand as we approach a group of his teammates. Jack opens the circle to let us in. A few guys I've met, but several others, I haven't, and they eye Declan and me carefully.

"This your girlfriend?" one of them asks.

"My wife," Declan corrects him, and a thrill shoots through me at the hint of pride in his voice. Or maybe I'm imagining it.

Declan introduces me to each guy, never letting go of my hand. They're talking hockey, camp stories mostly, but even when Declan's not speaking directly to me, he makes sure to let me know he remembers I'm here by the little circles he traces on the inside of my wrist and the small, quick smiles.

I consider leaving him alone to talk sports, but then he uses our joined hands to pull me in front of him and wraps both arms around me, so anyone talking to him has to literally speak over me. I lean back into his strong chest and he rests his chin on the top of my head. I have never felt like a more ridiculous couple. Or more wanted.

At that thought, unease settles in the pit of my stomach. It only feels like we're a serious couple because of our fake marriage. Our actual relationship is new, and I need to pump the brakes on my feelings before they get away from me.

I pull away, missing his touch immediately.

"Need something?" he asks, searching my gaze. "Want to go?"

"No." I force a small laugh. It sounds brittle, even to my own ears. "I am gonna hang with the girls. All this hockey talk is making me sleepy."

A flash of hurt in his eyes makes me regret the words, but I walk away anyway.

CHAPTER TWENTY-FOUR

Jade

PLEASE DON'T STAY QUIET

The party continues well into the night, with more people trickling in the later it gets.

"It looks like Jack called in every hot woman he knows," Scarlett says.

"He's trying to show the rookies a good time." Dakota takes a drink from her cup. "But I swear if that chick takes one step closer to Johnny, she's going to find herself in the pool."

Piper and Scarlett laugh. I attempt a smile, but my jealousy burns just as bright. Declan steps away from a girl that leans a little closer, and I feel so unworthy of his loyalty. It'd serve me right if Declan decided hooking up with a random chick was far easier than me running hot and cold on him.

I look away and turn the conversation to Scarlett. "Didn't you say there's a lake at the back of the property somewhere?"

"Yeah," she says the word slowly. "You want to see it?"

I stand, eager to get away. "Yes, definitely."

"Let me just tell Leo."

"They'll be fine. We'll just be gone for a bit." I take one more peek at Declan, this time he's looking my way and our eyes connect for the briefest moment. "Come on. We'll be back before they even realize we're gone."

I know that is unlikely, but I need more space between Declan and me. Why did I have to start falling for my husband?

We all crowd onto Leo's golf cart, sitting on laps in the front and the back, as Scarlett drives us down a path, toward a private lake on Jack's property. She parks under a tree that has an old, weathered Wildcat jersey hanging from a branch.

"This is it," she says, locking the brake.

"Wow." Kota mouths. "I had no idea this was back here." She lifts up on her toes and points. "I think I can see my house from here."

She and Maverick bought a house not far from the street that Declan, Ash, Leo, and Jack live on. I haven't seen it in person, but the pictures look gorgeous. It still trips me up that me and all my friends live in these big, beautiful houses that I only ever dreamed of as a kid.

My mom always managed to put a roof over our heads, but we stayed in a lot of places that were no bigger than Declan's living room.

We turn on some music and sit on the grass near the water, and the conversation flows from Dakota and Maverick's house remodel to Scarlett and Leo's wedding date (they still haven't nailed it down) to Piper and Tyler's planned elopement next spring.

I'm happy for my friends and happy to talk about all that's going on in their lives instead of mine.

Our happy bubble is invaded by the sound of another vehicle approaching. We turn to see some of the guys heading down on golf carts.

"Looks like we brought the party to us," Scarlett says, happiness evident in her smile and the way she stands to greet Leo.

Sure enough, the guys have blankets and coolers and a couple of speakers that quickly drown out our music. Tyler and Maverick, even Ash, hop off the carts and start toward us.

Each of my friends gets up to say hello to their guy. In the distance, a couple more carts are coming, and I hold my breath as I wait to see if Declan is with them.

When it's clear he isn't coming, I stand and go to Scarlett. I tap her shoulder to get her attention.

"Can I take your cart back to the house?"

"Yeah. Is everything okay?" Her brows knit together.

"Yeah." An excited smile pulls my lips apart. "Everything is great."

"Keys are in it." She reaches out and squeezes my hand before I jog off.

My heart races as I head back to the house. *Don't be gone. Don't be gone.*

The sun has set, but Jack has lights strung up around the yard, giving me enough light to search for his dark head.

I find him in a circle of young guys, not far from where he was standing when I left. His back is to me, so he can't see me approach.

Even so, when I get within six feet of him, he turns like he knew I was coming. A hint of surprise crosses his face as his lips pull into a smile. He takes a step in my direction, but then pauses and lets me close the space between us.

He didn't come after me. He knew I needed space. Maybe what he said about knowing exactly the kind of woman I am was true. He always seems to know what I need even before I do. The man has the patience of a freaking saint, and I'm tired of overthinking it. I like him. He likes me. And I want to jump his bones immediately.

Stepping to him, I cup his cheek and lift up on my toes to bring my mouth to his. His surprise is short-lived and then he's kissing me back like he hasn't seen me in days, instead of hours.

Dropping back to the heels of my feet, I open my eyes and look up at him. "Hey."

"Hey." His voice is gruff but laced with humor. "What was that for?"

"For being you."

One side of his mouth lifts higher.

"Having fun?" I ask.

"Yeah. I'm having a pretty good time. You?"

"Yeah, but…" Anticipation builds even before I say the words. "I wanna go home and have sex in every room of your house."

His brows rise.

"If you need to stay a little lo—"

My words are cut off as he picks me up and tosses me over one shoulder. Through my laughter, I think I hear him call, "Later, boys."

He doesn't put me down until he's taken me through the house and out the front door. My feet hit the ground, and before I know which way is up, his mouth is on mine, kissing me in a way that has my toes curling.

He lets out a pained groan as he pulls away, then laces our fingers together as we hurry back to his house.

Once we're inside, he wastes no time. His hands frame my face, and his lips are back on mine. He picks me up again, not breaking the kiss, and I wrap my legs around him as he walks us upstairs.

He lays me on his bed and then stares down at me so long, I start to worry he's changed his mind.

"Everything okay?"

"Fuck yeah. I've been picturing having you naked in my bed for weeks."

He still doesn't move, just continues to look at me.

"Should I just sit here quietly while you have a moment?" A humored smile tugs at my lips. I don't know how he continues to make me feel so wanted.

"Oh no, baby. Please don't stay quiet." Finally moving, he climbs onto the bed and invades my space until I'm forced onto my back. "In fact, feel free to scream all you want."

We're a tangle of eager limbs and a clash of hungry lips after that. His palms slide up my calves to my thighs and then under the skirt of my swimsuit cover. I fist his shirt in both hands so he can't leave me.

Hooking one arm around me, he pulls me to a sitting position and works my swimsuit cover over my head. Dark eyes drop to my lips, which already feel swollen from his hard kisses. It's my mouth he watches as his fingers pull the knot of my bikini top free. I toss that to the side too and reach for the hem of his T-shirt and tug it up.

An involuntary sigh escapes at the sight of his chest and stomach muscles. His lips pull up into the tiniest of smiles at the sound.

"Not a scream," I whisper, scraping my nails over the dips and ridges of his upper body.

"Not yet, but we're just getting started." He nips my lower lip. "Lie down, baby."

Goosebumps dot my skin as I follow his instructions. He starts at my ankle, pressing his lips tenderly to the skin and then gliding his mouth up, letting his tongue peek out and his teeth lightly graze my flesh.

His hands and mouth caress me in the most adoring way. He's as thorough in his kissing my body as he is in everything else he does. The ache in my core is almost unbearable when he finally grips the fabric of my bikini bottoms in his teeth and tugs them down.

I'm all too happy to help get them off. Declan lets out a tortured groan when I'm bare to him.

"You're so wet." He drags a finger over my center.

"You were walking around all day without a shirt on."

"I do that a lot of days. At least at home."

I give him a coy grin.

"Ah, fuck," he mutters when he realizes the implication of my words. Then he covers my pussy with his mouth. My hips arch, but he keeps me pinned in place.

Gone is the slow and patient guy I've come to know. He's a man on a mission. He has my first orgasm hitting in seconds, and he doesn't stop, even when I scream out his name.

His talented mouth continues to lick and suck, and he adds a finger and then two, until I am chasing that release a second time.

He kisses up my body and he takes a nipple into his mouth. I am so overcome with sensation that tears prick behind my eyes. With a hand, I push at his chest until he sits back. His gaze searches my face for understanding.

"My turn."

One side of his mouth lifts.

"Stand up," I order in a bossy and playful tone that has the other side of his mouth pulling up.

"Yes, ma'am." He gets to his feet next to the bed, and I walk forward on my knees to get closer.

I'm eye level to the serious bulge in his trunks, but I keep my eyes on his. I untie his shorts and push them down, trying to go slowly, but I'm far too excited to be patient. "You are seriously sexy."

"Right back at ya."

"You make me feel sexy in a way other guys haven't."

A flash of anger creeps into his gaze, but then he reaches out and caresses my face as he dips his head down to kiss me. I get lost in it for a moment, then pull away, smiling. "It's supposed to be my turn."

"Sorry." His voice is gruff as he stands tall. "Where do you want me?"

"Here will do." I scoot another inch and then wrap a hand around the base of him.

Every muscle in his body tenses as I close my lips around the head of his dick.

"Oh, fuck, Jade."

The gravelly tone of his voice and the look of exquisite torture laced with happiness on his face encourage me to keep going.

Taking a page out of his book, I force myself to go slow. I open wider, taking all of him in, and then glide back up, swirling my tongue around his piercing as I do.

He threads his fingers through my hair and tugs gently, but lets me keep up my own pace. Only when I take him all the way in again, does he hold me in place. I suck a little harder, tears pricking my eyes, before he pulls me back.

I glance up at him to find his eyes locked on me. Bringing this beautiful, strong man pleasure is my new favorite hobby.

Pausing, I wait for him to take over again. He gets the hint and uses the hand tangled in my hair to guide me over him, picking up speed. It's my turn, but I love letting Declan be in control.

When I'm sure he's seconds from coming, he pops me off him and climbs over me, forcing me back. Opening his nightstand, he takes out a condom.

"Still want to do this?" he asks.

Is he serious?

"If you don't fuck me, I will do it myself." I bring my hand between my legs and circle my clit. I'm so wet and so turned on, but I need him to get there.

He watches with dark eyes as he covers himself with a condom, then captures my wrist in one hand to stop me from touching myself. He brings my fingers to his mouth and sucks each one. *This guy. This fucking guy.*

"Tonight, all your orgasms are mine," he rasps.

Without another word, Declan pushes inside me. The time for slow and controlled is over. He moves at a pace that has him driving hard and deep. I lose track of the number of times he brings me over the edge while he chases his own release. The man has the stamina of a god.

I want so badly for him to find the same bliss washing over me.

"Declan." It's half-scream, half-plea. Those dark eyes lock onto mine, and finally, he lets go.

As night creeps into early morning, I lose track of how many times we have sex. We never leave the bed, though. We'll have sex in every room of the house another day.

I'm curled up on his chest, so satiated that I drift in and out. Declan lifts me into his arms. I'm so tired, I don't want to move. It takes me a second to realize he's taking me somewhere. Does he want me to sleep in my own bed tonight? Maybe I've been spending too many nights in here.

"Sorry," I say, opening my eyes, "I didn't mean to doze off in your bed. Put me down. I can walk back to my own room."

"You want to sleep in your bed?" His brow creases in confusion.

"I thought…" My sentence trails off as he carries me into the bathroom and sets me down, then turns on the water.

"I thought we could take a quick shower before bed. We're a mess."

"Oh."

Declan steps in and adjusts the water, then reaches a hand out to me.

It feels amazing. Even more so when he wraps his arms around me and lets me lean the bulk of my weight on him. I can't bring myself to look at him as I say, "I don't want to go back to my room."

He tips my chin up with a finger, then brushes his thumb against my cheek. "Good. Shower with me, then sleep in my bed tonight?"

I nod, and the smile that I get in return makes my stomach dip.

CHAPTER TWENTY-FIVE

Declan

MINE, BUDDY

The following Saturday, I wake up in my bed alone for the first time in a couple of weeks. Not a fan.

Usually, Jade sleeps in well past my alarm, but the bed is cold, and I can't hear any movement in the house.

I get up and take a quick shower, then head downstairs. Today I need to finish a few odds and ends around the house. It's mostly done. I'm waiting on a couple of things for the upstairs bathroom, and I still want to switch out the cabinets in the kitchen, but summer is winding down and I need to start putting all my focus on training and getting ready for the upcoming season.

While I eat a bowl of cereal and down a protein shake, I keep expecting Jade to turn up. Maybe she's working? She didn't mention it last night, but then again, we've done a lot less talking and a whole lot more making out this week.

I have two texts. One from Maverick, a group text reminding

us all that his one-year anniversary party is tonight. He and Dakota did a Vegas quickie wedding last year, so Mav is going all out on the anniversary party. Should be fun.

The second text is from Ash, saying he and Leo are skipping our usual morning run. I fire back a response, letting him know I think they're both slackers and then head out.

I only get as far as the driveway when I spot Jade's red Volkswagen coming up the street. I pause and wait for her to pull in. She refuses to park in the garage. I have yet to figure out how to force her into it. Maybe shoveling herself out from under a few feet of snow this winter will do the trick.

Who am I kidding? That's going to be me. I like doing shit like that for Jade. She always looks at me in awe over the simplest considerations.

She's sporting an ear-to-ear grin, which I find myself replicating until I notice the truck pulling in behind her. Jade hops out of her car and heads toward the guy parking behind her. *What the hell?*

A young guy gets out and looks at her in a way that makes me want to pummel him.

"What do you think?" Jade asks, and it takes a second for me to realize she's talking to me.

"What?"

"The chair." She points as the guy pulls down the tailgate and climbs up into the bed of his truck. My gaze jumps from the chair to the guy unhooking the straps and stealing glances at Jade.

"I found it at a little thrift store. It's in practically new condition."

"Where do you want it?" he asks her.

"Living room," she says at the same time I finally snap out of it.

"I got it." I step forward and take the chair from him. It's a puke-green, velvet-upholstered accent chair with a round back. It's heavy as fuck and smells musty as hell.

I try not to breathe as I lift it down from the truck. "You paid money for this?"

"She got a great deal on it." The dude jumps to the ground and continues to beam at Jade.

"Who are you?" I ask him.

"Declan," Jade admonishes me and sends an elbow into my ribs. Like I care if this dude thinks I'm rude. I think he's rude for gawking at my girl.

"Yes, *wife.*" I look at the guy as I speak, sending him a silent, *Mine, buddy. Capisce?*

"This is Elton," Jade says. "He works at the store and offered to bring the chair himself."

Yeah, I bet he did.

"Thanks, man. We've got it from here." I motion with my head for Jade and step toward the house. "Show me where you want this, wife."

This time she rolls her eyes at the endearment. "Okay, *husband.*"

She might be patronizing me, but I still kinda dig it.

Jade holds open the front door for me, and I walk through and head toward the stairs. "Your office or room?"

Walking into the living room, she attempts to move my favorite recliner. Attempts because it's heavy and doesn't budge. "I thought it could go here."

"Where will the recliner go?"

"I'm not sure." Bringing her thumbnail to her lips, she scans the room.

Since it doesn't look like this ugly thing is going upstairs, I set the chair down next to the couch. The rest of the furniture is a dark gray.

I bought it all new when I moved in here, so it fits the space perfectly.

"If you don't like the furniture pieces that are in here, we can go pick out new stuff together."

"I like them," she says, moving to stand on the opposite side, like she's trying to get a read on the room from every angle.

"Then why the sudden desire to wake up at the ass crack of dawn and buy an old chair?"

Her gaze snaps to me. "I want to contribute something. Everything in this house is yours."

She didn't have a lot when she moved in, but I guess I see her point.

"This chair smells like fifty years of ass."

"It's vintage."

"Uh-huh."

"You don't like my chair." She crosses her arms over her chest.

"I didn't say that. Don't care for the smell, but I've got a bottle of Febreze around here somewhere, or I can stop by Ash's and see if he has some Axe body spray. That shit masks everything."

Her smile slips, and I want to kick myself. Fuck, this really means a lot to her.

I close the distance between us and take both her hands in mine. "The chair is great. Thank you."

"You hate it."

"Nah. It's growing on me. I'll move the recliner into my office, and it can go right there." I point to the spot.

A pleased smile curves her lips. "It matches the little flecks of green in your eyes."

"That right?" I dip my head lower and brush my lips across hers.

"Mhmm."

She pulls back and looks to the chair. Saying my apologies to my recliner, I take it into the office, and when I return, Jade is pushing the green chair into its spot.

"What do you think?" She plops down in the middle of it and grins at me.

I think it looks a fuck of a lot better with her sitting in it.

Later, we get dressed up and go to Maverick and Dakota's anniversary party. Mav did not disappoint. It's as over the top as I would expect from the dude. He loves the same way he does everything else—big and wild.

The party is out back of his new house. A huge white party tent is set up, and there are a million lights strung all around, inside and out. A live band is playing and people are already dancing. There's also a huge buffet of food and tables set up inside the tent for people to sit and eat and relax.

"Congratulations," I say to him, when Jade and I make our way around the party to the happy couple.

"Thank you." Mav pulls me into a bear hug while Kota watches on and laughs.

He goes to Jade next, giving her the same enthusiastic embrace. "Thank you for all the tips."

"Tips?" Jade asks, looking confused.

"He's been reading your articles for the past year," Kota answers for him.

"Are you serious?" I ask with a chuckle.

"You haven't?" He fires back at me.

I've read through the ones Jade sent me for approval, but outside of those, I haven't. And now I wish I had because she aims a pleased smile at him. "I love that. Thank you. I thought those table decorations looked familiar."

"All you," he confirms, then bobs his head in time with the beat. "But this playlist is all me. Dance, wifey?"

After they go, I hold out my hand to Jade.

"Dance, wifey?" I ask, mimicking Maverick.

With a giggle, she puts her palm on top of mine. When we get to the dance floor, she's quickly pulled away from me and into a circle with Scarlett and Piper, along with some of Dakota's friends from college.

Maverick introduces me to some of his old Valley U teammates that made the trip up, and we hang back, watching the girls, talking hockey and other bullshit to pass the time.

It reminds me of a hundred other nights where Jade and I were at the same event. I hung with the guys, while she was the life of the party. We'd maybe catch each other's line of vision once or twice, and on a couple of occasions, we even said a few words to each other.

But I don't want to be that guy anymore. I like spending my evenings with her a whole lot more than standing on the sidelines like I have most of my life. The music changes to a slower song and I take that as my sign.

Stepping forward, I wrap both arms around her waist. She glances up over her shoulder and smiles at me.

"Still want your dance?" She leans into my chest.

"Definitely."

Jade turns to face me and drapes her arms over my shoulders. I tighten my grip to eliminate the space between us. I wouldn't call what we're doing dancing, more like hugging and swaying ever so slightly.

Tonight, she has on this sexy black dress that ties around her neck and leaves her back bare. I glide my hands over her soft, warm skin.

"You look gorgeous tonight."

"You already said that."

She's right. I did. She still grins at me, though.

"You are pretty sharp, yourself. I could get used to seeing you in a suit."

"I wear them for every game, so you're in luck."

"Oh, right." Her eyes light up, which makes me chuckle.

She tips her head up to kiss me. "I need a drink. Wanna come with me?"

"Always."

Jade leads me to one of two bars set up for the party. She orders for us and then hands me a glass filled with something blue.

"What is that?" I ask, taking a sniff.

"Mad Dog, what else?"

I chuckle at the mention of Maverick's favorite liquor. He's always drinking this shit. I take a small sip and then grimace. "I have no idea how he drinks this."

"I kind of like it." She takes a bigger drink and then grins. "It's strong."

"Easy, baby. You have plans later."

"I do, huh?" Her brows lift.

"Someone left me hanging this morning."

She sticks out her bottom lip. "How do you think I feel every morning?"

The thought of Jade wanting me that way when she wakes up alone on every other day of the week when I get up early to work out has my blood pumping faster.

"Sounds like we need to sync our schedules."

"Oh no. You get up way too early for me."

"The early bird gets the worm and all that."

"The early bird gets no sex, apparently."

A chuckle shakes free from my chest. "Touché."

"This is really growing on me." She takes another drink and stares over at the house. "Have you seen inside?"

"Yeah." I nod. "I helped him move."

"Of course, you did. You're such a good guy."

"That almost sounds like a bad thing coming out of your mouth."

"No, I like it. You're a gentleman in the streets but a freak in the sheets."

I bark a laugh into the night. She's too fucking much. "Come on. I'll give you a tour of the house."

"Oooh." She has an extra pep in her step and I'm not sure if it's her excitement to see the house or if she's already feeling the effects of the stupid-strong alcohol.

I'm a crappy guide, but Jade doesn't seem to care that I lead her straight to the powder room at the front of the house.

"Oh, this is so nice," she says, turning in a circle. "I can't get over everyone's houses. You should see some of the dumps I lived in growing up."

An ache forms in my chest at her admission. She doesn't talk about her childhood or her mom a lot, and I haven't pushed because I know what it's like not to want to relive painful memories.

"Don't look at me like that," she says. "It wasn't that bad. I had a home and food, and my mom was great most of the time."

"But not all the time?"

"Is anyone great all the time?" she asks.

I stay quiet. I don't know the answer to that, but she knows my story points to the same conclusion.

"Except you. You're always great." She steps back to me and places a hand on my chest. "Why are you always so great to me?"

"I like you."

"I guess no one has liked me as much as you, then."

"I guess not."

She grips my shirt and tugs me to her. She tastes likes Mad Dog, and I'm suddenly thinking it's not so bad anymore. I back her up against the vanity and then lift her onto it.

"Is this okay?" she asks, glancing back at the door.

I walk over and shut and lock it. "I'd say we owe them after they were getting it on at our wedding reception."

"Oh right. We totally do." She reaches up and unties the top of her dress. The material pools at her waist. "Why are you still wearing pants?"

Laughing, I go back to her and stand between her legs. "I like it better when you undress me."

I cup her boobs, running my thumbs over her perfect pale nipples as she undoes my pants and pushes them down, with my boxer briefs, far enough that my dick springs free.

I'm already hard and leaking for her.

"Do you have any condoms?"

"Dammit, no." I jut my chin toward the medicine cabinet. "Maybe Mav has every room in the house stocked?"

"We don't need..." she trails off and then restarts, "I'm on birth control."

I nod.

"You still want to check to see if he has every room stocked, don't you?"

I slide my palms up her thighs. "Later."

She scoots to the edge and pushes her panties down, then pulls them off and slingshots the lacy material at my face. I catch them in one hand and shove them in my pocket.

Leaning forward, Jade grabs me by the shirt—something I've learned to love because it always means she's about to kiss me.

Our position has my dick at the perfect level, rubbing against her slit as her lips crush mine. Her body shutters at the contact, so I do it again, this time pushing in just a fraction.

I'm too turned on, too impatient. The next time, I bury myself inside her. Jade whimpers and tightens her grasp on my shirt.

I'm never gonna last like this, but she doesn't seem to mind.

"It's never been like this." She drops her head to my shoulder. "You're either very good at this or…"

Her body tightens around me, and she finds her release. Three more thrusts and I follow her, biting down on her shoulder to keep myself from asking her to finish that statement.

We get cleaned up and head back to the party, hand in hand. My mind is still stuck on Jade's words; it's never been like this for me either. Is it the circumstance or is what we have just more? Somewhere along the way, I stopped being able to picture going to parties or even home without Jade by my side. Is she feeling that too?

She swings our joined hands between us and smiles up at me. "How much do you hate the chair?"

"What chair?" I ask, playing dumb and fighting a grin.

"You need more color in your house. You're all grays and blacks with wood accents."

"I don't hate the chair."

"Good." Her smile gets bigger.

"It needs to be cleaned though. It stinks something awful."

She buries her laugh into my bicep. "It really does, doesn't it?"

CHAPTER TWENTY-SIX

Jade

BOY TALK

As I'm walking out of the office Thursday evening, well past sunset, I get a text from Scarlett, *9-1-1 My place. Bring wine.*

My stomach drops. Oh no. I hope everything is okay. I abandon my plans of going home, showering in Declan's life-altering shower, and then continuing my binge of *One Tree Hill*, and send a reply to let her know I'm on my way.

When I arrive thirty minutes later, two bottles of wine in tow, my best friend meets me at the door.

"What's wrong?" I ask as she takes one of the bottles from my full hands and then hugs me tight with one arm around my neck. She has a solid hold for such a small chick.

"Nothing. We just missed you." She frees me from her vise-like grip but grabs my arm and pulls me with her into the kitchen. Piper and Dakota are sitting in chairs in front of the island. Music is playing from one of their phones and two charcuterie boards are laid out with meats, cheeses, nuts, and chocolate.

"You scared me." I swat at my best friend's hand. "Do not use 9-1-1 when it isn't an emergency."

"I'm sorry," she says as she grabs an empty wine glass. "But we haven't seen you in weeks."

"You saw me yesterday."

"Work doesn't count."

"Fine. I saw you last weekend at their anniversary shindig." I wave to Dakota. "Great party by the way."

"It was, wasn't it?" Dakota beams.

"That doesn't count either," Scarlett says. "We needed girl time."

I smile as I take a seat in a chair between Dakota and Piper. Now that I know everyone is okay, I'm happy to see them. "And the wine?"

Scarlett pours me a glass and then refills everyone else's before she leans on the island. "We figured the best way to get you talking about Declan was to liquor you up."

"I'm gonna need way more wine than this," I mutter, only half-kidding.

"Are you together now?" Dakota asks.

"We got married, remember?" I shove a hunk of cheese in my mouth.

"You know what she means." Piper nudges me with an elbow. "Spill the details. We need some new gossip around here. It's all 'Leo's so great. Maverick's so amazing. Tyler's so hot.'"

She grins big as she says the last part, and we all laugh.

"You guys are all very predictable and boring now, but I am not going to be your entertainment with my messy love life."

The truth is I'm jealous of how happy they all are. Their relationships are unshakable, and Declan and I are somewhere between faking a marriage and being seriously into each other. He does these nice things for me: going to events, building me an office, and so, so many more little things.

I can't help but wonder if he really likes me as much as it seems or if he's just holding up his side of our agreement. I don't doubt that he likes me, but it's hard to gauge which actions are because he wants to spend time with me and which are because he agreed to be my fake husband. It's a lot. The best way I've found to navigate it, is to not think too hard about it. And kissing. Lots of kissing.

"Where are the guys if you're all together?" I ask, pointing between the three of them.

"At Ash's house," Dakota answers. "Did Declan go over?"

"I'm not sure."

They all look at me like they think it's weird I don't know Declan's minute-to-minute schedule. Is that odd? Should I have texted him to tell him I was coming here? Sam never really cared unless it impacted plans we had made together.

I stare at Scarlett as I say, "I came straight here from work because someone said it was an emergency."

"What do you two usually do at night?" Piper asks.

"I work while he does stuff around the house. He's removed so much wallpaper, he should get some sort of award. The place is looking really great." A brief image of him, shirtless and blasting rock music while he works around the house comes to mind, and it's a pretty great image, too.

"What's that smile?" Scarlett never misses anything. Especially if it has the potential to embarrass me.

"I was picturing Declan shirtless and sweaty."

"And on top of you?" Dakota clinks her glass against mine.

Warmth spreads through me. "That is also a great visual."

Piper's responding squeal of excitement makes me lean away from her. "Ah, I love it so much. He is so smitten. You two are adorable."

Damn these girls and their ability to get me talking.

"He's contractually obligated, not smitten."

"It is possible to be both." Scarlett's brown eyes are warm and sympathetic.

"I don't know, but it doesn't matter. We're in this for a year and we've decided to make the most out of it. He's great and I like him. There. That's all I'm giving you."

"For now." Piper's lips twitch with amusement over her wine glass. "Soon enough, you'll be just like the rest of us, in love and unable to shut up about it."

"I'm happy for you guys. Truly," I say, "but I'm just having fun while it lasts."

"Why wouldn't it last?" Dakota asks.

"Yeah. I mean, you've already survived more drama than most couples and look at you." Piper isn't wrong, but it's not that simple.

"That's because we spent the first month avoiding each other. We haven't even had a fight yet."

"So?" Scarlett's brows rise with the question. "Couples fight. It isn't a death sentence."

"Not for you, maybe." I've seen enough guys walk out on my mom after an argument to know that sometimes that's all it takes. Scarlett and Leo, Piper and Tyler, Dakota and Maverick, they are so deep in love that they can survive a fight over who has to take the trash out, or whatever it is they argue about, but Declan and I aren't in love. What's going to happen when we disagree about something?

My phone buzzes in my purse. Declan's name flashes on the

screen, *Dinner out tonight? I can pick you up from the office.*

"It's him. Isn't it?" Scarlett asks. "You're smiling."

I hadn't even realized I was, but of course, she's right. I dig in my purse for the chocolate bar I also picked up for this so-called emergency. "Shut up."

I toss the chocolate at her and then reply, *Can't. I'm at Scarlett's house with the girls.*

Before I can set my phone down, he sends another text. This one is a selfie. It's Declan making a frowny face at the camera.

I run my finger along the screen. Even making a goofy face, he's undeniably handsome. I fight the urge to say goodbye to my friends and go hang with him. We're going to another event for the magazine tomorrow night, so he should enjoy a free night where he isn't obligated to hang out with me. *The guys are at Ash's. You should go hang with them. I'll text you on my way home. We have two bottles of wine and a lot of boy talk to do still.*

CHAPTER TWENTY-SEVEN

Declan

YOU'RE JADE FREAKING DAVIS

I pace the living room, looking out the front window at the street as I call Jade. We're supposed to be at an event in fifteen minutes. Another magazine thing at some museum. I didn't get a lot of details, but I was promised food.

"Hey, where are you?" I ask when she answers.

"Still at the office. I'm going to have to meet you there." In the background, I can hear people talking and things shuffling around like Jade is searching for something on her desk.

"I could pick you up on my way."

"The event is closer to you than me."

"Yeah. So?"

"That's silly. It's out of your way."

I run a hand through my hair. Telling her I don't mind going out of my way to pick her up won't convince her, that much I know. Jade might very well be the most stubborn woman I've ever met. If I order takeout, she demands to pay me for half. Like I need twenty bucks. And after every event I attend with her, I wake up the next morning to breakfast or coffee made for me.

The day after I showed her the office space, she cleaned the kitchen, like super cleaned, even mopped the floor, and she made homemade blueberry muffins. I don't even really like blueberries, but I ate every single one, afraid that if I didn't, she'd do something else to repay the favor. God forbid, she bring home another piece of furniture that smells like a nineteen nineties pool hall.

I like doing things for her, and with her. I just like being around her. But man does she make it difficult to do nice things, knowing it's going to make her feel like she needs to repay the favor. A part of me recognizes that her need for there to be an equal amount of give and take is a defense mechanism, but the other part of me, the more selfish and impatient part, knows what it really means is that she doesn't fully trust me.

"Okay. I'll meet you there," I relent.

"Oh shoot. I need to change, and my dress is at the house. I'm leaving now. I'll hurry."

"Take your time."

She ends the call before I can get the full sentence out. Twenty minutes later, Jade comes through the front door like a tornado. She tosses her bag on the floor and sprints up the stairs yelling, "Five minutes."

I expect it to take much longer, but exactly five minutes later, she jogs back down, holding her shoes in one hand and lifting the hem of her red dress up with the other.

"Woah." I'm frozen in place as she continues to rush around, getting her shoes on and shoving her phone and lipstick in a small black purse.

"Sorry, sorry." When she finally looks up at me and finds me staring, slack-jawed, her expression morphs into something like confusion. "What?"

"You look…" I struggle to put together words. So fucking hot is what I'm thinking, but I temper my response. "Wow."

A smile curves her painted red lips. "This old thing?"

"Price tag's still on it."

Gasping, she lifts both arms and swivels to find the nonexistent price tag.

"Kidding." I step forward and offer her an arm. "Ready?"

She swats at my chest and then lets out a small laugh. "Yeah. I'm finally ready. Are *you* ready to go to this thing? I overheard some girls at work today saying it was a total snooze fest last year."

"Yeah. I'm excited."

She cuts me a glance that calls bullshit.

I lead her out to the car and open the passenger door. "I'm starving. Plus, I get to walk around with a *super-hot* chick all night. I think I'll live."

She laughs again. I fucking love making her laugh.

An hour into the most boring event ever, I'm second-guessing my earlier statement. I have had to sit through some really stuffy, boring team events, but this one beats them all. We're seated at a table with four older men, who haven't stopped talking about politics since we sat down.

"This is awful," she whispers, "and the food is terrible."

After I shove another piece of stale roll in my mouth, I nod. I'm about to ask her if she wants to make an escape when one of the men, I think he said his name was Dave, turns his attention to me.

"Tough loss last season." He rests an elbow on the white tablecloth, flashing a Rolex.

"Yes, sir. It was."

"How's the wrist?"

I make a fist, instinctively, checking for any discomfort. Late last year, I broke it during a game and had to have surgery. Longest six weeks of my life.

"All good. I'm ready."

Dave grins. "Is it true you stayed in that game against Tampa after you broke it?"

"I heard you stayed in the game and scored two goals," the guy next to Jade leans over her and pipes in loudly. He's had four glasses of scotch in under an hour, but he started out being loud, so I'm not sure his booming voice can be blamed on the alcohol.

"Don't believe everything you hear." I drop a hand on Jade's thigh, and she jumps with surprise.

"I think I see an old friend across the room. Come with me to say hello?" I stand and offer her a hand.

She gets to her feet quickly. "Of course."

Clutching her fingers in mine, I head across the room as she expects, but then duck out into the hall.

"Where are we going?"

"No idea."

"You didn't see an old friend, did you?"

Giving my head a shake, I come to a stop next to the wall and lean my back against it.

Jade places both hands on my chest as she invades my space. "You aren't very good at being the center of attention, are you?"

"Tonight isn't about me." I cover both her hands with one of mine.

"It isn't really about me either. I was hoping I'd get a chance to talk to Robin. She's an editor that's been with the company for like twenty years. She's a legend. But she isn't even here. I'm sorry I made you come for nothing. I owe you."

"No, you don't. I signed up for this, remember?"

I get an almost imperceptible nod. "Did you really play with a broken wrist?"

"Two games."

"Why?" Both brows shoot up as she searches my face for understanding.

"The team needed me."

Pushing off me, she takes a step back and glances down the hall in both directions. "Let's get out of here and save whatever's left of this evening."

"Are you sure? I can go back in and booze and schmooze some more if it'll help."

"I'm positive. Those guys at the table don't even know who I am."

"You're Jade freaking Davis." I raise my voice and lift my arms over my head.

"And you're ridiculous," she says, but the smile it gets out of her is worth the stares in our direction. I'll shout her name from the rooftops if it'll make her happy.

When we get to the car outside, I go to the passenger side to open her door. That happy look is gone and replaced with a sort of somber expression.

"Thanks for tonight. I'm sorry it wasn't very much fun."

"I always have fun with you." I wink at her.

"I can think of a lot funner ways we could have spent tonight." Heat sparks in her eyes.

"Let's get home and see if we can salvage the night then, huh?" I pull my keys from my pocket, then dangle them in front of her. "Wanna drive?"

"Really?!"

Fuck, the way her face lights up steals the breath from my lungs. I'm a total goner for my wife.

CHAPTER TWENTY-EIGHT

Jade

HIDING FROM YOUR HUSBAND

"Honey, I'm home!" I call, walking through the front door. I set my laptop bag and purse on the entryway table.

"In the office." Declan's voice carries through the house, along with the faint clink of metal.

When I get to the room he calls his office, he's mid-set, squatting with a barbell along his back, holding what looks like a lot of heavy weight.

He smiles at me in the mirror in front of him, then racks the bar.

"Hey." He steps to me and drops a kiss on my lips. "I thought you were going out with the girls."

"I was, but Scarlett wasn't feeling well, so we rescheduled."

"Lucky me." He scoops me up and I wrap my arms and legs around him. We kiss all the way to the kitchen, where he sets me on the counter. "What do you want for dinner?"

I love that he asks me the question, even though he is planning to eat one of his healthy pre-cooked meals that he's been devouring five times a day since he started prepping for the season.

Training camp and the official start of team practices aren't for another month, but all the guys have been getting together to work out and skate every day. I don't think I truly appreciated how much time and effort goes into what he does. Not just during the season, but year-round.

"I don't know. I'll make myself a sandwich later or something."

He holds up one of his food containers.

"You would share your precious, pre-made meals with me?"

Smiling, he tosses them both in the microwave. "You can't live on peanut butter and jelly."

"Not true."

He comes to stand between my legs.

"What are your plans for tonight?"

"I was planning on watching the baseball game in front of the TV, passing out, and letting you wake me up all drunk and giggly."

"I guess I could go upstairs and down what's left of that bottle of vodka in the freezer and reappear in an hour or two."

"Something to look forward to another night."

The microwave dings and Declan grabs our dinner and two forks. We take it into the living room, where he turns on the baseball game.

"Wow. This is good," I say, after taking a bite of the chicken, sweet potato, and broccoli meal. Honestly, my expectations were low. I take another bite to make sure I'm not just really hungry. I worked through lunch today, rewriting an article with Melody's notes.

"I've been telling you. Way better than PB&J three times a week."

"Let's not get carried away." I love me some peanut butter and strawberry jelly on wheat bread with the crusts cut off.

"How was work?" he asks, between bites.

I love that he asks. Sam was completely disinterested in hearing about my work. In fact, he hated my job, which I guess was fair, all things considered.

"Really good. By the way, have you heard of the Hat Tricks and Puck Bunnies podcast?"

"Yeah, definitely." He looks intrigued. "Why?"

"They invited me on the show. Well, us, actually. They want to do an entire show on us and two other couples. It's a whole off-season, 'man behind the helmet' angle. You tell them how you're spending the summer, and I add in fun tidbits."

He drops the container on the coffee table. "Jade, I don't think that's a good idea."

"Why not?" I prepared myself for this outcome, but it still stings. A big podcast like this would get me in front of a whole new audience. If even a fraction of those listeners decided to read my articles, it'd mean a huge jump in numbers.

"Hockey is my job. Even if it's a one-off, shooting the shit type interview, it's still a part of that."

"Okay," I say, trying to figure out his real concern.

"I don't want to spin a story to people that weigh in on my professional life. I know these guys. I respect them."

"And you don't want to flaunt our fake marriage in front of them," I state matter-of-factly. Things have been going so well, the lines have blurred for me.

"I'm sorry," he says.

"No, of course. I'll tell them no." For reasons I can't fully articulate, I feel hurt and silly because I'm hurt. Of course, he has boundaries. It's just, this man has gotten so far under my skin in such a short amount of time, that it doesn't feel like we're flaunting something fake anymore.

I'm still thinking about it the next morning, when I send an apologetic 'no thank you' email to the podcast.

"It's done." I blow out a long breath after the whoosh sound, indicating the email has been sent.

"Sorry," Scarlett says. "But you're getting a ton of media requests. Another one—a better one—is right around the corner. I can feel it."

We decided to work from our favorite coffee shop this morning instead of at the office. My phone buzzes on the table between us and she smiles. "See?"

I hold up the screen so she can see it's my mom calling and not my next big interview request, then I hit ignore. My friend doesn't comment on the way I dodge my mom's calls. Talking to my mother requires an all-day buildup.

"Hey, do you want to get out of town this weekend?" I ask.

"And go where?"

"Anywhere."

She purses her lips and arches a brow. "Hiding from your husband?"

"No," I say automatically. "Maybe. I need a breather. We're dating but married, living together and always in each other's space. It's a mindfuck." It's going so well that it's freaking me out.

"Yeah." She nods in agreement. "I get that."

"We could road trip to Chicago or rent a house on the lake for the weekend."

"I can't." Her lips pull into a half smile. "I am doing two engagement shoots tomorrow and I promised Cadence I'd come by on Sunday to have some adult conversation."

Scarlett's sister, Cadence, had a little boy two months ago. I don't generally say this about babies, but he's the freaking cutest.

Scarlett has to go into the office a few hours later, but I stay at the coffee shop, downing copious amounts of caffeine and trying to write. Trying because not a whole lot of words are being written.

When my mom calls a second time, I decide that talking to her is slightly less painful than staring at a blank screen and answer. "Hey, Mom."

"Hi." That one word, or rather the way she says it, has me immediately on high-alert. "Am I too old for pink walls?"

"What's wrong?" The only time she gets a burning desire to paint the walls or buy new bedroom furniture is when she's single.

She huffs a little laugh. "Can't a mother just call to check in on her daughter?"

"Yes, you're too old for pink walls."

"I figured as much."

"What happened with Kenny?"

"He moved out last week."

"Why didn't you call me?"

"I'm calling you now." Translation, she's spent the past week playing Fleetwood Mac records and burning sage in the house.

"I'm sorry."

"It wasn't meant to be." She says it like it's the universe's fault, instead of hers or Kenny's. "What are you up to?"

"Working."

"Still?"

I check the time. It's only five. She'd probably be appalled to know

I work most nights until six or seven, and that's just the hours I put in at the office. "I'm almost done."

I close my laptop and stand and stretch.

"Big plans this weekend?"

"No. Probably just working."

"You shouldn't work so much. You're young. You should be out, having fun."

I make a noise that isn't exactly agreement.

"I miss you," she says.

"Maybe we could meet up for lunch sometime this weekend?"

"Or you could come here and I could make something for us."

"Yeah," I say, not exactly on board, but then I think through what my weekend will be like if I stay. Hanging with Declan and working on the house. Lazy mornings and late nights. It sounds great, which should have me rushing home to him right now, but I still can't get a read on this situation.

I like him. I like him even more than I thought possible. And I think he genuinely likes me too, but we're only two months into this thing. When we got married, I thought the worst possible outcome was us hating each other by the six-month mark. Now I'm more scared I won't want it to end.

"You know what. How about I come for the weekend?"

"Seriously?" The last time I stayed overnight at my mom's house, I think I was nineteen, so the surprise in her voice is warranted.

"We can paint and shop for new bedding and furniture. We'll go all out."

And maybe while we're doing it, I can figure out how to date my husband.

When I was young, my mom and I bounced around apartments and houses to live with her boyfriends. Things would be stable for six months or so, then they'd break up and mom and I would be back out on our own. I was ten when I realized this was going to be a constant cycle of my life and begged my mom to find a house of our own.

I thought that it'd be better to have her boyfriends move in and out, then us always being the ones hopping around, but I'm not sure that was actually true. This house is tainted with memories of all her past boyfriends.

Still, it was nice that we stopped having to pack up and go. My old bedroom was turned into a craft room about a month after I left for college. I wasn't offended. It's a small house and I had no desire to return, not having a room made it an easy excuse not to visit.

But as I toss and turn on the sofa, I'm seriously wishing my old twin bed was still in the spare room. Or that I was back at my current residence.

My phone buzzes on the coffee table and I reach for it; Declan's name is on the screen, along with a picture I took of him at Jack's pool party. The man really looks great in a pair of trunks.

"Hi," I answer, keeping my voice quiet.

"Hey." His deep reply sends goosebumps racing down my arms. "Are you busy?"

"No. Getting ready for bed."

"Did you have a good evening with your mom?"

"Yeah. We prepped her room to paint tomorrow, picked up supplies and then went out to dinner."

"Sounds nice."

"It was…mostly."

He stays silent, giving me time to add more.

"She's so happy for me. For us. I hate lying to her. She may not have been the world's greatest mother, but I still love her and hate keeping something like this a secret."

"So don't."

I laugh at how quickly he says it, and at how simple it seems to him.

"Too many people know already. If this got out, it would be bad for both of us."

"She's family," he says. "My family, my friends on the team, all know. It makes sense for you to be honest with yours too. She wouldn't really sell out her own daughter, would she?"

"No," I say without hesitation. She's been selfish and inadvertently callous, but never intentionally.

"Then tell her. I'm fine with it. I trust you."

Something in my chest twists at how freely he's given me that trust. I have to wonder if I deserve it.

"Anyway," he says when I don't respond, "I was just calling to make sure you got there safely and that everything was okay. I didn't realize you were even thinking about going to your mom's this weekend."

That twisting sensation tightens.

"Everything is fine. She called this afternoon and sounded kind of upset about her latest breakup."

He makes a noise that doesn't sound like he completely believes that's the entire story, but again, he doesn't push.

"I'll be back Sunday, and, in the meantime, you have the house to yourself all weekend."

"A few months ago, that would have sounded nice."

I squeeze my eyes shut. My voice trembles as I say, "I'll see you Sunday, okay?"

"Yeah," he clips.

"Bye."

He waits a few beats, like maybe he's hoping I'll say more, then says, "Night, Jade."

The next afternoon, while we're repainting my mom's bedroom, I decide to broach the subject of my marriage.

"How come you never got married again after Pat?" I ask her. Pat was husband number three. It lasted a month.

While I wait for her answer, I keep my gaze on the paint roller. She decided on a soft white for all the walls, except one, which is, of course, pink. She chose a dusty, light pink, and it actually turned out really nice. It turns out, pink has no age limit.

"You wish I'd gotten married again?" she asks, disbelief making her voice lift several octaves. "To which guy? I thought you hated them all."

"I didn't hate all of them." I finally look over at her. She's stopped painting and is arching a brow at me. "Okay, I didn't really like any of them either. But you did. Some of them you even dated for a year or more."

"None of them asked," she says. "And even if they had, I'm not sure I really saw myself saying yes."

"You don't want to get married again?"

"No, I guess I don't. Maybe if I meet the right guy. Someone I can see myself with forever. It's been a while since I felt like that. Like with you and Declan. You must have known pretty fast that he was the one."

I know this is my opening to tell her the truth, but I grapple for the right words. "Not exactly."

Her mouth pulls into a frown. "You couldn't have dated for more than a month before you got married."

I set my roller down in the paint tray. "We didn't date at all."

My pulse quickens and I take several quick breaths before adding, "Sam called off our engagement the week of the wedding and Declan stepped in to save my job."

I think I've stunned her. She just looks at me with wide eyes, her mouth opening and closing, but no words come out.

"I know it sounds bad."

"How could you do something like this?"

"It isn't that big of a deal. And now we really are dating, so it isn't a complete lie."

"But you're not dating, Jade. You're married. Marriage is a beautiful, sacred thing."

"That ends in divorce half the time."

"So that's your plan?"

I nod. "Melody said we needed to give it at least a year and that works for Declan too because he'll be in the off-season next July. It'll give things a month or two to quiet down before hockey starts again."

"I cannot believe this." She shakes her head and looks down at the floor. "I'm really disappointed in you."

"That's rich, Mom. You've dated a dozen or more guys over the years, moving them into this house, into our lives, like they were going to be around forever when you admittedly knew they weren't, and you're disappointed in *me*?"

"You are deceiving people. It's wrong."

"We're really together now. I like him a lot."

"You can't start a relationship like this."

"Says who?"

"It isn't right. This isn't healthy for you or him. How do you expect him to respect you after the choices you've made? You can't really think he'll want to be with you after this is all over?"

It's all my worst fears spoken aloud, and icy dread washes over me. "Maybe you're right, but how could I possibly know what a healthy relationship looks like? I've avoided coming home for years because you're always so focused on whatever guy you're dating, that you lose sight of everything else. You don't even know who you are without a boyfriend. At least I can stand on my own."

Hurt flashes in her eyes, and I regret saying the words, even if they're true.

"I'm sorry," I say.

"No, I guess I deserve that. I know I wasn't perfect, but I did my best. I'm gonna get some air." She stares at me a beat, so much disappointment in her gaze that it makes my stomach uneasy.

"Fuck," I mutter when she's gone. "Fuck, fuck, fuck."

CHAPTER TWENTY-NINE

Declan

NEW MUGS

It's Saturday night, and I'm sitting at Ash's house, watching TV with him and Jack. Everly and her friend Grace are here too, getting ready to go out for the night.

"Where are you going?" Jack asks them as they start for the front door.

"To a friend's house," Everly retorts with all kinds of attitude. "I already told Ty and he's fine with it."

Jack grunts.

"Have fun," Ash calls after them. "Call if you need a ride or whatever."

"Will do!" Everly waves and heads out. Grace hesitates, then also gives a shy wave.

"Later," Ash says, smiling a little too hard at Everly's friend.

When she finally goes out after Everly, Jack elbows him. "Terrible idea."

"What?" Ash asks, like it isn't obvious he's into Grace. He looks to me for backup.

"I agree. Terrible idea."

"Whatever. She's cute and hella smart."

I shake my head. "Still, no."

He huffs. "We should go out."

I feel old as fuck. The last thing I want to do right now is go out. I want to go home, but I've been avoiding doing just that all day.

I used to love the peace and quiet of my own place, but now it isn't the same without Jade. Her stuff is everywhere. She's everywhere. And I've started to like it better that way.

"I'm out," I say.

Ash looks to Jack.

"Fine. I'm in," he says.

I stand to leave them to it.

"Are you sure?" Ash asks. "Nothing waiting at home for you."

He is right about that, but I still pass. "Have fun. See you in the morning."

I walk back to my place, second-guessing my decision a dozen times until I see Jade's red Volkswagen in the driveway.

My heart rate speeds up and I quicken my steps to get inside. I come up short when I spot her bag inside the front door.

"Jade?" I call, moving toward the kitchen, where the light is on. Her back is to me, and her red hair is pulled up in a ponytail. My heart fucking leaps at the sight of her.

"Hey. When'd you get back?"

She glances over her shoulder at me, then grabs a coffee mug from the cabinet. "A couple of hours ago."

"Oh, shit, sorry. I was just at Ash's, getting in a workout. You should have texted."

"No, it's fine. I know you're busy and I am behind on my article."

"Did you have a good weekend?" I ask, cautiously. She wasn't supposed to be back until tomorrow.

"Yeah. We finished painting and I didn't want to sleep on the sofa another night."

It isn't the enthusiastic, I missed you and couldn't wait another night to see you, that I was hoping for, but I'm still glad she's here.

"Where are the other mugs?" she asks.

"Oh, I got new ones while you were gone. Plates, too. Eight new place settings. I had no idea all that shit was supposed to match."

Jade turns and stares at me. Fuck, she's gorgeous. She makes my kitchen gorgeous. I take a step toward her, but she crosses her arms over her chest. "You bought new mugs?"

"Yeah. Those others were so old, I can't even remember where I got them. I think they might have been something my grandma sent me when I got my first apartment."

"And you just threw them out?"

"Y-yeah," I answer slowly. "I thought you'd like the new ones. They're red."

I feel like an idiot pointing that out when she can clearly see the color.

"Why haven't you told me about Crissy?"

My mind spins, trying to figure out how we went from mugs to this. "Crissy?"

"Yeah. Your ex-girlfriend. You've never once mentioned her."

"She was never my girlfriend. We hooked up occasionally over the years, but it's been over for a while now. How did you hear about her?"

"Dakota mentioned her. She thought I knew."

Jade's eyes blaze with hurt or maybe anger, but I'm struggling to understand why. I haven't given Crissy a second thought since the wedding. Then it hits me, and I feel all the mistakes of my past hit me full force. If she knows about Crissy, she knows about the post that got her fired from her internship with the Wildcats.

"I didn't cheat on her. She posted that picture because she was pissed at me for going out with someone else, but we didn't have that kind of relationship. We went weeks or months without talking." I'd never cheat on Jade, or anyone for that matter.

"I still don't understand why you wouldn't tell me about her. When is the last time you were together?"

I'm starting to feel like whatever is bothering her isn't really about the damn mugs or Crissy, but I'll tell her whatever she wants to know. Maybe then she'll really understand that what we have is different than anything else I've had before.

"March."

"And you haven't talked to her at all since?"

"She texted a couple of times. I told her it was over. She was struggling to accept it."

"When?"

"The last time I talked to her was the night of your bachelorette party. She was calling and texting. I finally blocked her."

Her gaze narrows, and she studies me for a long moment. "So you agreed to marry me hoping it would help get her off your back?"

"Of course not. It wasn't like that. I saw an opportunity to help you, and I took it."

"Why?"

"I wanted to. We've been through this."

"I know, but *why*? Why me?"

I'm not sure how to answer that, and I don't want to bullshit her.

"This was a mistake," she says.

A cold sensation ripples down my spine. "What was a mistake?"

"Us. Me and you." She motions between us. "We were stupid to agree to this arrangement and even stupider to get involved while we're in this temporary marriage."

"Is this because I got rid of the mugs? I don't even know why you use them. Yours are much nicer."

"I use your old mugs because I like them!" She yells as she throws her hands up in the air. Silence falls between us after her outburst, then she whispers, "I'm gonna go."

Jade takes off out of the kitchen and up the stairs.

"Go where?" I ask, following a few feet behind.

"Back to my mom's for now, then I'll find a place. No one is going to check up on us to make sure we're living together. We have nine more months and then we can go our separate ways and forget all of this. I'm sorry I dragged you into my mess."

"Wait a second." I jog ahead of her. "You didn't drag me into anything. I was a very willing participant in all of it."

"You're a good guy, Declan," she says like that's the problem, then pushes past me.

I stand dumbfounded for a few seconds. What the hell is happening?

CHAPTER THIRTY

Jade

WE AREN'T OVER, SWEETHEART

Tears fall down my face as I shut the bedroom door behind me. So stupid. He looked so happy to see me. And I felt such relief to have somewhere safe to go after the fight with my mom, and now here I am leaving. I've screwed everything up so badly this time. No, I screwed this up months ago, by allowing him to step in and take Sam's place.

My mom is right. You can't start a relationship like this.

At least now, it's over. There's a comfort in the certainty of messing something up so badly you know it's irreparable. I know how to be alone. It's something I've prided myself on, never allowing a man to change me or get so deep that who I am revolves around him.

I loved Sam, or at least I thought I did, but I never worried about losing a piece of me with him. But with Declan, I feel like I'm in real danger of letting him in so deep that when it ends, I'll never recover.

He knocks twice before opening the door. My back is to him, but

I can tell he's hesitating before stepping into my space.

The words that come out are harder and louder than I expect from him. "What the hell, Jade?"

He's pissed. I stop packing. Fuck it, there's nothing here I need. I put my half-packed bag on my shoulder. I swipe at my tears before looking at him. "Don't worry. I'm going."

"Like hell you are." He stands in the doorway, blocking my exit. "Not until you tell me what the fuck is going on? You leave Friday without warning, then come back early and pick a fight over mugs and a girl I don't give two-shits about."

My throat is thick with emotion and more tears threaten to spill over if I speak.

He takes a step closer, and his voice is softer when he asks, "What happened with your mom?"

"I told her about us. We got into a fight, so I came back early."

"And now you're going back there because we got into a fight?"

I bite on the corner of my lip.

"You aren't really going to your mom's, are you?"

"I can stay at a hotel for a day or two until I find an apartment. It's no big deal."

"You'd rather stay at a hotel than here?"

Frustration bubbles up inside me, taking over the sadness. Why is he acting like he still wants me here after I just yelled at him over freaking mugs?

"I thought that's what you would want?"

"You think I *want* you to go?"

"Yeah. Why would you possibly want me to stay? I've been hot and cold. I'm a freaking mess, and I can't seem to stop screwing things up with you." Even though it's the last thing I want to do.

"I like you."

"But I yelled at you."

"What do you think I did when I stormed in here and told you that you weren't leaving?"

"You're just further proving my point. We're terrible for each other."

"Fuck that noise."

"You're a great guy, but I'm a horrible wife/girlfriend/person. You don't want to be with me."

"I think you can let me be the judge of that."

He takes my bag by the strap and pulls it off my shoulder and then throws it onto the bed.

"Why do you like using my old mugs?"

"I don't know. I just do." A little defensiveness works back into my tone. "I don't want to fight with you."

"Couples fight, Jade. That doesn't mean that it's over."

"Is that what we are?" I whisper.

"Yeah, baby. Whatever you think, whatever anyone else thinks about how this started, my feelings are now real." He lifts my chin up with a finger, so I'm forced to stare into his dark brown eyes. "Why do you like my old mugs?"

"Because they're yours." I liked using them, picturing Declan having coffee out of them a million times before. His hands around the same handle. His lips touching the mug in the same spot. I know it's silly, but I wanted that connection to him at first. Now I'm afraid it's that connection that's going to burn me alive.

His lips cover mine in a hard kiss that earns a squeak of surprise from me. My hesitation only lasts a second before I'm kissing him back with all the emotions swirling inside me. Declan keeps his mouth pressed against mine as he scoops my legs out from underneath me and falls onto the bed with me.

My heart is racing when he pulls back and stares at me.

He slides a hand around my waist. His calloused hands slipping under my tank top and skimming over my skin. "We aren't over, sweetheart."

I shut off my brain and all the negative thoughts that have been nagging me all weekend and surrender to him.

Pulling at his T-shirt, I get it over his head, then help him get my tank off. We're undressed so quickly and then he's pushing into me, filling me so fully that I can't tell where he ends, and I begin.

He isn't gentle, but I don't want him to be. Every thrust, every searing kiss, reminds me how good we are together, despite the circumstances or the reasons we got into this.

As my orgasm gets close, Declan pulls out of me and moves down, covering my pussy with his mouth as I fall over the edge.

He doesn't stop after one orgasm. He pushes for another, until I'm chanting his name in a nonsensical string of sentences. "Declan. Oh, stop. Don't stop." and "You. Amazing. So good."

When he pushes inside a second time, I am so ready for him. Nothing feels as good as when he's inside me.

He slows his pace and says, "Look at me."

My gaze snaps up to his. He pulls out almost completely, then inches back in, all the while staring down at me. "Say it."

When I don't immediately reply, he pulls back out. I whimper and a grin tugs at the corners of his lips.

"Say it, Jade."

"We aren't over."

He slams into me. Pleasure twists his features as I cry out. "Not by a longshot."

CHAPTER THIRTY-ONE

Declan

I'M NOT PLANNING ON DECKING ANYONE

In mid-September, training camp finally arrives. There's a different air in the locker room already. Losing so close to holding up the Cup, has us all hungry and focused. Even the new guys seem to feel it.

I pull off my sweaty T-shirt and shorts and head for the shower. Today we finished up with a weight-training session that has my muscles quivering. I'm gonna be hurting later. Jade's been taking care of me in the evenings with epic rubdowns that undo the knots, though the best part is that they usually (always) end in sex.

Things with us have been good. She's still fighting with her mom, which I know has her uneasy, but she hasn't picked any more fights or tried to leave. Though if she does, I'll happily remind her that we aren't done. There are so many more things I want to do and see with her.

For the first time ever, I'm starting the season eager but also excited for the little breaks where I can take her on vacation, make love to her on the beach or get cozy in a winter cabin. I'm even excited about Thanksgiving—a holiday I haven't celebrated in years. Maybe I'll invite the guys over to our house. Our house. I like the sound of it.

When I get out of the shower, Jack is sitting at his stall waiting for me.

"Hey." He tips his chin in greeting. "Wanna grab a beer and look over some film from today's scrimmage?"

"I can't. Jade and I made plans to get dinner at that new Mexican place down the street."

"I could eat." He turns to Ash. "Do you want to get dinner with us?"

Fortunately, or unfortunately, I'm not sure yet, Jack is the only one that's free. We swing by and pick up Jade, then head to the restaurant.

After we sit down at the table, I rest a hand on her thigh and lean close to kiss her temple. "He invited himself."

She laughs lightly and her red hair catches the light. "I think your teammates are jealous you're spending so much time with me."

It's my turn to chuckle. "Maybe so."

Her phone rings in her purse, and when she looks at the screen, she sighs. "It's work. I better make sure something isn't wrong with my article. It needs to go to the printers tonight."

"Go. I'll order you a margarita."

"A strawberry one," she says, standing and putting the phone to her ear.

"You two seem happy," Jack says when she's gone.

"Things are good."

"I'm glad." He fiddles with a coaster on the table, then adds, "I don't have to tell you that it was risky getting involved. Your contract might be secure, but I've seen less exciting drama than this take guys out. If people found out—"

I hold up a hand to stop him. "I appreciate your concerns. I knew them months ago. What's really on your mind?"

"I just want to make sure your head is right. Leo told me the guys at HTPB wanted to interview you and Jade."

"Yeah, that's right." I still don't see where he's going with this. "She turned it down."

He sighs. "I'm sorry. I don't want to sound like a dick. I don't know Jade that well, but I worry this situation is going to get you in trouble, or worse, impact your game. Relationship drama is the worst kind of distraction."

I nod. I don't doubt the truth of his words.

"Is she worth it?" he asks.

It's only because I can hear the real concern in his voice that I don't feel like hitting him. "Yeah, man. She is."

He sighs. "Then at least promise me you'll give me a heads-up if anything should happen. I'll do whatever I can to have your back."

"Thank you for that."

A smile finally lifts the corners of his mouth. "You're different with her."

"Yeah?"

He nods. "Yeah, you've got that same dopey-ass smile Leo's had on his face since he met Scarlett."

"It worked out for them," I point out.

"I think you're forgetting the part where he got his A stripped and spent an evening in jail."

"I'm not planning on decking anyone. Except maybe you." I grin, so he knows I'm only half-serious.

Jade comes back and the conversation flows easily. Despite Jack's concerns, he's all smiles and laughs at dinner. He asks her about what she's working on, then she asks us about camp today, and pokes fun at Jack's newest commercial—an ad for a local barber shop. Jack can dish it, but he takes it well too.

By the end of the night, any weirdness between me and my long-time teammate has passed.

"See you in the morning," I call as he drops us off.

"Later. Bye, Jade." He lifts a hand in a wave.

Inside, Jade and I head straight for bed. She's been putting in even longer hours than usual at the office, and I have to be back at the arena early tomorrow.

Climbing under the covers, she snuggles up to my side and rests a hand on my chest, then yawns. "I might be too tired to be your personal masseuse tonight."

"That's all right." I knead at the knots in her shoulders and neck. "Feels like you need it more than me."

She moans. "Never stop."

"What'd work need earlier?"

She glances up at me and her expression grows serious. "Melody wasn't happy with my piece for the print issue next month. Even though I spent all day rewriting it."

"I'm sorry. You're a great writer. Don't let her get in your head."

I've started reading everything she publishes—online and in the magazine. She's smart and witty. I can see why podcasts and other media have reached out to her. Her personality comes across so vividly in her writing that you can't help but think, I want to know that person.

"It isn't the writing she had a problem with exactly. It's the content. She wanted me to write about the start of the Wildcats season and how it's impacted our marriage, time together, etc. I guess people find the lives of hockey girlfriends and wives especially fascinating. Anyway, I tweaked it to add in more details about how it changed my life, but she still wasn't thrilled. I think she was hoping for more of an inside scoop."

I keep rubbing circles over her smooth skin. I think of Jack's earlier concerns. Since our initial conversation about keeping my job out of it as much as possible, she's done just that. I appreciate it. Especially because I know it's caused some tension at the office.

"Thank you for doing that and I'm sorry she's giving you a hard time."

"It's no big deal. She's just still salty that I turned down the Hat Tricks and Puck Bunnies podcast." She lets out a loud sigh. "Sometimes I think it'd be easier to walk away and deal with the consequences."

This is the first I've heard her say anything even remotely close to wanting to quit. I've thought it a million times, but I know what her job means to her.

"I bet a thousand other magazines would be thrilled to have you."

She yawns again. "Melody would lose her shit. I have no idea what she'd do to us."

"Hey." I squeeze her shoulder, bringing her tighter against my chest. "If you don't want to work there anymore, we'll deal with the fallout."

"Just like that? What about not wanting to create waves during the season?" She looks up at me, searching my face.

"I can ask my agent or Elyse in the front office. She deals with PR for the team. We can figure it out, if that's what you want."

A slow smile spreads across her face. "I don't know how you're real."

"James is probably still awake." I start to sit up, but Jade pushes me back down.

"Give me some time to think about it?"

"Of course." I roll on top of her. "Take all the time you need."

CHAPTER THIRTY-TWO

Jade

YOU CAN HAVE WHATEVER YOU WANT

On a chilly October night, the Wildcats have their first home game. I ride to the arena with Scarlett. I completely forgot about the WAG box until we're walking through the doors of the swanky suite.

It has a private bar, cushy seats, a large screen to follow the game closer, restrooms, a private nursing room, and even a playroom for the women with small kids.

The girls that know each other hug and catch up. Excitement hangs in the air for the game and season.

Someone thrusts a green beanie in my hand. It has Sato in white with the number seventy-seven.

"What is this?" I ask, glancing at my best friend.

"You're officially a WAG." Scarlett grins at me and then puts on her own beanie with Leo's last name and number. "Amalia owns an adorable clothing boutique. Mostly kid stuff, but she makes custom gear for the wives and girlfriends every year. I have a sweet leather jacket from the playoffs. She's married to Morrison. He's number twelve. They have a little boy named Johan. Cute but a total terror," she whispers the last part.

"I don't think I should be in here."

"Why not?" She ignores me and leads us to seats next to Piper and Dakota. "You're one of us now."

Declan told me that his team was his family, but I don't think I realized exactly what he meant until now.

"How's work?" Piper asks. "Loved your article on makeup sex, by the way."

"Yeah, that was gold," Dakota agrees. "Johnny and I don't really fight, but sometimes we pretend, just so we can have hot makeup sex."

"Work is…" I struggle to find the right word. "Challenging."

"Melody is on her ass," Scarlett answers for me.

"She wants me to push harder into the whole married to a professional hockey player angle."

"Makes sense. Hockey players are hot," Piper says.

Everyone murmurs their agreement. Me too. Declan's body is insane, which I already knew, but seeing him use it like this is definitely doing something to me.

The ladies continue to chat and they're all smiles and laughs until the puck drops. Then, all their attention is on the game. Some of the ladies are quiet, nerves making it hard to do anything but watch. While others, like Scarlett, are loud, cheering like she wants every person in the arena to know she's Leo Lohan's girl.

I'm caught somewhere in the middle. Not because I'm nervous, but because I feel the weight of everything hitting me at once. I know what family, or rather the lack of one, did to Declan. It sent him spiraling for years until he found it in the guys on the team.

I can't risk that for him. Which means I can't quit the magazine, no matter how much I might want to. Besides, it's my mess. Walking away feels like giving up. Even if someone else wanted to hire me, I doubt Melody would make that transition easy.

When Declan's on the ice, it's hard for me to focus on anything else. He skates hard and fast from one end to the other. On one shift, he slams a guy into the boards. On the screen, they capture Declan's half smile as he takes off in the other direction, leaving the other guy stunned for a second. I wince and my pussy throbs at the same time. Damn, that's hot.

I don't know a lot about hockey, though I should for as many games as I've watched with Scarlett over the years. Even before Leo, she'd occasionally drag me along to a game, so she could cheer on her dad.

Coach Miller. Another reason I can't risk everyone finding out that Declan got married to help me keep my job. Scarlett's dad is the closest thing to a father figure I've ever had. I don't want my mistakes to mess up anything for him or the team.

I can do this for eight more months. Maybe if Declan and I attend a few more events, that'll get Melody to relax a little on the articles.

At the first intermission, I spend a few minutes talking with the girls about the first period and then find a quiet corner and call my mom. We haven't spoken since I left her house, almost a month ago. I hurt her feelings, but she hurt mine too.

"Hello?" she answers, hesitation in her tone.

"Hey, Mom."

A few seconds pass in silence. "I wasn't sure I'd hear from you."

"You could have called me."

"When someone storms out of my house, I've found it best to let them approach me in their own time."

"Why didn't you try to stop me?" Like Declan had. It's bugged me for weeks. I expect men to walk away or let me walk away, but not my mom.

"I figured you needed some time to sort through things on your own. That's why you came home in the first place, right?"

I hadn't told her that, but I guess it isn't surprising she figured it out. "Yes."

"And did you sort through it?"

"Mostly."

"Good," she says. The buzzer sounds, signaling the end of intermission. "Are you at the game?"

"Yeah."

"Declan is playing well. Or that's what this announcer is saying."

"You're watching the Wildcats?" I got my love, or rather lack of, sports from my mom.

"It's on. I wouldn't say I'm watching it exactly. I started a new cross stitch. But I thought I should see if this new son-in-law of mine is any good."

A laugh slips free. "Yeah, he's pretty good."

The guys take the ice and Mom and I fall quiet again.

"I'm sorry for the things I said about you and Declan," she says when I'm sure the conversation is over and she's going to excuse herself and hang up. "You were right. I don't know anything about healthy relationships or staying married. I hope you two are really happy together for a long time."

"I'm sorry, too. I was awful to you. No matter what choices you made when I was a kid, I'm an adult now and I can't put this on you."

"No, you can't, but you weren't wrong. I gave up on finding love a long time ago. I've settled for companionship. But when I met Declan, I thought you'd found what I hadn't. I guess it was a little bit of a shock to find out it wasn't real."

"I think love is like the color pink. It's ageless. You can still have more than companionship, Mom."

She lets out a small chuckle. "Maybe you're right."

"I better go," I say, when the action starts back up on the ice. "Can I come back another weekend and see you?"

"It's your home," she says. "You're always welcome here."

I hang up and take my seat next to Scarlett.

"Everything okay?" she asks.

I nod. "Yeah."

"You don't look convinced."

"Do you consider home to be your parents' house or Leo's now that you live together?"

"Leo's house." She smiles. "Why?"

"My mom called her house my home, and it was strange. I don't feel like that's my home anymore. I guess I haven't lived there in so long anyway."

She bumps her shoulder against mine. "It isn't the house. It's Declan. He feels like home to you now."

After the game, Jack has a party at his house. Declan and I drive straight there, and it's already packed.

Declan guides me in front of him with a hand on my lower back.

"Who are all these people?" I yell over the music.

"I have no idea and I don't care." He pulls me backward into a corner of the living room and presses into me. His lips are on mine before I realize what he's doing.

I wrap my arms around his neck and smile into the kiss. His hands slide into the back pockets of my jeans and his fingers dig into my ass as he draws me tighter against him.

"Someone is feeling frisky." I nip at his bottom lip. "Are you always like this after games? Because I think I just found a new appreciation for hockey."

"It isn't hockey." His mouth slants over mine and he lets out a little growl. "It's you."

"Me?" I ask, when we pull apart a few seconds later. "You didn't greet me like that this morning."

"You wearing that hat with my name and number on it, cheering me on."

My fingers lift to touch the beanie still on my head. "How do you know I was cheering?"

"Just a guess. Were you?"

"Maaaybe." I draw out the word. I definitely was. It turns out, once I stopped freaking out about the lies we've spun and how they could hurt the people he cares about, I'm not that different from Scarlett when it comes to cheering on my man.

He lets out a low, deep groan. "I knew it."

"You looked real good out there. I got a little carried away."

"I'm about to get carried away here." One hand moves from my ass and slips under my shirt. His fingers leave a trail of goosebumps as they move up my spine and then wrap around the back of my neck.

"You know, we do live like a hop, skip, and a jump down the road."

"Can't wait that long. Come on." He's walking again, dragging me along as he weaves through people until we reach a closed door. Pushing it open like he lives here, he flips on a light and then shuts the door, pressing me against it.

Bookshelves grab my attention as his mouth descends and covers mine.

"What is this room?"

"Library," Declan says.

"Jack has a library?!"

"You want a library, baby?" He lifts my shirt and his lips graze over the top of my breasts.

"I didn't know that was an option. I don't even buy paperbacks anymore because I got tired of moving them from apartment to apartment."

He pulls back long enough to look me in the eye. "You can have whatever you want."

My heart pounds in my chest at the sincerity of his words. Declan is the kind of guy I have to remember to be careful sharing my dreams with because he's just ridiculous enough to try to make them come true.

"Right now. I just want you."

A slow smile pulls at the corners of his mouth. "If you weren't already my wife, I'd ask you to be my girlfriend."

CHAPTER THIRTY-THREE

Declan

GET A ROOM

On Sunday after practice, the guys and I head to Wild's to celebrate our goalie, Mikey's birthday. Ash and Maverick are counting as they make the kid chug for twenty-three seconds because that's how old he turned today.

"Remember your twenty-third birthday?" I ask Jack as we stand at the bar, leaning our backs against it and watching our teammates.

"Barely." He drains the rest of his glass and then turns and signals to the bartender that he wants another. "We were here. I remember that much."

"Yep. It was during development camp. We were only a few years older than most of the guys, but we took them out the last night, which coincided with your birthday, and they conned you into attempting twenty-three shots."

"Not attempting. I succeeded." He shudders.

"Does it count if you can't remember?" I turn to grin at him. I had to carry his ass out of the bar.

"I wished I hadn't the next morning. That part I remember well."

"We've had some good times in this bar. Lots of celebrations. Lots of booze."

He lifts his new beer toward me. "And many more to come."

I tip my glass in his direction.

"You want another?"

I glance down at my nearly empty beer. "I think I'm gonna head out after this."

"Aw, come on. It's early."

He'll have my balls if I tell him I'm itching to get home and hang with Jade. Things are good. No, things are great. I don't have a lot of free nights and I'd rather spend them with her than getting shitfaced.

I love my teammates, but I'm tired of the bar scene.

"Listen, if you go, then Leo will leave, followed by Tyler and Mav." He makes a rolling motion with his hand. "You catch my drift?"

"Yeah, man. It wasn't subtle."

"But you still want to go?"

"Mikey is already blitzed. He isn't going to notice if I leave."

"But I will. Don't I count?" He quirks a brow as he takes a long drink from his glass.

"You just want a wingman." I nod my head toward the guys. "You have Ash."

"He's a terrible wingman. He either ends up hitting on them himself or getting into deep conversations and killing the mood."

Chuckling, I nod. He isn't wrong about that. "I have beer at home, and I like my house."

"And the woman in it?"

I can only grin. Especially the woman in it.

"Another beer for my friend," he tells the bartender and then pulls out his phone.

Before I can object, he adds, "One more beer. If you still want to leave after that, I'll call you a sober ride."

"All right but get ready to call that ride."

"We'll see," he says, a little too smug.

A new glass is placed in front of me. I thank the bartender and resist the urge to chug it, like Mikey's been doing all night. Instead, I wander over to the rest of the team. Some of the guys are playing pool and others are throwing darts. I join in on the latter. One game of darts, while I finish my beer, and then I'm out. Maybe Jade wants to order takeout and watch something. She's been binging *One Tree Hill* and I'm reluctantly invested in the old TV series. Though if she asks, I'll deny it.

My mood gets lighter the closer I get to finishing my beer. I throw my final dart and reach for the glass at the same time the guys around me erupt in a chorus of cheers. I turn to see what the excitement is about and my heart lurches in my chest.

Jade. Jade is here in this bar. Damn, she's gorgeous.

I move toward her at the same time I realize she isn't alone. Scarlett, Piper, and Dakota are with her. Scanning the room, I find Jack watching me with a smirk. That fucker. I lift my beer to him and mouth, "Well-played."

"Surprise!" Jade says, meeting me halfway. She pauses a step away, like she's waiting for my reaction.

I close the space between us, framing her face with both of my hands and kissing her. She squeaks in surprise seconds before I feel her lips pull into a smile and her arms go around my neck.

I drop my hands to circle her waist and lift her. Someone, I think

Ash, calls, "Get a room."

That's exactly what I was planning on doing. Taking her to a room—mine, but now that she's here, the bar doesn't seem so bad.

"I guess that means you're okay with me crashing guy time?" she asks, when I set her down.

Her face is flushed, lips wet from our kiss, and her arms are still linked around my neck.

"Yeah. I'm okay with it." I drop another kiss to her mouth. "Want something to drink?"

She nods and I walk with her over to the bar and order her a seltzer and me another beer.

"Scarlett said you're celebrating someone's birthday?"

"Mikey." I point to where he's sitting. His loud, drunken laugh booms above the music. He's stayed upright longer than I expected.

"Looks like he's having fun." She takes her drink and stands so the left side of her body rests against mine. "It's nice you guys did that for him."

It is nice, and her pointing it out to me makes me feel bad for wanting to bail.

"So…" she starts and hits me with a smile. "Pool? Darts?"

"Your choice."

"If I'm playing, darts. If I'm watching, pool."

"Not a fan of pool?"

"I'm a fan of winning, and I'm terrible at pool."

"You've just had the wrong partners." I take her hand and lead her to an empty table.

Once I've racked the balls, I call to a nearby Leo, "Do you and Scarlett want to play us?"

He looks to his girl and she nods. Leo and I are pretty evenly matched, as are the girls, but Jade and I have something they don't—a hunger to win. Maybe it's because we're still in that phase of wanting to show off for each other, or maybe it's a difference in our base personalities. Fuck, maybe it's just that they're more interested in kissing than beating us.

I'll kiss my girl when I've earned it by destroying the competition. Jade seems to have the same mindset. She cheers as I sink each ball, and when it's her turn, she gets the most determined look on her beautiful face.

On Scarlett's next turn, she drops the last solid ball and aims for the eight ball. The angle isn't quite right, and she misses, making it Jade's turn.

My girl lets out a breath as she studies the table. One stripe left and the eight ball.

"You've got this," I say quietly, as I stand behind her and brush my hand over her hip. "Take your time."

She doesn't look at me, but nods. I step back to give her room and say a silent prayer as she aims and fires, sinking our last stripe ball like a shark. Without celebrating, she moves right into position to shoot the eight ball.

"Side pocket." She points with the cue.

I hold my breath, pulse racing. It's just a game. I know it's stupid, but I can't remember being more excited than when that final ball inches toward the side pocket and drops.

She whirls, jaw hanging open and eyes wide. "I did it!"

I drop my cue stick to the table and catch her when she jumps into my arms. I spin her around and cheer. Nobody gives a shit that we just won, but it doesn't matter. This moment isn't about them.

Our kiss is fueled by the adrenaline of winning and something even better, something I didn't even know I was missing out on—winning together.

We take on Piper and Tyler next, easily beating them. Then Ash and Jack try their luck but we're on a roll and can't be bested.

When no one else will play us, we finally take a seat at the table with Mikey and a few of the single guys. There isn't a lot of room, so Jade sits on my lap, and I wrap one arm around her waist.

"Happy birthday, kid." I lift my glass to Mikey. His drunken state is more subdued the later it gets.

"Thank you. Thank you." His stare holds on me and Jade. "My wish this year is to win the Cup and find a girl half as cool as yours."

I tighten my hold on her. Something else I didn't realize I was missing out on—being part of a couple that was so happy, people wanted to be me.

I clink my glass against his. "I wish that for you too."

CHAPTER THIRTY-FOUR

Declan

GUT PUNCH

"**N**ice game tonight." Ash lifts a wrist and I bump mine against it.

"Thanks. You too. That last assist was money."

"It was. Wasn't it?" He grins. "Are you coming to Wild's for a beer?"

"Not tonight." I stand and run a hand through my still-damp hair. I don't think I've ever cooled down and showered faster after a game.

"Where are you headed?" he asks, pulling on a clean shirt.

"I'm taking Jade to dinner."

"They have food at Wild's," he teases.

I stand and shoulder my bag. "Have some wings for me."

Jade is waiting for me near the doors to the back parking lot. When she spots me, she smiles and starts walking toward me. I pick up speed, and when she gets close, I drop my bag, so I can lift her up.

"You're killing me with all this team spirit." She's wearing that beanie with my name and number on it, along with a Wildcat jersey that I happen to know also has my name and number on it because I gave it to her.

I had no idea how good it would feel to have someone show up like that for me. Not the team. *Me.* It's a gut punch. My grandparents never saw me play professionally, and yeah, the team has become like family, but this is different. It makes me crave more.

"It's only fair. You in this suit does things to me." She kisses me, lips coated in some sticky gloss that I'm determined to have all over me before the night is over.

"Wait until you see what's underneath the jersey. I got new lingerie today."

"Oh yeah?"

Mischief glints in her eyes. "Green lace."

"Thanks for that visual," I grit out. "I'm gonna be hard all night. I want to take you somewhere."

She smiles at me, then places another kiss on my lips. "Home hopefully?"

"If we go home, we aren't leaving, and I owe you a real date."

"A date?" she asks, voice rising with excitement.

"Yep." I set her on the ground and pick up my bag, then lace our fingers together as we head outside. "I realized we haven't been on one."

Jade's grip on my hand tightens. "Where are we going?"

"It's a surprise."

"Well, am I dressed okay?" She pauses and glances down at her jersey, jeans, and boots.

Damn. I didn't even consider that. I wear a suit to the game. Most of the time, I change into something more casual after, but I put the nicer digs back on for the date.

A smile spreads across my face as an idea strikes. "Not yet."

Our options are limited on a Saturday night after ten, but I text Jack because he knows everyone, and sure enough, fifteen minutes later, a woman named Rose is opening her store so Jade can pick out a dress.

Rose makes me wait at the front of the store, while she dotes on Jade, selecting a dozen dresses and then ushering her into the back to try them on.

I wait for what feels like decades, scrolling my phone, leg bouncing, before Rose clears her throat.

I stand and slide my phone back into my pocket before I glance up. Then I swallow my tongue.

The black dress is somehow sexy, even though it doesn't show that much skin. It's long, with a slit showing off just a hint of one leg. The straps are thick, but hang off her shoulders, and her boobs are pushed up in a way that there's no way to not stare.

Jade's smile is tentative as she waits for my reaction. One hand goes to her stomach, and she takes a shaky breath. "Too much?"

I can't seem to speak. Rose laughs lightly. "That's exactly the reaction I was hoping for."

Handing Rose my card, I thank her, then turn to Jade. "You're a jaw dropper, baby. Wow. I think I had a mini cardiac episode."

Her responding giggle is a hit of dopamine. "This dress is the nicest thing I've ever worn. The fabric is so soft I feel naked."

"Later," I promise. I can't wait to peel her out of it very, very slowly.

Rose tells us to have fun and come back anytime, and I promise we will.

By the time we get to the restaurant, it's almost eleven. I'm always amped up on game nights. It's hard to get to sleep until early in the morning, as I come down from the high of pushing my mind and body, but Jade covers a yawn as our drinks arrive.

"Sorry," I say.

"Don't you dare be sorry. This is amazing. No one has ever done something like this for me."

"Still. Maybe we should order and take it home."

"I'll be fine with a little caffeine." She takes a sip of her Coke. "This is so nice. Seriously. I had no idea you had this in you."

I chuckle. "Yeah, me either."

"You've never brought a girl here before?" Her gaze narrows slightly as she waits for my answer.

"Definitely not."

"And the dress?"

"Didn't even know that was possible. You can thank Jack for that."

"I can't figure you out, Declan Sato."

"What's there to figure out?"

"You're so considerate and generous, plus ridiculously hot."

I smile at that. I don't think I'll ever get tired of her telling me I'm hot. Not that it's something I strive for exactly, but as long as I've been on the team, it's been Jack or Leo that girls are drawn to by looks alone. Ash picks up women because of his fun spirit and charm. I was the guy that sort of faded into the background. Happily, mostly. It was less drama, and my focus was on making something of myself.

But then Jade shows up and I want her to notice me. I think I always wanted her to notice me.

"Sounds to me like you already have me figured out. Considerate, generous, and hot. I can live with that."

She keeps smiling at me for a beat, then slowly it dims, and she gets serious. "Why me?"

Jade's the kind of girl who'd never ask to eat at a fancy restaurant or buy a nice dress, which makes me want to give her whatever she wants. But that isn't what she's asking. How do you explain being drawn to someone before you even knew them?

"I don't know. I'm not good with words like you. Making you smile and laugh is like watching the goalpost light up. It feels good, deep inside me."

"Wow." Jade's smile returns. "I think you're pretty good with words. Don't let Melody find out. She'll fire me to hire you."

"Doubtful." I stare at her over the candlelight. The lights in this place are dim and we're at a table far in the back to give us privacy. "How's work been?"

Her smile falls a little. "Okay."

I cock one brow. It's been tense. I can tell by the extra hours and stressful pacing she does every time she has to turn in an article.

"Interest in my online and print pieces have declined. It's been weeks since I've had any media requests. I'm afraid she's going to cut me completely."

"Fire you?"

She shrugs. "It's almost worse than if I'd said no to going through with the wedding. Who's going to hire a writer, who took a thriving weekly column and drove it into the ground?"

"I'm sorry. What can I do?"

"Nothing. I'll figure it out." She attempts a smile, but it's covering real fear. I can see it in her eyes.

The mood lightens over dinner. The food is incredible. We order steak and mashed potatoes and lasagna, sharing both, then top it off with chocolate cake.

I don't want the night to end, but Jade's covering more yawns the later it gets.

Back in the car, I rest one hand on her bare thigh through the dress slit, and she scoots closer to me and drops her head against my arm. By the time I pull into the garage at home, she can barely keep her eyes open.

"We're home, baby."

She hums and sits taller. I get out and open her door. She's still half-asleep, so I leave the rest of my shit and scoop her up.

She's so tired, she doesn't even protest as I carry her into the house and upstairs to my room. When I flip on the lamp on my nightstand, she lifts her head from my chest.

"Sorry. Too little sleep mixed with too many carbs."

"You're fine. I'll take any excuse to carry you to bed, baby."

"Set me down." She wiggles in my hold.

Once I do, a little more life flares in her eyes. Turning around, she asks, "Will you unzip me?"

It's almost a shame to see her take off this dress. *Almost.*

I tug the zipper down and the fabric gapes to show more of her back. Jade holds on to the straps, so it doesn't fall off her frame, then turns around to face me.

My dick is already tenting my pants before she lets the material pool at her feet.

"Fuck me," I mutter.

"That was the idea." She steps out of the dress, wearing nothing but a little green thong. "The matching bra didn't work with the dress."

"I'm not mad about it."

A coy smile plays on her lips as she reaches for me. She undresses me while I drop kisses to her shoulders and neck. When I'm naked, she tries to drop to her knees. My dick pulses at the thought of her mouth on me, but I pull her back up.

"Not tonight. I need to be inside you now."

She pushes her panties down eagerly and then we fall onto the bed. Jade wraps her legs around me and I push into her without waiting.

Her pussy squeezes me tight, and my heart is pounding in my chest. I still.

"Are you okay?" she asks, after a few seconds of me buried inside her, unmoving.

"Better than okay." I breathe her in and then slowly start to move.

Her eyes flutter closed, and she lifts her hips with each thrust.

There aren't any more words as I continue to drive into her at a slow, steady pace. Sweat beads on my forehead and my balls draw up. Jade's close, too, but I don't want to finish before her.

Leaning down, I kiss her on the mouth, then her neck, finally trailing down to her tits. She bucks as my tongue circles her nipple, so I do it again, then close my teeth around her sensitive flesh.

She cries out as she comes and I take her mouth again, finding my own release while kissing her like my life depends on it. In this moment, it feels like it does.

We lie there for a moment after, catching our breath. I'm starting to go soft until I pull out of her. Her pussy clenches around me like it's fighting to keep me inside, and it's so hot, I'm rock hard again.

Jade curls up on her side, eyes still closed. Another yawn escapes her.

"Want anything?" I ask as I start for the bathroom to clean up.

"Uh-uh," she replies, without opening her eyes, then groans. "I need to wash my face and brush my teeth. Stupid good hygiene."

Laughing, I pull her to her feet, and we get ready for bed together. She's brushing her teeth in a sleepy daze, looking so damn cute.

"I was thinking. What if we did the HTPB podcast?" I ask.

"Really?" she asks, mouth full of toothpaste. There's a trace of excitement mixed with confusion. "You want to do the podcast now?"

"If it will help." I lift one shoulder in a shrug. I still hate the idea, but maybe it's the right call. "You're too talented. I don't want to see you get fired."

"No, I don't think so," she says. "Thank you, but I can deal with Melody and whatever the fallout is from my boring articles."

I know it bothers her. She takes such pride in her work. I hate that she's in a tough spot.

She spits and rinses her mouth and toothbrush, then comes to me and cups my cheeks. "You're a very good man."

My throat feels tight, but I manage a smile.

We get in bed and Jade nestles into me, her head and one hand on my chest, like usual. My mind still races long after we've said good night. I want to fix this for her, but I don't know how. Her words keep replaying over and over. *You're a good man.*

The thing is, I'm not really sure I am. I'm all right. I don't kick puppies or make babies cry or anything, but the things I do are for her and the other people I love.

My chest squeezes.

"Hey, are you awake?"

She doesn't answer and her breathing is slow and even.

"I love you," I whisper. "I fucking love you, Jade."

CHAPTER THIRTY-FIVE

Jade

I'M PRETTY SURE I DREAMT IT

"**Y**our schedule is seriously hindering my sex life," I tell Declan, as he packs his bag for another away game. They've had three out of town games this week already. I've spent more time alone in this bed I'm currently sitting on while I watch him get ready to leave again, than I have with him in it the past five days.

He smiles, then his gaze drops to my bare chest. My body heats at the way he looks at me. I have no room for complaints, really. We were up late last night making up for his absence the two nights prior, but I do sleep a lot better when he's here.

I stand on the bed and drape my arms over his shoulders. "Call in sick?"

Laughing, he places a soft kiss on my lips and then circles my waist and pulls me off the bed. "I'll be back tomorrow. Quick trip and then I'm home for a whole week."

"Seven whole days," I mutter dryly. Though, truthfully, I'm

ecstatic. A month into the season and I don't know how he does it. I'm exhausted just trying to stay awake long enough at night to answer his calls after every game.

"I gotta go." He swats my ass playfully. "And you need to shower and get ready for work."

"I don't want to wash you off me yet."

He groans, drops his bag and picks me back up. The kiss is quick but still manages to steal my breath. Dropping me back on my feet, he says, "I gotta go. Call you tonight."

I don't follow him downstairs, but I wait for the sound of the front door announcing his departure before I head into the shower.

I use his body wash. If I can't smell him on me, then I'll have to settle for smelling like him.

When I get into the office, I've no more than set my purse on my desk when Scarlett appears.

"Is everything okay? You didn't show for coffee."

"I'm sorry. Declan and I started saying goodbye around six this morning, and, well…it went through coffee." I sit at my chair and get out my laptop.

"You're forgiven." She holds a coffee cup out to me with my name written in black Sharpie.

"Oh, you're the best." I take it from her and then enjoy a long drink.

"I know." She leans against my desk. "So? Did he say it again?"

My face grows warm. "No. I'm pretty sure I dreamt it."

"You did not dream it." Scarlett shakes her head and laughs. "He is in love with you. Everyone can see that."

"Then why hasn't he said it? It's been weeks since that night." I was almost asleep. It's possible I didn't hear him right.

"I'm not sure," she says. "Maybe he knows you heard him and he's waiting for you to bring it up."

My skin feels tight, and the back of my neck gets hot. There is no way I'm bringing it up.

Changing the subject, I ask my best friend, "Did you read the interviews I sent you earlier this week?"

"Yeah." Her face lights up. "I can't get enough. Leo, too. Who is it? Someone we know?"

"I can't tell. It's anonymous." I started reaching out to friends of friends, old colleagues, and classmates to see if any would be willing to answer questions about their marriage. I've received a wide variety of responses. A few that have been married less than five years, several in the five-to-ten range, and one couple that's celebrating their twentieth anniversary this year. I don't know what it all means or where it's going, but it's been fascinating to read their love stories.

"Ugh. I want to know! They are so sweet. I hope Leo and I are like that in twenty years. When do we get to read more?"

"That's all I have back. I'm waiting on five more to respond, but who knows if or when they'll get it to me. And I still have to figure out how to use the individual interviews from divorced couples."

She pouts.

"You'll be the first to know when I get more. Promise."

"I love it. You're turning into a total romantic. Who would have thought?"

"It isn't about romance. It's figuring out why some people make it work and others don't."

"It's a little about romance."

Melody's office door opens. Scarlett straightens and we both look over to see our boss standing three feet away.

"Jade, can I have a minute?" She smiles, but I still get an uneasy feeling low in my stomach.

"Of course." I stand on wobbly legs.

Melody disappears back in her office and I shoot Scarlett a nervous glance.

"Lunch?" she asks.

"If I still work here," I whisper back. "No, I take that back. Lunch either way. But if I get fired, I'm drinking my lunch."

"She wouldn't," Scarlett says, then adds, "she better not."

I take several deep breaths and smooth out the invisible wrinkles on my skirt on the short walk to Melody's office.

As I take a step into her space, she glances up and says, "Shut the door, please."

My pulse quickens as I close us in and then take a seat in front of her desk.

She's smiling at me again, and for some reason that has me even more nervous than if she were frowning.

"I got an interesting call this morning," she starts, leaning back in her chair.

My first thought is that someone has figured out the truth about Sam calling off the engagement and me marrying Declan to save face (and my job). But why would she be smiling about that?

"Oh?" I try to ignore the way my voice wavers.

"Do you remember Olivia Benton? I believe you met her at the charity event back in July."

"Of course."

"She is doing the PR for a new reality show. It's still in the conceptual phase, but if everything moves as fast as she thinks, they'll begin filming in a few months."

I stay quiet, brain churning to figure out where this is going.

"Think Real Housewives meets NBA Wives, but make it hockey."

"Hockey WAGs?"

"Precisely. They already have three other wives signed on. She couldn't say who, but I know she wouldn't be involved unless it's going to be huge."

"That's great," I hear myself saying. My mind can't seem to process the information fast enough, because I still have no idea where this is going.

"She is hoping for one more. You."

"Me?" I croak.

Melody nods. "She's a big fan of the magazine and of you."

"I'm flattered," I start, and Melody jumps in.

"You'll film for a few months. You can continue your regular life, including working here, but we'll have to figure out what kind of access to give them and if we want to tweak your angle to include the show." She sits forward. "Those are things for me to figure out." She pushes a card toward me. "This is Olivia's number. She'll go over everything else in more detail."

I take the card and run a finger over the gold lettering of Olivia's name. "This is so flattering, but I don't think this is for me."

"Jade, I don't think you understand what a huge opportunity this is for you."

"No, I do." Adrenaline pumps through my veins. It's the kind of publicity that could mean hundreds of thousands more people might read my words. But Declan would hate this. Cameras following us around and invading our lives? No way. "I'm sorry."

I start to get up, but she levels me with her next sentence.

"Twenty-five thousand per episode with a signing bonus of five hundred thousand."

I sort of fall back in my seat. "How is that possible?"

"It's an invasive process. They understand that it needs to be worth your while, and they feel confident that it's going to be a hit."

Holy shit. Five hundred thousand dollars?!

I could quit this job and take time to write a book or... anything. The sky is the limit with that kind of padding in my savings account.

Melody stands. "Olivia pushed hard for you. At least take a day or two and think it over."

Numbly, I nod and get to my feet. My hands start to shake as I get back to my desk. I stare down at Olivia's card. I can't say yes. I start to toss it in the trashcan but can't bring myself to let go.

Declan will never agree, but maybe it wouldn't hurt to have all the information.

CHAPTER THIRTY-SIX

Declan

THIS IS REAL

We lose in regulation to Boston, giving up two points. It's our second loss this week to teams we should have easily beaten, and when I step on the team jet to head home, the mood is thick with frustration. We want to send a message this season. *We're out for blood. Get the fuck out of the way. It's our year.*

Jack is sitting in my seat. He and Tyler are watching film from the game.

"Sorry, man. Two seconds," Jack says to me, holding out a tablet between him and Tyler.

"Nah, it's good." I pass by them and stop next to Morrison a few rows back.

He looks up from his phone and nods his head.

I drop into the seat next to him and glance at his screen. His little boy has his face smushed up close, talking, though I can't make out what he's saying.

Smiling, I pull out my phone to text Jade, then realize how late it is. Every time we lose on the road, she sends me a single message with only the middle finger emoji. It cracks me up.

Morrison says his goodbyes to his wife and son and then turns to me. "Sorry, man. I couldn't find my headphones."

"Nah, you're cool."

He sets his phone on his lap. The wallpaper is a picture of him and his family. The three of them are all smiles.

"Isn't it late for him?" I ask.

"His sleep schedule is all fucked up," he says, like I know what a sleep schedule is.

Even though most of my friends have settled down, and some are even engaged, their lives don't feel that different from mine. Kids. That's a whole other level.

It makes me wonder what the future might be like with Jade. We could travel in the off-season. I can take her to all the places she's ever dreamed of going. More weekends and fun with our friends. Maybe kids at some point. I've never really let myself daydream about all that—my own family, but I like the idea a whole lot.

I can't sleep on the plane, even though I'm dog tired. I'm too anxious to get home. By the time we land, and I make the drive to my house, all I want is to see my girl and then sleep for twelve hours. In that order.

I pull the Ferrari into the garage and cut the engine. My muscles protest as I unfold myself from the car. Everything seems to hurt worse after a loss.

The house is quiet, and I move softly, so I don't wake her. I took a puck to the side of the leg last night and it left a nasty bruise.

I find her in the bedroom, but pause when she isn't asleep like I expected. Her laptop sits in front of her, and she has on headphones. My movement startles her, and she jumps, then hits me with a big smile as she tosses her computer and headphones to the side and scrambles up to say hello.

"Hey, baby. You're awake."

"Of course." She climbs me, wrapping her arms around my neck and her legs around my waist. "For seven whole days you're mine!"

She squeezes me and her hands dig into another sore spot on my body. I don't manage to cover my wince and Jade immediately drops down. "Are you okay?"

"Little banged up. Nothing a hot shower and ice pack won't fix."

"Are you tired?"

I shake my head. The last thing I want is to go to bed. I'm so excited to be home for the week. Leaving Jade gets harder each trip. Each time I'm a little more eager to come home to her.

I think of Morrison and his little boy. That has to be brutal, not seeing your kid every day. Though there are probably perks too. I see how the guys with families light up on family skate nights, watching their kids take the ice, knocking a puck around together.

"Good." She kisses me and I pull her down onto the bed. We make quick work of our clothing and then Jade pushes me onto my back and scoots down my body.

"Whatcha doing, baby?" I ask, voice gruff as she kneels between my legs.

"Making sure you get a win tonight." Her lips curve into a smile and then she's taking me into her mouth before I can tell her that finding her in my bed waiting for me is all the win I need. Though, I'm not opposed to another.

Jade makes the sexiest noises while taking me to the back of her throat and swirling her tongue along my piercing. Her mouth is perfection, and I don't want to stop her, but I can't wait another second to be inside her.

Lifting her, I bring her on top of me. She eases down on my dick and then stills.

"Always so good," she whispers, staring down at me. "Are you sure you're real?"

"Pretty sure." I lean up and lightly bite her nipple. She moans, so I do it again, then give the other one a little nibble too.

I can tell she wants me to continue, but she pushes me back down to the mattress and starts to ride me. Slow at first, driving me to the brink of insanity with the need to come. Her fingers dig into my chest as she increases the pace.

Only when I can tell she's close, do I take over, sitting up again and kissing her while I use my hold on her hips to drive us both over the edge.

"Declan," she mumbles as her orgasm continues to send spasms through her body.

"Jade." I nip at her shoulder. "Baby. I'm real. This is real."

The next morning, I wake up at my usual time, despite wanting to sleep in. Jade's in the shower, so I get dressed and head downstairs to make breakfast before she has to go to work.

I don't have to go to the arena today. My plans are to put the finishing touches on the upstairs hall bathroom. I need to switch out the faucet, change the doorhandle, and touch up the paint in a few places. I bought a clawfoot tub that should be here any day, and then it will be complete. Jade almost always uses my bathroom now, but I couldn't resist getting her the tub of her dreams.

I scramble eggs, fry the turkey bacon (Jade replaced the real stuff), make some toast, and then cut up a cantaloupe. I'm more of a protein shake guy most mornings because it's faster, but I could see myself making breakfast for her like this on all my days off.

When everything is ready, Jade still isn't downstairs. I make coffee, grab a cup, and move toward the living room. As I pass by the counter, a stack of papers catches my eye.

The contract format makes me do a double take. I set my mug down next to it and pick up the papers. I scan quickly, brain racing to figure out what it is I'm reading. Then, flip back to the first page and start over. *The hell?*

"Good morning!" Jade's chipper voice behind me catches me by surprise and I whirl around, contract still in hand.

"What is this?" I hold up the papers.

Her eyes widen and her smile falls. "I was going to talk to you about that."

She takes the papers from me and moves into the kitchen to get her own mug of coffee.

"A reality show?" I ask, following her.

"Do you remember the woman, Olivia, we met at the charity dinner we went to with Leo and Scarlett?"

"Yeah, vaguely."

"She's the publicist for the show and thought I'd make a good addition." She takes a sip of her drink before facing me.

"You're not going to do it, right?"

"I said no," she says, but something in her tone still has me on guard.

"But you want to do it?"

"It's a lot of money. Plus, the possible exposure."

I brace my hands on the counter. "We don't need the money."

"*You* don't," she clarifies. "But I barely make enough to cover my monthly expenses."

"I can cover whatever you need."

"For now, but what about in seven months when this is over?"

When it's over?

"I wasn't aware we had an expiration date." My pulse is racing and my body tenses.

"You know what I mean. We agreed to stay married for a year. After that, even if we're dating, I wouldn't expect you to pay my way."

I have no idea what to say. It feels like a punch straight through the chest. I've fallen in love with her. I'm not looking at the end of our agreement like my out. I'm in this.

"Say something, please," she says.

"If you do the show, what does that look like?" I wave a hand around the room. "Cameras following us around everywhere we go and in our home?"

"Just me, but yes."

"Like I don't live here too," I mutter. I'd have to tiptoe around my own damn house.

"We can set boundaries. Olivia promised that you wouldn't need to appear in any shots if you weren't on board and that it wouldn't disrupt your schedule."

"Jesus, you're seriously considering this?"

"No." She shakes her head. "Yes. I don't know. It feels like I should if you're not completely opposed."

My brain spins, trying to decide if I'm wrong for not wanting her to do this.

"I know that you don't like it, but can you at least think about how good this could be for me?"

"What about your job at the magazine?"

"I would keep it, at least until I figure out my next move."

"I'll give you the money right now. Take time off, write a book or whatever you want. You don't need to do this."

"I don't want your money." Her voice rises. "I want to do this on my own. I want to be something. This feels like my shot. I know you don't want this thing between us to interfere with hockey, but maybe we can work it so that it doesn't?"

I turn and run a hand through my hair.

She circles around me. "You're telling me that you didn't make sacrifices to get where you are?"

"It isn't the same and you know it."

"I can't take back the mistakes I've made. I'm here and I'm just trying to make the most of it."

"We're a mistake now?"

"No." She reaches for my arm, but I pull away.

"You're choosing to let someone else help you, when I'm offering. I don't get it. I *want* to help you and I'm not going to make you sell your soul or dignity to do it."

"My dignity?" She looks downright pissed off. I guess that makes two of us.

"I love you!" I basically bellow the words at her.

Her wild eyes grow larger, and her mouth hangs slightly open, but she says nothing.

Fuck. Fuck. Fuck. This is not how I saw this morning going. It isn't how I wanted to tell her that I love her and want to plan a future together. But from the look on her face and lack of response, we aren't on the same page anyway.

Letting out a breath, I say, "I'm gonna take a walk."

"Wait." Desperation clings to her voice.

I stop in my tracks and look back at her. Her eyes plead with me, but she doesn't say anything else.

"You can do whatever you want, Jade. You obviously have a plan for your life. Just do me a favor and figure out if I'm in it."

CHAPTER THIRTY-SEVEN

Jade

LET'S RENEGOTIATE

arrive at work, numb, but thankful to have something to do. When I get to my desk, Scarlett is waiting for me with two coffees. Wordlessly, she hands me one.

"Thank you."

"You're welcome."

I start to sit as she adds, "We need to hustle. Your photo shoot for the six-month follow-up two-page spread is in an hour."

"Oh, crap. I completely forgot."

She smiles. "At least we get to work together today."

That is something. I take my laptop with me and check my email while I'm in hair and makeup. The article I wrote for today's photoshoot is in final edits and I look over the proofreading copy I was cc'd on last night.

My stomach dips at the sight of the new headline: *My Life Married to a Wildcat.*

Work used to be the place that I felt like my most true self. Even when I was engaged to Sam, for the purpose of writing the articles, it was me. My life, things that interested me. It was honest, if not completely truthful. But with Declan, we're trapped in this lie that has become so massive I can't see around it. I know that everything he's done has been to help me, but I'm just really tired of being the girl that needs saving.

I can't help but wonder if the reality show would give me a chance to show people who I am. Yes, the show is centered around the life of a hockey wife or girlfriend, but the guys aren't the stars and hopefully it would funnel people to my writing. And I guess I want to be the star of my career again. Maybe this gives me that first step. Plus, I'd have the signing bonus to fall back on if I needed it.

We start the shoot with a series of shots of me sitting in a big emerald chair with my laptop resting on my crossed legs.

Scarlett comes over to me when Janet, the head staff photographer, calls, "Let's take five."

I stand with my computer.

"Those looked great," she says.

"Not like I wanted to go back to bed and forget this day happened?"

She leans into me and wraps an arm around my shoulders. "You had a fight. You'll work through it."

"I don't know." She didn't see his face when he yelled that he loved me. It was almost like he was mad that he'd fallen for me. I don't believe love is enough. I've seen too many people walk out on my mom after claiming to love her. Either that or people use the word far too generously.

And the truth is, when I look at the future, of course I want to be with him. So much that it scares the crap out of me.

We do two more wardrobe changes and more photos in a variety of poses before Janet calls a wrap. My cheeks hurt from smiling and I'm bone tired from acting so opposite of how I've felt all day.

I'm far too exhausted to even think about going anywhere but home after work. The front door is unlocked, and Declan is sitting in the living room staring at a TV that isn't on.

"Hey." He stands when I linger in the entryway.

"Hi," I reply tentatively. Even though I'm tired of being the person needing a rescue, there's still a part of me that wants nothing more than to go to him, to have him wrap his big arms around me and tell me it's all going to be okay.

Declan stays rooted in his spot six feet away. He glances at his feet and then slowly lifts his face to look at me. "I'm sorry I was an asshole this morning."

I'm moving to him before I realize it. I hug him around the middle. "Me too."

His arms circle my waist and the knot in my stomach loosens for the first time since this morning.

"I was going to talk to you about the show. I knew you wouldn't like it, but I wasn't trying to hide it."

"I know," he says quietly, then repeats it a little louder, "I know."

"This situation is tricky and I'm trying to navigate it the best way I know how. I have to be smart. When this is over..."

He pulls back and stares down at me in confusion. He takes a seat back in the same spot he'd been sitting when I walked in, and I move into the living room and sit on the vintage chair I bought. He had it cleaned at some point and it no longer smells like cigarettes and dust.

"I mean when our contract is up. I like you. I like you so much, but people break up. It's just a fact. You can't predict what might happen between us."

"Then let's renegotiate."

"What?" I feel my brows pull together in the middle.

"You want assurances. I can't give you that, so I had my lawyer draw up a contract." He stands and moves toward the kitchen.

Confused, I go after him. He hands me an envelope and then gets a beer from the fridge.

My heart rate speeds up, and my stomach does about a million somersaults as I read it. It says I can do the show, but in exchange, he wants to dissolve the prenup and stay married.

Stay married??!!

"Declan—" I start, and my voice breaks.

"There's one more thing." He stares at the ground. "I want to have a kid with you."

The world tilts.

"I love you. I'm sorry I yelled it at you earlier, but it's true. I want you to be my wife for real and I want to have a baby with you. I want us to be a family."

In a million years, I never saw this coming. My voice barely works as I say, "We've never even talked about kids."

"We're talking about it now." He leans a hip against the counter. "Do you want kids?"

"Sure, but…" I trail off. Not like this. Not as part of some agreement like we're bartering one kid in exchange for me doing the show.

"I can't sign this." I set the papers down and take a deep breath. "I won't do the show. You have been great to me and I respect that you don't want to be a part of it."

He runs a hand through his thick hair. He looks more confused than before. "I can't figure out what it is you want."

I swallow. "I want to get divorced."

So much hurt crosses his face that I can hardly take it. "As long as we're married, things are complicated," I explain.

"What about your job?"

"I will deal with Melody and the fallout."

"What about us?"

"After the dust settles then maybe we can figure out where that leaves us."

"So we're breaking up? This is just over?"

"No, not over."

He invades my space, and those brown eyes search my face. "Forget everything. The job, this marriage, everything I said tonight. Do you want to be with me?"

"Of course, I do."

"But you want to get divorced?"

"I don't want us to be together because we're legally obligated."

"Fuck, Jade, I didn't think we were."

"You're misunderstanding me."

"Maybe, but it still fucking hurts." He starts walking. I'm not sure where he's going, but I follow him to the front door. Panic washes over me. I have royally fucked this up.

Stopping, hand on the doorknob, he looks back at me. "I asked you to figure out what you want. You want to get divorced? That's your answer."

"Yes, but please don't go. I'm doing this because I care about you. It's the only way I can think to move forward without destroying both of us. It frees us to figure things out in our own time without all the pressure."

He nods. "There's another envelope on the counter for you. Sign the papers and I'll take care of everything."

With that, he turns and walks out the door.

CHAPTER THIRTY-EIGHT

Jade

CAN'T A GIRL WALLOW IN PRIVATE?

"**A** million dollars?" Scarlett's eyes bug out of her head.

"Yep."

That's how much he's giving me in the divorce papers he left. I'm entitled to nothing according to the prenup. A million freaking dollars. All I have to do is sign.

Piper, Scarlett, and Dakota sit in the living room. I don't know how they knew, but thirty minutes after Declan walked out, the three of them showed up with hugs and wine.

"I'm not taking it," I clarify. "He's already done enough. I don't want his money. I never wanted his money."

"We know that," Piper says.

"Did he say when he was coming back?" Scarlett asks.

I hold out my empty wine glass. "No, but I don't think it'll be tonight. He probably wants to wait until I move out. I should probably start packing."

Dakota fills my glass but shakes her head. "I don't think he expects you to move out. He said he wants to have a kid with you."

I swallow a large gulp of wine. "I can't stay here. Not now. It doesn't feel right."

I glance around the house. I've never thought of it as mine, but it is my home, nonetheless. It has little touches of me everywhere. The green chair, the red mugs and plates, a collection of my scarves and hats by the front door. But it's the reminders of Declan everywhere I look that make it hard to breathe.

"Do you know where he is?" I finally ask them.

"He was at Ash's," Piper says. "They were talking about heading to the lake for the weekend to cheer him up, but they were still there when I left."

The thought of him being hours away makes my chest tighten. I lie back on the floor and stare up at the ceiling.

"What do I do?"

"We can't answer that, honey," Scarlett says, coming to lie next to me.

"What do you want to do?" Dakota asks.

"Right now, I want to find him and climb into his arms. Even when we're fighting, I just want him. Is that weird?"

"No, that's something else," Piper says.

"It's love. You love him." Scarlett threads her fingers through mine. "He's your person."

"Was my person. Now he's my ex-husband."

"Not until you sign the divorce papers," Dakota pipes in.

Piper moves from the couch to sit on the floor at my feet. "Are you really going to go through with it? If you love him and he loves you, there has to be another way."

"If I don't, I'll either sit around wondering if we ever would have worked out if it weren't for the circumstances or counting the days until we've reached the one-year mark and he's no longer contractually obligated to be with me. I can't live like that, waiting for the worst to happen."

"There are no guarantees. Not even if two people get into a marriage with the best of intentions." Dakota's words settle like a rock in the pit of my stomach.

"How do you get through the day like that?" I rub at my chest.

I've watched so many men walk out on my mom. She's not perfect, but I saw how much she cared for them. Yet, they still left.

The girls stay late, but Declan doesn't come back. At two in the morning, I have to push Scarlett out the door. She's the best friend a girl could ask for, but I just want to sleep. I have a long day ahead of me tomorrow. Ugh. I can't even think about packing and moving. Where am I going to go? Back to my mom's?

I climb into Declan's bed and breathe him in. I can't believe it's really over. I fall into a dreamless sleep and wake up, what feels like minutes later, to banging on the front door. When pulling the covers over my head and ignoring it, doesn't stop the pounding, I stomp downstairs.

Can't a girl wallow in private? I'm sure it's Scarlett, or maybe Piper, possibly both of them coming over to make sure I haven't crawled under the bed and started belting Taylor Swift songs at the top of my lungs (though I definitely felt like it last night).

My legs are bare. I slept in Declan's jersey (Don't judge me. I'm wallowing), and my hair is up in a high ponytail that shifted while I slept and is now a messy side pony. The tangled ends slap me in my face with every stomp.

I'm cursing Scarlett and her loyalty as I pull open the front door. "Do you know what time it is?"

Only, it isn't Scarlett.

A large guy in his mid-to-late forties, by my best guess, stands on the other side. He has a thick gray beard and matching hair. His brows lift and his stare drops to my legs and then quickly up to meet my eyes. He clears his throat, then lifts his left arm to look at his watch. "Ten o'clock on the dot."

I cross my arms over my chest. "Can I help you?"

"I'm Rick. Can you let Declan know I'm here with the tub? The guys and I will get it unloaded." He takes a step away from the door.

"Wait," I call after him, "he's not here."

"Oh." His stare narrows. "I thought I confirmed the delivery with him."

My face heats. I'm sure he did, and the fact Declan isn't here means he didn't want to face me.

"I'll give him a call," Rick says.

While he goes to his truck, phone to his ear, I run back upstairs and put on shorts and a bra. When I get back downstairs, he's coming to the front door again.

"Are you all right with us bringing it in this morning?"

"Yeah." My voice is squeaky. Oh, how I wish I'd heard the conversation between him and Declan. Where is he? What did he say?

With a nod, he and his guys get to work. I leave them to it and head for the kitchen to make coffee. I find one of the old mugs. Declan put them back in the cabinet after I had my meltdown over them. I do like the red ones, but somehow using the ones he's had forever makes me feel closer to him.

With my coffee in hand, I go sit in the living room. I can hear the guys working upstairs and I keep glancing toward the front door for Declan. I pull back the curtain and look toward Ash's house. It looks quiet over there. Maybe they went to the lake after all?

I've had my second cup of coffee by the time Rick comes downstairs with his men. They pull up the drop cloth they placed on the floor when they carried the tub upstairs.

"Do you want to take a look and make sure it's okay?" Rick asks.

I hesitate. I am so not the right person to be checking on home projects, but he stares at me so intently, I find myself agreeing and following him.

The light is on in the bathroom. He steps in first and then moves to the side to let me look. My breath catches and the back of my eyes sting. A stunning clawfoot bathtub sets in exactly the spot I said it should go under the window.

"What do you think?" Rick asks.

"I love him," I say, then catch myself. "I mean *it*. I love the tub."

CHAPTER THIRTY-NINE

Declan

MY FRIENDS ARE ASSHOLES

The morning after I walked out on Jade, Ash finds me in the kitchen under his sink.

"Do I even want to know what you're doing?" he asks, shuffling past me.

I finish tightening the nut under the sink and slide out of the small space. "I fixed the water pressure. It was like a fire hose."

"I could have done that," he says.

"It's been like that for as long as you've lived here."

He pulls a Gatorade from the fridge and leans against the counter. "Could have, but never would have."

"Now you don't have to." I test the faucet and then wash my hands and dry them on a towel. "Give me five to change and then I'll be ready for a workout."

"Dude, chill. It's Saturday."

"We work out on Saturdays sometimes."

"That's really what you want to do today?" His expression is filled with a kind sort of pity. The guys spent most of last night sitting with me, trying to get me to talk to them or brainstorm ideas to fix things with Jade. They mean well, but I don't want to talk to them about how I'm feeling, and this isn't about a grand gesture. I want her to want me in the ordinary moments. So, I'm staying busy.

"Yeah, it's really what I want to do." Lie. I want to go home, but since I can't do that, I have to keep moving.

Because Rick called me this morning when he went to deliver the tub, I know Jade is still there. Or was. Is she waiting for me to come home or is she packing up and just hasn't left yet? Not knowing is torture.

The front door opens, and a second later, Jack appears. When he sees me, one side of his mouth lifts in a grin and he nods to Ash. "I told you he'd still be here this morning."

He holds out a hand. Ash frowns then turns and pulls a bottle of Macallan from the cabinet and gives it to Jack.

"Thanks." Our captain smiles big.

"Wait," I say, when I figure out what's happening. "You bet on how long I would be here?"

"More like how long until you went back to Jade," Ash clarifies. "I had you pegged for less than eight hours."

"My friends are assholes," I mutter. The truth is, I haven't gone back yet because I'm a coward. I don't want to know if she signed the divorce papers and is making plans for a future that doesn't involve me. Not yet. I need a little more time to live in the uncertainty.

"Ah, cheer up," Jack says. "I gave you until at least tonight. I figured anyone could hold out one night, but two?" He shakes his head dismissively. "Want a drink?"

"It's not even noon."

"Like you have anything better to do," he quips back.

With a grin on his face, Ash watches us banter. "We were just talking about getting in a workout. You in?"

Jack looks like he wants to do anything but that, yet he nods his head. "Sure. Why not?"

Tyler and Leo have joined us by the time we're ready. Ash has a pretty sweet home gym in his garage. He blasts the music, and we fall into a rotation of cleans, deadlifts, and pull ups, followed by sprints between Ash and Jack's houses. The burn of my muscles helps, but it doesn't completely alleviate the desire to run across the street to see if Jade is still there.

I can't quite see the spot she usually parks in from Ash's driveway. I pause for a moment and stare hard at the house. Is she in there hoping I'll walk through the door or is she long gone?

Walking out on her nearly killed me. I know she's used to people running and I hate that I fed into her deepest fears, but I don't know what else to say to her. I want to give her everything she needs, but I guess I was hoping that all she really needed was me. In the same way, Jade is exactly everything I want and need. The details don't matter as long as I have her.

It's the worst feeling to realize she might never feel the same about me. I can't live with that. She deserves to feel this way about someone, even if it isn't me.

I don't know how long we work out. The guys all seem to be waiting for me to call it. That's not likely. I want to go back into Ash's living room so tired and weak, it isn't possible for me to leave.

Everly is the distraction that finally stops us. She and Grace pull into the driveway in front of the garage. As soon as I see Everly's face,

I turn and glare at Ty. "You told Ev?"

He looks slightly embarrassed as he says, "I thought you might want someone to talk to."

"He has us," Ash says.

"Someone who knows what girls are thinking," Ty says, then looks at Leo. "And someone more impartial than Scarlett and Piper."

"Big Sato," Ev says, stepping out of her car and closing the door.

"Hey, Little Sharpie."

She walks through the garage, Grace on her heels, and comes straight to me.

"How are you?" she asks, hugging me quick, then pulling back and searching my face. "Never mind. I know the answer to that. I'm sorry."

"Thanks." I don't want sympathy. That means they all think it's really over and I haven't quite accepted that yet.

"Anyone hungry?" Ash asks.

We go inside and while the guys and Grace linger in the kitchen, Everly and I go into the living room.

"How's school?" I ask her.

"Good." I get a genuine smile out of her. "I'm a straight A student. Proud?"

"Always," I say. "Having any fun?"

"Yes." She laughs lightly. "Grace and I are going to tailgate this afternoon before the football game."

"Be careful."

Her laugh gets louder.

"Just when I think you're cool, you break into big brother mode."

"Can't help it. I remember being an eighteen-year-old boy."

"I know they're all trash."

That makes me chuckle. "Good. They are. But still, be careful. Text one of us if you need anything."

"I'll be fine. Don't worry so much." She bumps her shoulder against mine. "Want to talk about Jade?"

"Not really," I admit.

"All right. Let's talk about you then."

I shake my head at her, but Ev isn't that easily discouraged.

"Okay, let's start small. How long are you planning on crashing on Ash's couch and not showering?" She sniffs my shoulder and makes a face of disgust.

"I don't stink." I drop my face to my chest. "Okay, fine, I do, but it's only because we just worked out. I showered this morning."

"Maybe you should go to your house and shower now." She sits forward like she's going to get up.

"No. Not yet."

She sinks back into the seat next to me. "What are you waiting for?"

"I'm not sure."

"If you don't want to see her, then maybe you should text her."

"And say what?"

"I don't know. Doesn't matter. Most of the joy of receiving a text from someone you like is just seeing their name light up the screen."

I pause a second to imagine what it'd be like to see Jade's name flashing on my screen right now. My chest tightens.

"I can't go home or text her until…" I trail off. "Until I can live with the consequence of her decision. Whatever it is."

"You're a good guy, Declan," she says. "And Jade is great. I'm rooting for you two."

"Thanks, Little Sharpie." I wrap an arm around her neck and bring her in for a quick hug.

When we break apart, she stares toward the kitchen. "I better go. You're sure you're good?"

"I'm fine." I tip my head. "Get out of here and go have fun."

I walk with her to join the rest of the group.

"Ready?" Everly asks Grace.

"Yeah."

The girls say their goodbyes and start for the door. Ash pulls a beer from the fridge and offers it to me.

I shake my head. "No, thanks, but is it cool if I use your shower again?"

"Don't even need to ask," Ash says, still staring after Grace.

"Thanks." I slap him on the shoulder. "Could you be a little less obvious?"

"Huh?" He glances at me. "What do you mean?"

"Nothing, man." I fight a smile.

Upstairs in the guest bathroom, I strip down and step into the shower. There's some girly smelling body wash from when Everly lived here. I open the bottle and squirt some in my palm. Jade started using mine since she moved in and I love that. It's like I'm with her all day long. Another pang of sadness slams into me. Fuck. Is every little thing going to remind me of her until the end of time?

I'm shampooing my hair when I think I hear my phone ringing. I pause and stick my head out of the shower. My heart leaps when the ringtone plays again. I jump out of the shower, wet and sudsy.

Nobody calls me, and the ones that might are all here. All but one.

I wrestle the device from my sweats pocket, while soap streams down my face and into my eyes. It stings. Fuck does it sting. I let out a scream as I widen my blurring eyes. Jade. Holy shit, it's really Jade.

Panic has me frozen for a split second. What if she's calling to tell me it's over? I guess at least I'd get to hear her voice one last time.

I swipe to answer and reach for a towel. "Hello?"

"Declan." My name comes on a sob that has a whole new kind of fear screaming through my veins. Something's not right and I have a bad feeling it has nothing to do with me. "C-can you come to the house?"

"What's wrong?" I ask, already pulling my sweats on, skipping the boxers because it'll take too much time. I grab my shirt and bolt for the door.

"I…" She sniffles and takes a second to compose herself. I don't know why. I'd take her snot-nosed, red-eyed over any other girl in the world.

"I—" she starts again, her voice quieter, "I need you."

CHAPTER FORTY

Jade

BIG AND GENEROUS

Tears pool in my eyes, and I breathe through the pain shooting through the top of my right foot. I'm pretty sure it's broken.

Within a minute of calling Declan, I can hear him coming through the front door.

"Jade?" he calls, concern evident in his tone.

"Office," I croak, and more tears fill my eyes. He came. He said he would, but it still fills me with so many emotions, it's hard to breathe.

He races into the room with a wild look that softens when he sees me on the floor. Kneeling in front of me, he scans me from head to toe. His shirt is on inside out, his hair is wet, and he smells like someone else's body wash. Even with the throbbing in my foot, the jab in my heart is more unbearable.

When he sees the red, and already swollen, top of my foot, his face twists like he can feel my pain. "What happened?"

"You came."

"You called," he says, like it's just that simple.

I swallow around the lump in my throat. "I was trying to move the recliner back into the living room for you."

His brows furrow, but then he stands.

"Don't leave me. Please." I reach out and grab his forearm. I watched him walk away before. I don't want to do it again.

He kneels back down and brings one of his palms to rest on my cheek. His thumb glides across my skin, wiping away a tear. "I'm just going to get an ice pack. I'll be right back. Okay?"

I nod, but it takes another few seconds to loosen my grip. "Okay."

He leans forward and presses his lips to my forehead, lingering there for just a moment before he stands and leaves me on the floor.

When he comes back, he has an ice pack that he gingerly places on my angry, swollen foot.

"Hold this on there," he instructs, and then lifts me into his arms.

I don't ask where he's taking me until we get outside, and I realize he's heading for his car in the garage.

"I'm taking you to the emergency room to get an X-ray," he says. "Do you want me to call Scarlett or your mom to meet us there?"

"No. I'll call them later."

He nods and sets me in the back seat of his SUV. "Knew this vehicle would come in handy. Good thing I didn't sell it."

He gives me a playful wink that does wonders for easing the tension between us.

"Thank you for coming."

Hesitating with his hand on the door, he stares at me a beat before saying, "Always."

The ride to the hospital takes less than fifteen minutes. Declan pulls up outside the ER, puts the SUV in park, and hops out. Instead of going in to get a wheelchair, he scoops me up again.

"Your shirt is on inside out and backward," I tell him.

"Free-balling it too." He grins, but keeps walking into the ER.

"What?" A small giggle escapes with the word.

"I was in the shower when you called. I threw on my sweats and shirt as fast as I could."

Warmth spreads through me, but I don't have time to dwell on it because Declan storms up to the front desk. He tells the receptionist who I am and what's wrong with me. She wants him to fill out paperwork for me, but he shakes his head. "I'm not putting her down unless it's for a doctor to look at her."

She flushes. "Sir, I understand you want to stay with your girlfriend—"

"Wife," he corrects her.

There's some back and forth before she finally agrees to let him carry me to the back and fill out the paperwork in a chair next to my bed.

He's focused hard on the task of answering a million questions about me, my health insurance, and medical history. Surprisingly, he knows most of it, without even asking. I lie back and watch him. Being with Declan just feels good. Even with a broken foot and fluorescent lighting.

When a doctor finally comes in, Declan stands.

"Hi," she says, looking from me to him, then back to me. "I heard you hurt your foot."

"Yes," I say, and remove the ice pack. It's started to turn an ugly black and purple and is somehow more swollen, making it twice the size of my left foot.

"Ouch." She sanitizes her hands and then steps toward me. "What happened?"

"I dropped a recliner on it, while I was trying to move the chair into another room."

She presses only lightly on the top of my foot, but I gasp at the pain that shoots up my leg. Declan stands and comes over to take my hand.

"Sorry," I tell the doctor. I'm a big baby when it comes to pain, but damn, that hurt.

"You don't need to apologize," Declan says. Then to the doctor, "Wouldn't an X-ray be better, so you don't hurt her again?"

"I'm okay," I say.

She smiles at him and steps back. "Can you put weight on it?"

"I haven't really tried," I say at the same time Declan says, "No, she can't."

The doctor looks between us again. The man played hockey with a broken wrist two games last season and he's treating my broken foot like it's going to be the death of me.

"I'm going to order an X-ray now. The swelling and tenderness indicate it's likely broken, but let's see exactly what's going on and then we'll figure out how to get you fixed up. Okay?"

"Thank you." I give her an extra broad smile to make up for the grumpy man next to me.

"It shouldn't be long," she says, and returns my smile.

Declan frees his right hand from mine, gives me his left, and extends the right to her. He still looks like he wants to tear the hospital apart to get my care expedited, but he finds his manners somewhere under all that protectiveness. "Thank you."

With a nod, she leaves us. A nurse comes next to give me some Tylenol for the pain and a fresh ice pack. Whether it's because of

Declan's insistence or not, I can't be sure, but it's less than five minutes before I'm wheeled to another room for an X-ray.

By the time we find out that it is broken, in two spots, the pain medicine is working and I'm getting tired from the crash of adrenaline and the emotional rollercoaster I've been on for the past twenty-four hours. I just want to go home.

I try to listen to the instructions as they put me in a boot for discharge, but my eyes are heavy. They wheel me back out to the vehicle and Declan lifts me into his SUV.

"Can I sit in the front?" I ask, not lifting my head from his chest.

He shuts the back door and instead takes me to the passenger seat. "You need to keep it elevated as much as possible."

"I will when we get home," I promise.

While he drives, I lean over to rest my head on his shoulder. I must fall asleep because the next thing I know, he's got me in his arms again.

He climbs the stairs with me in tow and then heads to his bedroom. Laying me down, he asks, "Do you need anything?"

I shake my head as a yawn keeps me from speaking.

He shifts his weight from one foot to the other. "Is it okay if I stay in here with you for tonight? I don't want to be far, in case you need something."

I scoot over to make room for him. He kicks off his shoes and lies down with his back up against the headboard.

"Thank you for being here."

"You can always call me. No matter what."

I close my eyes again as another yawn escapes. "The pillows smell like you."

"I would have taken you to the other room but…"

When it seems he isn't going to finish that sentence, I glance up at him. "But what?"

"I didn't want to see your stuff all packed up." His jaw tightens.

I'm so tired it takes my brain a second to process. "I haven't packed anything."

"But the green chair is gone, and you were moving the recliner." His dark eyes scan my face for understanding. "I thought you were putting it all back like it was before you moved in."

"The green chair will look better in my office, and I was moving the recliner back because you love it. I never should have made you move it in the first place."

"It's just a chair. I don't care where it goes."

"I know. That's why I wanted to move it."

"I don't follow."

I've never been one for grand gestures, or really gestures of any kind. I've always loved simply and selfishly. Declan showed me that there was another way. His love is big and generous. And I want to love him back in that same way so that he can feel how good it is to be loved that way.

I swing my legs to the side of the bed and stand, wincing only a little as I put weight on my right foot.

"What are you doing?" Declan is by my side in a flash, circling my waist and taking the pressure off my right foot.

"I need to go downstairs."

"Lie down. I'll get whatever you need."

"No. I want to get it myself."

He looks exasperated but picks me back up again.

"No." I wiggle to get him to put me down. "I need to walk by myself and get it."

A deep growl rumbles in his chest, but reluctantly, he sets me down. "Why can't you let me take care of you? That's all I want. Whatever it is you need downstairs, it isn't an inconvenience for me to get it."

"I know, it's just..." If stomping wouldn't hurt, I'd do it now. "I love you, and I wanted to get the divorce papers you left and rip them up in front of you."

He looks stunned.

"I was moving the recliner back to show you that I want to be here with you. It was dumb, I know. It wasn't the sexy or grand gesture you deserve for all that you've done for me, but it was all I could think of at the time. I never wanted to get divorced, not really. But I thought it was the only way to know that we were both in this because we want to be."

"I want to be," he says.

"Me too." I take a step closer to him. "Six months ago, I didn't believe in the idea of marriage. Then you came along. Now I can't imagine life without you. I am so in love with you, Declan. Crazy in love. I want our happily ever after, if you'll still have me."

He takes me by the upper arm and pulls me back to him. His mouth descends on mine, and he kisses me, while taking my feet out from underneath me.

I wrap my arms around his neck and kiss him back like my life depends on it.

"You love me?" he asks, out of breath.

"Yes." My heart beats wildly. "So much. I'm sorry about the stupid reality show, about all of it, really. None of it matters without you. Of course, I love you. How could I not?"

He kisses me again, and it lights up my insides.

No one has ever loved me as well as he does. Losing boyfriends in the past was hard, sad even. But losing him for good would be devastating in a way that terrifies me.

He rests his forehead against mine and nips at my bottom lip. "I love you too." Another nip. "*Wife.*"

CHAPTER FORTY-ONE

Declan

I'M LOSING MY TOUCH

I wake up early Monday morning alone. I sit up and look for any sign of Jade. Stubborn woman is going to give me an ulcer. She refuses to stay off her feet. Yesterday, I only succeeded by giving her multiple orgasms every time she tried to get out of bed.

After pulling on sweats and a T-shirt, I head downstairs.

"Hey," she says, glancing up from her laptop. Her fingers continue to fly over the keypad. "Coffee is made, and I cooked you an omelet."

"You should be resting," I remind her as I kiss her good morning.

"I am." She points to her right foot propped up on a chair.

"Uh-huh," I say, not at all convinced. "What are you doing up so early?"

"I haven't been to bed yet."

One brow lifts. "No? I seem to remember someone that looked a whole lot like you screaming out my name minutes before I passed out."

Her face flushes. "You passed out, but I did not."

"Damn. I'm losing my touch," I mutter as I walk over to the stove to get my food and a cup of coffee. I take both back to the table and sit across from her. "After breakfast, I'll have to try again."

Smiling, Jade looks up and takes a sip from her mug. "You were amazing. You're always amazing."

"Mhmm. Obviously not, if you had the energy to stay up all night."

"I couldn't sleep. I had a new idea for the article I wrote on our first six months together, and my brain wouldn't rest until I got it out. I rewrote the entire thing. It's either the best thing I've ever written or I'm delirious from lack of sleep. Can you drive me into the office on your way to the arena?" Her words come fast and bubbly. She's so amped up.

Yep. Definitely losing my touch.

"You're going to work today?"

"I know what you're thinking," she says.

"You need to rest. Can't you work from here for a day or two?"

"And I will. I promise. I just need to go in this morning."

I grind my back teeth. "Yes, I will take you, but the rest of the week, you're staying home, even if I have to skip practice and hold you down."

"Ooooh. That sounds promising." She grins at me playfully.

I'm thankful our game this week is at home or I'd be tempted to sneak her onto the team jet.

"Dinner tonight?" I ask. "I'll pick up something and then we should probably talk about a few things."

Her smile dims. "Right."

I reach across the table and take her hand. We spent yesterday naked and making each other feel good, and as much as I'd love to live like that forever, there are things we need to figure out to truly move forward.

"Can we talk earlier in the day? Lunch?"

I do a quick mental run through of my schedule and then nod. "Yeah. I have a break around noon."

"That's perfect." She beams.

I drop off Jade at the curb outside of her work. "If you're foot starts bothering you at all, call me or have Scarlett run you to the house. If I don't answer, call the arena and tell them it's a family emergency."

"I am fine."

"You're not fine. You have a broken foot."

She leans over and cups my cheek as she brushes her lips over mine in a quick kiss. "In a few hours, you can whisk me home where I promise to rest."

"I'm gonna make sure of it." I nip at her bottom lip before she pulls away.

When I get to the arena, I find Leo and Ash in the weight room.

"He's alive!" Ash calls when he sees me. "How's Jade?"

"Stubborn. I'm considering tying her to the bed to keep her from overdoing it."

"I'd go with a couple spreader bar restraints," he deadpans. "Just as effective, but more fun."

"Oh geez," Leo mutters with a laugh. "Not a visual I needed this morning."

I shake my head at him, but it feels good to be laughing with them.

"Things are good, though?" Leo asks.

"Yeah, things are good. We tore up the divorce papers yesterday."

"I'm happy for you." Ash lays a hand on my shoulder and squeezes. "But if you need to borrow the spreader bars, just say the word."

CHAPTER FORTY-TWO

Jade

MOM JEANS

Melody stares at me from her pink, plush chair, hands crossed at her waist.

"You know I can't print this." Her gaze briefly flicks to the computer screen in front of her.

"Why not?" My voice quivers just slightly. I knew it wasn't going to be easy to convince her to make a last-minute switch on my article, but it's my favorite thing I've ever written. I took bits from all the interviews I've done with other couples and from my own experience these past six months with Declan and compiled them into a sort of lessons in love piece.

"Our readers are expecting an up-close and personal detailing of your marriage to a pro-hockey player. This is the kind of crap a million other magazines are publishing every day. It's played out."

Her words sting, but I keep my head held high. Maybe it is played out, but there's a reason that people love reading about romance. It gives us hope. Relationships aren't always easy or pretty. In fact, the one thing every couple I talked to had in common were the trials and tribulations along the way. Love is coming to a crossroads and deciding that the other person is worth the fight.

"My personal life isn't up for grabs. Not anymore."

She leans forward. "Your personal life is what keeps you in a job."

"Then I guess it isn't a job I want anymore."

She laughs, like she thinks I'm joking, but when I don't join in, she stops. "You can't be serious?"

Staying quiet, I hold her stare.

She looks away first. "We can publish this on the website as a one-time special feature, but your regular article will publish as is. You have to trust me, Jade. This is going to be good for the magazine, and for you too. Look at the exposure it's already given you. Your writing is good, but you need a point of view that sells. I gave you that."

"You did and I appreciate it. I learned a lot about publishing and myself."

A pleased smile lifts her pink-painted lips.

"When I took this job, I was so willing to do anything to be successful. Deceiving people didn't seem so bad because I didn't even believe in a happily ever after, not really."

"You don't have to believe it to sell it. Look at me. I've been divorced twice."

"You're right. I think we proved that."

"Continue the articles for another six months, completing your first year of marriage, as scheduled, and then we'll find another place for you. The beauty department could use an additional strong writer."

"No, thank you." Even if I believed she'd keep her word, which I don't, I know that I can't stay here. I stand and clasp my hands in front of me to keep them from shaking and showing how nervous I am. "I quit."

"Where will you go?" She stands behind her desk.

"I'm not sure yet," I say honestly.

"I have connections all over the city and the publishing industry. Not to mention, I know your big secret. What would the media think if they found out that your husband was in a fake marriage?"

It's a low blow to threaten Declan's reputation, but it has it's intended impact. I'd rather die than see him take the backlash for my mistakes.

Steeling my voice, I rest one hand on the door handle and look her straight in the eye as I say, "I don't know, but I doubt it would be as bad as if they found out the Editor-in-Chief of *I Do* was using a fake marriage to sell magazines."

With that, I let myself out. Scarlett pops up from her cubicle and rushes to my side.

"Are you okay?" Her brown eyes are wide as she studies my face.

I manage a nod, too afraid to speak. I'd already packed up the things at my desk, so I grab them and keep my chin lifted as I walk to the elevator. A few people whisper and stare, but I try not to show that I'm anything less than confident in my decision.

When the elevator doors close me and Scarlett inside, I finally breathe.

"Holy shit." The words come out with another whoosh of air.

"I'm so proud of you." She hugs me. "I wish I could have seen her face."

"No, you don't," I tell her. "It was scary. She threatened to go to the press and out me and Declan."

"Let her try. No one could ever see the two of you and not know you're crazy about each other." Her grip on me tightens. "Whatever happens, I've got your back. A lot of people do. She doesn't want to mess with your family."

"I know." I squeeze her back. "Thank you for always being there for me, even when I didn't know how to appreciate it."

Declan's Ferrari pulls into the parking lot as we walk outside, and my heart beats a little faster.

"Your husband is here," Scarlett says in a playful tone.

Declan stops in front of us, and Scarlett opens the passenger door for me. She leans down to wave at Declan. "Hi."

"Hey, Scarlett." His deep voice rumbles in response, but his eyes are on me.

Scarlett turns back and hugs me one last time. "Love you. Check in later and let me know how you're doing."

"I'm going to be just fine," I tell her, before sliding into the seat with all my stuff.

She closes me in, and Declan glances at the box in my lap.

"Hey, thanks for the ride." I lean over to kiss him.

"You're welcome." He jabs a thumb toward the box. "What's all that?"

"Notebooks, pens, some photos, and a cactus that might be dead."

"O-kay."

I thought I'd be more scared, but I feel hopeful and excited about what's next. A smile spreads across my face. "I quit."

"Seriously?" Both of his dark brows lift.

Nodding quickly, I talk at a rapid pace. "I realized that I was never going to get to write the things I want while working there. I'll be thirty and still writing about my life married to a Wildcat. And I guess I realized that I don't want to share that part of my life anymore.

You're all mine."

"Should have borrowed the spreader bars," he mumbles.

"What?" I ask with a giggle.

"Nothing. That's amazing news."

"Really? You're okay with this? It might take me a little while to find another job." Letting another person take care of me isn't easy, but no one ever has, or will, love me as much as he does. It seems like the perfect time to take a leap of faith.

"Really, really. You're too talented to be writing about me. I'm not that interesting."

"Oh, I beg to differ." I drape a hand behind his neck and thread my fingers through the hair at the nape of his neck. "But thank you. I'm excited. Maybe I'll try to write a book or something while I look for another job."

"I can think of all sorts of ways to keep you busy." His mouth slants over mine and his tongue sweeps into my mouth.

We make out in the parking lot until the windows start to fog and Declan complains his sweats are feeling tight in the crotch.

"One more thing," I say, while catching my breath.

"What's up, baby?" He tucks a lock of hair behind my ear.

"About having a kid."

He looks like he wants to interrupt, but I keep going before I lose my nerve. "I do want kids, but not yet. Is that a deal breaker?"

"With you, nothing is a deal breaker." He drops another kiss on my lips and brushes his thumb across my cheek. "You were worried about this?"

"I know how important family is to you. It is for me too, just not yet. Maybe in a year or so."

"I want kids with you, if and whenever, you're ready. I'm sorry you felt pressured. It was never a deal breaker. I knew upping the stakes and asking you to have a baby would force you to figure out what you wanted, but it was still a shitty thing to throw at you." His grip is firm on my neck, and he ducks his head, so we're inches apart. "You're my family. If it's just the two of us, that'll be enough."

My stomach dips and I lunge forward and capture him in a tight hug. "I love you so much."

"I don't think I'll ever get tired of hearing that." His hand cradles my head. "I love you too. But just so we're clear, I think you'd be sexy as hell in some mom jeans with a baby on your hip."

"And you with a dad bod, making pancakes for a couple of twin girls." I sigh at the image, then press my lips to his.

"Twins? Girls?"

I smile at the slight panic in his voice.

He swallows the laugh that slips from my lips. "Boys. Maybe one girl. Fuck it, let's have a dozen of both."

CHAPTER FORTY-THREE

Jade

I HAVE A WIFE

"**O**h my gosh, it's gorgeous!" Piper holds my hand in place and looks at the ring from every angle.

"What did you do with the other ring?" Dakota asks.

"I think I'll donate it. There are a lot of charities that take old engagement and wedding rings." Something I only know because of all the bridal research I did over the past two years. "Fresh start, new ring."

When Piper lets go, I raise my hand and admire the new bling. It's exactly the ring I wanted, oval cut, and twice as big as the last. And best of all, I didn't wear it while engaged to someone else. Declan surprised me with it this morning. He got down on one knee and everything. I finally got the kind of dream proposal I used to write about.

Knocking on the plexiglass in front of me gets my attention. Declan stands on the other side, stick in one hand.

"Hey." I quit admiring my ring and admire him. Wow, he looks good. Up in the box, it's hard to fully appreciate just how handsome he is in that uniform. I step forward and place both hands on the glass. "Got a girlfriend, number seventy-seven?"

"Nope." He flips a puck up and catches it on the end of his stick. "But I have a wife and if she sees you talking to me, who knows what she'll do."

"Better get back to work then."

He winks and then takes the puck in one gloved hand and makes a motion like he's going to toss it up and over the plexiglass. I nod eagerly, and he throws it over to me. Cradling it in both hands, I purse my lips and bring them close to the glass and make a kissing sound. "Good luck."

He winks again as he skates backward to rejoin the team warming up.

"This was such a good idea sitting down here," I say, still staring after Declan. "Up close, my husband is even sexier."

Everly wanted to bring some friends to the game, and Scarlett's sister, Cadence, brought Sebastian. Since we couldn't all sit up in the WAG box, we decided to watch the game from the lower level. Best decision ever.

My husband is fast and brutal on the ice. I love listening to the crowd around me cheer him on. But no one yells louder than me. Baby Seb sleeps right through it in Cadence's arms. He loves to be held.

At the first intermission, Cadence stands. "My arms are going to fall off."

"I'll take him," Scarlett says, and her sister passes him to her.

"He's pretty cute," I say, looking at his little pouty mouth and dark lashes. He's in a little Wildcat onesie and a beanie similar to the one I wear to every game with Declan's name and number.

"He is the cutest baby in the whole world," she coos at him, then looks at me. "Want to hold him?"

"Oh, I don't know. What if I drop him or…break him?"

Scarlett chuckles softly. "You won't."

I still hesitate, but then Scarlett is bringing him closer, and I find myself raising my arms to take him. Panic courses through me as his soft, but surprisingly heavy, little body nuzzles against me.

"Look at you," my best friend says. "How's it feel?"

"Terrifying, but also…nice."

"Ready to have a couple? Me and you. Our babies could be like siblings."

I have to admit, it would be fun to tackle motherhood with Scarlett, the same way we've tackled everything else life has thrown at us. "I'm going to need you to give me a year or two."

"The best I can do is seven months."

"Seven months?" I ask. "Wait. You're pregnant?!"

"Shh!"

I glance down at Sebastian and whisper sorry to him, then to Scarlett, "You're pregnant?!"

"Yeah." She's positively giddy as she smiles back at me. "We just found out yesterday."

"And you waited twenty-four hours to tell me?"

"I think I was in shock. I took like five tests to be sure."

"Oh my gosh, Scar. I'd hug you, but my arms are full. Does Cadence know?"

She shakes her head. "You're the only person that knows. We're telling my family tonight after the game."

"Oh man." My lips pull wider. "I'd love to see the look on Coach

Miller's face when he finds out Leo knocked you up."

"Leo's definitely sweating it, but Mom and Dad love him."

"I'm really happy for you." I lean my shoulder against hers and let my head fall against hers.

We stand like that until the team is coming back out. Cadence is still missing. I hope she's getting herself a big glass of wine. She deserves it. Holding this little chunk is more work than it looks. My arms are going to be sore. I might need to start working out before I think about having kids.

Declan skates onto the ice. He takes a puck to the net and then moves around it, scanning until he finds me. A slow smile spreads across his face when he sees me with Cadence's baby.

"What's the male equivalent of ovaries exploding?" Scarlett laughs. "Your husband is having a whole moment imagining you with his kid. Are you sure you don't want to do this together?"

I look away from Declan to my best friend. "I will be with you every step of the way, and someday, when I pop out a couple of cute little babies, you'll be able to coach me through it with all your wise motherly knowledge."

"Love you," she says.

"Love you, too."

When the game is over, I head to the back doors to wait for Declan. Staring at my mom's contact in my phone, I pace. I haven't talked to her again since we made up. I think part of me has been afraid that letting her in will just lead to future disappointment, but if loving Declan has taught me anything, it's that you have to fight for the family you want.

My pulse races as the phone rings, but it goes to voicemail.

I consider texting, but Declan appears, and I put my phone in my pocket and go to him.

"Hey." He leans down to kiss me.

"Nice game." I hold up the puck he gave me. "Think I could sell this and make a little fast cash?"

"Maybe if I sign it."

"Oooh. You'd do that?"

He grins at me fangirling. Maybe he doesn't realize it, but I'm hands down his number one fan.

"Ready to go home?" he asks.

"So ready. I've been picturing you naked for three hours. Tell me, do you get to bring the uniform and all that padding home?"

Chuckling, he wraps an arm around my shoulders and leads me out to his car. Back at the house, a familiar vehicle is parked in the driveway.

"Is that my mom's car?" I ask. It's too dark to make out the person sitting in the driver's side, but I'm positive that's her black Toyota.

"Don't be pissed," he says, once he shuts off the engine, "but I invited her."

"Why?"

"Because I know that it's been weighing on you and that you want to have a better relationship with her. And maybe I'm projecting my own shit, but if my mom were here, I'd want someone to push me to work things out with her. I'm just so damn happy. I want you to be too."

"I am. *So* happy. Ridiculously happy." I wave my hands around for emphasis. "But thank you for loving me so well."

"You're welcome." He gets out of the car and comes around to open my door. Leaning down, he whispers in my ear, "And I absolutely can bring my uniform home."

CHAPTER FORTY-FOUR

Jade

WHAT'S MINE IS YOURS

"**W**e're going to be late," Declan calls from the living room.

"I know. I'm hurrying." I clasp the necklace and grab my purse. With a glance out the window, I come up short and curse the blanket of white covering the ground. Late February in Minnesota is still cold and snowy. Every year I pray for an early spring. "I forgot to park in the garage again."

My handsome husband stands by the door, wearing the hell out of a suit and a smile. "Your car is cleaned off."

"What did I do to deserve you?"

His arms glide around the silky material of my dress and draw me closer. "Must be your charm and wit."

"Or my ass," I say as he grabs a handful.

"That too."

He helps me into my coat, and we head outside. The wind blows freezing air into my face and makes my eyes sting. I nuzzle into his shoulder, which is why it takes me longer than it should to realize it isn't my Volkswagen sitting in the driveway.

Declan pauses and waits for my reaction as we stand next to a shiny, red Mercedes SUV.

"What is this?" I ask, eyes growing wide as I take in the beautiful car.

"I finally sold the old Mercedes, and I bought a new one. For you." He holds the key up to me.

"Shut up."

His chest shakes with silent laughter at my response.

"You did not buy me a vehicle."

"Technically, we did. What's mine is yours, and all that. Do you like it?"

"Like it? It's gorgeous." I run a gloved hand along the red paint. "Are you sure we can afford this? Your wife is still unemployed."

His smile doesn't waver. "Good thing your husband's stock is up then. I got the endorsement campaign."

"Oh my gosh, really?" The Wildcats are having a great season and a lot of it is thanks to him. He's had so many offers for endorsements, but he was holding out for the one he really wanted – a well-known footwear and apparel company that has other professional athletes from a variety of sports.

It's a huge get for him, not only financially, but it pushes him into the limelight and gives him a little more of the respect he deserves. I'd like to think I helped with that part. Nobody puts Declan in the corner. Except me, and that's just so I can make out with him.

I stop admiring my new vehicle to hug him. "Congratulations."

Then it hits me. "You got a big check and bought me a car with it? Why didn't you buy yourself something?"

"I bought exactly what I wanted."

I still can't believe this man is real.

"Ready to test it out?" He opens the driver's side door for me.

I glance down at my shoes. "Actually, can you drive us tonight? These heels look great, but they're not very functional."

He scoops me into his arms and takes me over to the passenger side. It smells like new car and the leather feels cool through my thin dress.

While Declan drives us, I test out all the features of the car. When he finally pulls up to the event, I have the music cranking and the seat warmers going.

"Welcome, Mr. and Mrs. Sato." The valet opens my door and helps me out.

The Wildcat Foundation is hosting a casino-style event tonight at the arena. The entire team, including the coaching staff and front office, are here with dates, and fans were able to buy tickets to get up close and personal while they support a great cause.

We walk a red carpet, posing for several pictures on our way inside. Declan stops to sign autographs and take a few selfies.

Food, drinks, and games are set up all around the third floor of the building. Each member of the team has to work one of the games at some point during the night.

Declan's shift isn't until later, but he's pulled to take some group photos and I wander over to the girls. We're huddled up several times too, by photographers wanting to capture a WAG shot. Then we get drinks from the bar and roam around the big event area to check out the games.

Every thirty minutes or so, I feel Declan's gaze on me and scan the room until I find him. Each time our eyes meet, my stomach flutters.

This time, when I locate him, he's standing behind a blackjack table. His suit jacket is off, and the sleeves of his white shirt are rolled up, showing off his forearms.

Taking my champagne, I head closer. I hang back and listen to him interact with the people sitting at his table. He looks directly at me as he laughs at something someone said.

I want nothing more than to go to him, kiss him, and steal all his attention. Nothing feels better than being loved by him. But I don't do that. I blow him a kiss and head for another table. He'll find me when he's done.

In the meantime, I'm happy that he's putting himself out there more. People deserve to know him like his teammates and I do. He's the best and people love him. Just not as much as I do.

I don't get far before his muscular arms wrap around me from behind and stop me in my tracks. "Where do you think you're going?"

"To find the girls. I didn't want to interrupt."

"Please, baby, interrupt." He ducks his head to kiss my neck, sending goosebumps racing down my body.

"Aren't you supposed to be working?"

"Yep, just came to bring you back with me."

I turn to find the entire blackjack table staring at us. "Everyone is looking this way."

"Of course, they are. You're gorgeous."

"I don't think it's me they're looking at. Those women are hoping you toss me aside and take one of them home."

"Zero chance of that, baby. I'm all yours." He takes my hand and kisses the top of it, before threading our fingers together and leading me back to the table.

He introduces me as his wife, and I feel a rush of pride. I can't imagine being married to anyone else.

Chance, luck, divine intervention, or whatever it was that brought us together, I'm just happy I found him. I've made a lot of mistakes, but he is not one of them. He's my person, my soulmate, my forever.

And we're going to live happily, wildly ever after.

EPILOGUE

Declan

TO US

I'm having the best dream ever, when the sun coming in through the window threatens to pull me awake.

Wait, no, definitely not a dream. Jade is lying on top of me, kissing my neck.

"Morning, baby," I say, eyes still closed.

"Happy birthday." Her lips press against mine.

"Thank you."

She scoots down my body and disappears under the covers. She pulls my boxers down on her way and takes me into her mouth. I don't know how long she's been lying on top of me, kissing me, but I am more than ready for her.

"Oh, damn." I tangle my fingers in her hair as she sucks me all the way to the back of her throat.

My wife likes to go down on me, and I am not complaining. I like returning the favor two-fold. I warn her I'm close and then I'm coming hard way too soon.

"Fuck, baby, what a way to wake up."

Jade shimmies back up and falls onto the bed beside me, while I'm still catching my breath. "Birthday blowies, didn't you get the memo?"

"Best birthday present ever." I let my head fall to the side to kiss her.

"That's just present number one."

"Give me five minutes and I'll be ready for number two." I put two fingers in the air.

Her soft laughter tickles the side of my face. "Present number two doesn't include sex, sadly, but I still think you'll like it."

"Exactly how many presents are we talking about?"

"You'll just have to wait and see." She gets up and walks around the bed, completely naked, and heads into the bathroom. "Shower?"

"Never gonna say no to that." I'm on my feet and chasing her as fast as I can move.

I get present number two and three in the shower and then we head out to my favorite breakfast place. Leo and Scarlett meet us there.

"How are you feeling?" Jade asks her best friend.

"Awful. I'm pretty sure this baby is trying to kill me."

My wife hugs her and then leans down to talk to her stomach. "Be nice to your momma."

Leo drapes a protective arm around Scarlett's shoulders. "Let's see if we can find something for you to eat that the kid doesn't hate."

We have breakfast, and then Jade and I drive out to her mom's house. Momma Davis gives me a hug and a dozen homemade chocolate chip cookies. Things have been better between her and Jade. I'm not sure if that'll stand when or if she starts seeing someone new, but I'm gonna keep pushing Jade to have a relationship with her.

Birthdays are always weird. I haven't celebrated the day in years. When the person who brought you into the world isn't around, it feels sort of pointless. Or it always has to me. But with every stop on Jade's agenda, I'm starting to realize the pattern.

When we walk over to Ash's house that night, I am looking forward to a fun night, kicking back with my friends. We have a game tomorrow night at home, so we won't be getting too crazy, but it should still be a good time.

"That's my favorite dress," I say, glancing over at Jade in her little green dress. The same one she wore the night of her bachelorette party.

"Is it?" she asks with a mischievous smile. She knows damn well it is.

"Thank you for today." I circle her waist and bring her body to mine on the stoop outside of Ash's house. "It's the best birthday ever."

"You have a lot of people who love you. A big, slightly dysfunctional, but truly loving family."

"I know."

"None more than me, though. Don't forget that." She raises one hand above her head. "I'm way up here and everyone else is like, way down here." She leans to the side to put that same hand down by the ground.

"So basically, everyone else just sorta, kinda loves me?" I tease.

"Oh no. They really love you. I just love you that much more."

Her arms drape around my neck and she tips her face up in that way she does when she wants me to kiss her. I press my mouth to hers.

"Your mom would be really proud of the man you've become. Your grandparents, too."

Warmth spreads through my chest. I don't have the words, so I kiss her again.

Practically the whole team is here tonight. Even Everly and Grace stop by to wish me a happy birthday.

I spent a lot of years perfectly content to hang in the background and let life happen around me, but Jade pushes me to be present in moments like these.

After making a lap around the room to say hi to everyone, we pause in the doorway between the kitchen and living room.

"Who should we pretend to be tonight? Scarlett and Leo are sweet. He keeps rubbing her belly. Tyler and Piper disappeared, so they're probably in some corner making out. Then there's Dakota and Maverick getting a little handsy while talking to people." Jade lifts a brow in question. "Or we could stare at each other longingly across the room like a number of others hoping not to go home alone."

I step in front of her and place my hands on her hips. "I don't want to be anyone else. Not tonight. Not ever again."

She links her arms around my neck and stares into my eyes. "You want to go home and have sex, don't you?"

I nod. "Yeah, immediately."

Laughter lights up her face. I love these guys, our friends and family, but my very favorite place is home with my wife.

Before we can make our exit, Ash claps me on the shoulder. "Happy birthday, man."

"Thanks. Appreciate you hosting."

"Always happy for a reason to throw a party," he says, and hands me a glass of whiskey.

Somewhere in the room, someone whistles, and then Jack commands everyone's attention by stepping onto the coffee table and lifting his glass. "Happy birthday to one of the greatest guys I know. I hope it's the best year yet, buddy. To Declan."

Everyone tips their glass toward me. "To Declan."

I lift my drink to them in return. I get a chorus of happy birthdays shouted my way.

"And to my gorgeous wife," I say, after swallowing down the dark liquor. "Because of you, last year is going to be hard to top."

Jade smiles and clinks her glass lightly against mine. "To us. The best is yet to come."

PLAYLIST

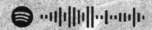

2 Be Loved (Am I Ready) by Lizzo

Bad Idea by Dove Cameron

I Like You (A Happier Song) by Post Malone feat. Doja Cat

Eyes On You by Nicky Youre

Uh Oh by Tate McRae

Bad Habit by Steve Lacy

Betty (Get Money) by Yung Gravy

Nonsense by Sabrina Carpenter

I'm a Mess by Avril Lavigne feat. Yungblud

Bones by Imagine Dragons

Disaster by Conan Gray

So Good by Halsey

Brutal by Olivia Rodrigo

Don't Come Back by Tate McRae

Midnight Rain by Taylor Swift

10:35 by Tiesto feat. Tate McRae

Wait for U by Future feat. Drake and Tems

Can we Pretend that We're Good? by Daniel Seavey

Ender Will Save Us All by Dashboard Confessional

ALSO BY REBECCA JENSHAK

Wildcat Hockey Series
Wildcat
Wild About You
Wild Ever After

Campus Wallflowers Series
Tutoring the Player
Hating the Player
Scoring the Player

Campus Nights Series
Secret Puck
Bad Crush
Broken Hearts
Wild Love

Smart Jocks Series
The Assist
The Fadeaway
The Tip-Off
The Fake
The Pass

Standalone Novels
Sweet Spot
Electric Blue Love

ABOUT THE AUTHOR

Rebecca Jenshak is a *USA Today* bestselling author of new adult and sports romance. She lives in Arizona with her family. When she isn't writing, you can find her attending local sporting events, hanging out with family and friends, or with her nose buried in a book.

Sign up for her newsletter for book sales and release news.